HIGHWAYS

The Last Days in May

D. S. ROBERTS

A Dallas S. Streeter Chronicle

Archway Publishing books may be ordered through booksellers or by contacting:

Archway Publishing
1663 Liberty Drive
Bloomington, IN 47403
www.archwaypublishing.com
1 (888) 242-5904

ISBN: 978-1-4808-5529-8 (sc)
ISBN: 978-1-4808-5530-4 (e)

Library of Congress Control Number: 2017918521

Print information available on the last page.

Archway Publishing rev. date: 12/12/2017

Prelude

Somewhere in the desert, headed south, trouble was on the road. And it was hot. *"Thirsty", "Thirsty"*... His mind was swimming on the hours past, and pass they did. The three large bullet holes in the lid of the trunk were his only link with the outside world. The only light, the only air, the only contact to the outside. Through them, the sun lit up bloody hands and forearms. It was then he realized where he was and what had happened. "There is a lot of desert between the beginning and what will be the ending" was his last thought before passing out into a restless nightmare that had only just begun.

Foreword and Dedication

I am D.S. Roberts and smuggling is in my DNA. It is, or must be, because it's how my maternal grandfather, who came to America in the early 1920's not speaking a word of English, got started by working for the "Purple Gang" in Detroit, driving boats across the Detroit River filled with booze for years.

He quietly walked away from that life, much as I have, when he had made enough to start building his dream of opening a German Bakery. He ended up owning three, along with a fleet of six trucks to make deliveries. He was never busted, never had the problems that his grandson encountered in a very complicated updated version of the same game. While he had to learn English, I had to learn Spanish, as well several dialects of, well, let's just call it "Island speak" for now…

Yeah, I was a smuggler. An adventure that started in the 70's and ended in the mid 90's. The years passed by fast, my friends and enemies passed just as fast. HIGHWAYS, "The Last Days in May," is Book Two of The Dallas Streeter Chronicles; a glimpse into one month of what really has been a life lived, and lived well. And isn't that what life is for? To be lived...Fully? I do hope you enjoy this novel. It is dedicated to all the old Water-Buffaloes who stomped the tundra to make our lives different, if not better, during the times of our "freedom," when

> *"Freedom was just another word for nothing left to lose."* –
> Janis Joplin

Contents

Chapter 1

D allas Steven Streeter and Martin (the Chief) Harvey had not seen nor spoken to each other in almost a year. At least since the Port Royal debacle. They both figured that with as much money as they had split-up between them (courtesy of Carlos Ochoa) that they should lay low and avoid the ever-curious. Whoever they were, it just made good sense. So Dallas and Janis, now married almost a year, had bought an estate on one of the many out islands N.E. of Trinidad. The Chief bought out a retiring Charter Boat operation. He bought out the whole lot. A nice 52' Hatteras Sport Fisherman only a few years old, the guy's private slip and the rights to the old guy's established clientele. He lived aboard it with his girlfriend Sonata. It was Sonata that introduced the Chief to the old owner. At the time, he wondered if the women came with the deal, but alas, no, she was just the broker that made a substantial amount of money on the deal. The Chief took her out a few times and that was it. She moved in and was handling all the Charter Boat end of the business. Some of the clients came from as far away as Germany, France and England. She was an equal in many respects, and the Chief trusted her. But he never discussed his past with her and never let on that he was anything but another charter boat captain. Not that he didn't think that she could handle the truth, but he lived by the golden rule: "Don't ASK, Don't TELL." And she never asked anything about him or his personal life before Trinidad. He liked this understood boundary – it brought them closer.

Dallas ambled around the upper floor of his half-moon-shaped house. He walked into the master bedroom and out the French doors to the upper deck. From here he could see for what seemed like a hundred miles. Dallas had bought the house, which was last house on the left, in some wacky silent auction. Not cheap, but easy as far as his privacy went. On this island, there are only six estates, two of which belonged to some Rock & Roll bands. One belonged to some new Internet geek that was always telling Dallas to get into it because it's the way of the future. Dallas humored him as best he could, but made no promises. The other ones belonged to a Saudi Prince and two Euro-Trash types. Maybe that was too kind; they were Frogs, plain and simple. They tilted their great big noses in the air whenever they saw Dallas. NOT even a hello from these bastards when Dallas drove by, waved, and said "Hello!" So whenever the rock band or bands were in-island Dallas always sent Janis over and invited them out in one of the boats. In return, the party started and lasted days. With all the groupies and hanger on-ers, the music was set up and turned the whole little island into a private rock concert. The bands, which I can't say much about, were no garage bands to say the least, between them if put in a room, the Gold albums alone would fill an entire wall. Then the Platinum albums would do the same. Oh, and then there's the statues... Golden Globes, the MTV's and on and on around the room they would go, all the way back to the late sixties. Yeah, these bands knew how to throw a party. So once or twice a year, whenever the whole band or bands were on island together, The Frenchie's crawled the walls vertically, and spit every time they saw one of the (Rock & Roller) scum's. For Dallas, these times kept the cabin fever down for weeks at a time. He relished it. And he reveled in it!

Along the way, he met some cool people during these times, starting with the owners. Janis was (Cause' Celeste!), the women of the manor so to speak. But it was the slow season; the island was almost empty except for the computer geek and the guy that takes care of the Little Store/Fuel Pump. He walked around the deck and down a flight of stairs to the pool deck. He ran into Olivia the live-in maid, she was on her way out with a large salad bowl of greens and mixed fruit for the native Iguanas that have made the half-moon shaped pool and two-tiered waterfall that fed it home. She hated this job. She called them great beasts and freeloaders. On more than one occasion Dallas was summoned into the house to chase one of the errant beasts out. It was usually Goliath - He was the largest at just over four feet. If it was up to Dallas they could have the run of the house, but Janis and Olivia wouldn't have any of it. The previous owner had imported Carolina River Rock installed as a pool deck and Goliath and his harem loved to sun themselves on it, and climb the waterfall for the view. Sea grapes grew thick around the whole pool area, except for the gated hole that led down two flights of stairs to the boat dock. The first flight of stairs was about thirty-five feet down to an eight by eight platform. At the far-right corner was the second thirty-five-foot section that ended at the dock. The dock itself ran out about seventy-five feet. On the port side was a 51' Morgan Out Island sailboat, (the first one had fell victim to the rocks in Great Iguana, Bahamas, and sank with over a thousand kilos of coke on board. And rogue DEA agent named Ernie Skeet handcuffed and tripping on mushroom juice just as the DEA Blackhawks descended.) Dallas had to let this one go in exchange for his one-hour head start for a new life with about 4.7 million in cash (courtesy of Carlos Ochoa). On the starboard side was that very same 42' Scarab with three 200 hp. Johnson Ocean Runners on it (Of course it had a new paint job and decals, along with new registration numbers on it) that got his crew off that floundering sailboat and to safety. Behind that boat was a flotilla of toys, a couple jet skis, a Zodiac dinghy and a couple of kayaks.

As Dallas stood looking out at the pool the urge to break radio silence and call the Chief overcame him. Olivia walked back in speaking in some native tongue that Dallas only recognized as being pissed-off. He gave her a look and smiled. She looked back and didn't. He turned on his heels and headed towards his desk. Since the whole house was built into the side of the cliff, his desk was a high polished slab of coral. Even the bookcases and shelves were built into the coral rock face with glass doors on each. Above his head was all his electronics - stereo's here, radios there, and over to the far right closest to the coral wall was a knob. He pulled out and up and a single-side band shortwave radio slid out on casters, the top sliding backwards into the wall leaving only the knob showing.

Dallas reached under the desk and found a piece of paper that he had stuck there almost a year ago today. On it was only a set of random numbers. Random if you didn't know what you were looking at, that is. "Ya Mon! It's still here," Dallas whispered. He reached up the main single side band radio, ran his finger along the numbers and punched the numbers into a keypad, lighting up each empty box on the display. As he finished the last two numbers, he counted backwards the sequence, and then forward. "OK," he thought, "this looks correct." Adjusting the volume and the gain, he spoke into a handheld microphone "This is base station SAFE HARBOR calling charter fishing vessel ON-LINE, over." Dallas repeated this twice, until a clear voice came ringing back, "Go ahead! This is Charter Fishing Vessel ON-LINE. Please go to pre-designated radio frequency, over!" Dallas smiled as he realized that the Chief was still on top of his game, and didn't need to be reminded about changing frequencies.

Dallas reached up again and pushed in a red button on a box with a row of green to yellow to red lights that flicked on when he pushed in the button. This box sat directly on top of the single sideband radio, and as he spoke back into the microphone the row of colored, lights undulated back and forth. The Chief had done the same thing on his Sport Fisherman. Now a conversation started as the scramblers were doing their thing, which is to change frequencies with every word spoken on either end. There are sixteen lights and ten thousand possible chances that somebody else could be using the same custom-made scrambler, at exactly the same time as they were, were nil. Therefore, it puts the real chances of interception being on or around sixteen million to one chances of even one word slipping out side this chosen frequency. As Dallas once said to The Chief, "Hey when it comes to our safety, if we can afford it, let's spend it!"

"Hey, SAFE-HARBOR? How are ya, Buddy? Long time well! Well, almost a long time… Anyway, what's up Dal?" "Well Chief it's been almost a solid year, and what do you think? Think it's cool enough to get together for a day, take out that nice-ass boat of yours out and catch some fish and catch up on a year's worth of lies?" "That sounds great Dal. Yeah I think we can get together fer a day and do some fishing." "Great Chief! Then I'll jump in my Scarab and zoom on over and . . . "Oh NO, NO, NO Dallas! That's the last thing I want is you zooming up in that fat Scarab with six hundred horses pushing it. Might not look right to my neighbors if ya know what I mean? No, I'll get everything together here, and it will look just like any other charter I might have. Things on the Big Island are a little strange at present." "What do ya mean strange, Chief?" "Well, a lot of in and off island traffic lately. I'll explain tomorrow OK?" "Yeah, OK Chief." "Then let's say about 8:30 am." "Yeah, sounds like a plan ta me Chief, I'll be ready at 08:30 am. So until then my brother, have a nice Sunday, er, what's left of it." "Roger! Charter vessel (ON - LINE) off the air, Ciao Dallas!" Dallas reached up and turned the radios off and the scrambler too. He slid the unit back into its hole and pulled the knob that closed the radio off from the world and view.

Just about the same time Janis showed up, and announced "Hey, Wonder Boy, we need some beer and I'm dying fer a cigarette. Would you please go to that place that doubles as a store and fuel

pump and get us some? Please Honey? Please!" "Of course I will,
I have a bit of cabin fever anyway, and it will let me see if any of
our Rock & Roller buddies are in island. I'll do it in a couple mins,
OK?" "Sure baby." Janis smiled and walked out the pool doors
and dove in. Dallas had his back to her and heard "GODDAMN
IT DALLAS! Come here and get this friggin dinosaur out of the
fucking pool!" "Yes honey, right away honey, but I think Goliath
likes you." "I don't care if he thinks I'm his mother! Get this fuck
out of the pool! NOW! I mean it DAL! NOW!" "Jeez, woman,
what do you want worse, the Cigs and Beer OR the dinosaur out?"
"BOTH ASSHOLE! Now get it out. And get out!" Janis, now with
a rumble in her voice, which means NOW!

The Chief stood up and turned off the radio and its scrambler.
He twirled the numbers on them both. This he did merely out of
habit, thought the thought Old Dogs & New Tricks tripped through
his mind as he put on his deck shoes. "Ah, shit," he mumbled as
he headed out the salon cabin sliding glass doors. "Jesus H. Christ!
It's hot as Hades out here today, and it's May 7th, which when you
are this far south the Equator starts to come in to play. It should
be getting cooler out, not hotter! Then settle in at a nice 78 to 82
degrees for about six months. If this keeps up it will kill my summer
charters. Fucking global warming!" This set the tone for his head as
he stepped over and on top of transom with one more step to the
pier-slip boards. He walked to his gate at the end of his boat slip
and gave the handle a hard-downward turn. It opened and re-locked
itself as it closed behind him. Directly overhead was his claim to
legitimacy - A curved sign with two Marlins doing a Tail Walk, one
at each end. In the Middle were the words

(ON–LINE)
BIG GAME / OPEN WATER CHARTER$, Ltd.
Ph # (869) DREAM–FISH
Trinidad & Tobago

Not a lot of information, but enough for the kind of people he wanted on his boat. Meaning smart, experienced, and above all rich! Not like some whom if they don't hook-up on the first day try and wriggle out of the minimum three-day contract. On a three-day run, the chances go up crazy so that when you do hook-up, it's gonna be what you came the six or seven thousand miles for. Big Game, Trophy Fish! So that's why the Chief's pre-configuration is in the shape of the ($) sign, and not one of these (?). The Chief was so expensive that if you did not catch your fish, you could later come down for a free one day. After all, as the Chief says, "It's called Fishing! Not CATCHING."

As he walked the length of the dock he heard a plane overhead on approach to the airport. He looked towards the direction of the noise and saw a plane he hadn't seen in a long time. It was an Aero-Commander, "Nice plane." he thought. These planes are unmistakable by their profile; they at one time were a high-end smuggler's plane. They are twin engine with the wings mounted above the fuselage and the engines mounted at mid-wing on each side. The fuselage itself was a long sort of torpedo-shaped deal. Its tail was tall and the horizontal stabilizers were mid-tail fin mounted. These planes had an incredible payload capacity, capable of carrying up to twelve hundred pounds, with a nice side door that allowed crew to kick out bales like on a bombing run. With the air intakes mounted so high, it could fly low, slow, and drop a load within a couple hundred

feet of a waiting Go Fast boat. Fly-out and never get caught in the radar net. Not only did it have fully retractable landing gear, but it could actually land on the water if it had to ditch and float for a respectable amount of time. Serious advantages for some unfortunate souls. If the seas were calm, they were known to be able to taxi around while calling for help. Or even, if close to an island, make it there under their own speed. But once in the water, that's where they usually stayed. Too much drag on too small a pair of engines. Most smugglers carried a small Zodiac inflatable with a fifteen-horsepower outboard. These weighed less than two hundred pounds, and it's been said they saved many a crew to fly again. (Lately the DEA had been using the ones they had confiscated - they liked them because they can carry at least eight men plus two pilots and all their supplies). They can land on short airstrips and take off from shorter ones with the right thermals. Anyway, the Chief looked at this one 'till it disappeared, and he continued to walk the street up to his favorite bait and tackle shop.

Dallas evicted Goliath from the pool and sent him scrambling into the Sea Grapes. Janis thanked him with a small kiss, and said, "Don't forget my cigs, OK?" "Yeah, OK, I won't. Or the beer." "Hmm, Hmm," Dallas hummed as he walked towards the garage door. Turning back, he yelled "Oh yeah, we have company coming in the morning! "Who?" Janis yelled back. But all she heard was the garage door slam. No cars are allowed on the island, so everyone used golf carts to get around. A self-imposed speed limit of fifteen miles per hour was the norm, but Dallas just couldn't deal with that, living all the way at the end of the island. So he imported a Polaris four-wheel drive ATV, with a custom built Cushman cover. This was no toy golf-cart, this little honey, while looking like a normal cart, could easily do fifty miles an hour on the straightaways. So instead of a twenty-minute drive, when the island was empty as it seemed to be now it was a seven-minute cruise. And fun at that. Nevertheless, he drove sanely and checked out a couple of the Rockers houses for signs of life. Not seeing any thing that indicated anyone was in-island, he drove on. Not even the Frogs were in-island. Every time he drove past those two mini-assaults on the senses he got mad. "Jeez just think, the whole island would look like this if the rest of the residents hadn't voted to stop the ambiguity on what was left of the tropical ambience of this island."

Dallas pulled in and parked in front of the little shack that served as Food/Liquor/Fuel dump and pump on the south end of the island. No one was in sight. He walked in the front, grabbed a case of Guinness beer and reached behind the counter for a carton of Marlboro Lights. Still no one appeared. Dallas walked out through the back door. Maybe the guy was filling up a boat or working on the pumps. Suddenly, he saw a person sitting in a swing, the kind made for two people and set so one could watch the sun go down. It had a thatched roof and a sturdy rope system for the swing.

Dallas walked over to the person sitting in the swing and heard a familiar voice, a voice he hadn't heard in almost a year. The voice clearly said, "Why hello Streeter! Been awhile hasn't it?" Dallas wanted to puke! COX! Dallas crisply said in return, "Yeah been a while. What the Fuck are you doing on my island?" "Oh Streeter, no man is an island! You know that!" "That didn't answer my question COX!" "Oh, that? Well I just thought I'd stop by and talk." "Talk?" Dallas said, incredulously. "You want to talk to me? You have no jurisdiction out here!" "What? Two old friends can't get together and talk out here?" "What two old friends?" Dallas asked. "You – Me – Us, WE aren't friends COX, you tried to screw me at the last minute, back when I gave you a serial killer named Skeets! Remember?" "Oh, that, well you were always one or two steps ahead of me Dallas, I had to make it look good, ya know, for the paperwork and all!" "Yeah I bet! COX," Dallas shot back. "Listen COX, get to the point!" "OK Streeter, the point is that . . . You mean you didn't get my message I sent out here?" "No. What Message?" "Well" Dallas, you probably don't know this, but our old friend Ernie Skeets – You remember him – Sycophant-Killer with a real hard-on for you by the way." "Yeah! What about him, Cox?" "Well when his old partner Henry McCluskey talked him out of that sinking sailboat, well, he didn't secure him real well. And Ole Skeets slipped his cuffs. We think that he had his own key hidden, and Henry didn't search him except for weapons, and with all that Cocaine floating in the water and the boat sinking . . ." "SINKING? Cox, it was in 4 feet of water. Jeez!" Dallas voiced loudly. "Yeah, yeah, we know that.

But everyone else thought different. "Therefore?" Dallas asked again. "Well Skeets slipped his cuffs and jumped out of the Black Hawk. "YOU have ta be shitting me COX!" "Nope, got clean away." "C'mon Cox, he was shot twice and tripping his ass off on mushroom juice!" "Oh that's what the stuff was!" Cox interjected. "Man, he thought we were aliens and taking him to a mother ship." "BUT HE STILL ESCAPED? "Yeah, poor old Henry, his old partner lost his pension behind this one." "Ya know something Cox? You guys are for real scumbags." "No Shit! Well that's not why I'm here." "Then why are you here?" "Got a beer?" "No," Dallas said, holding a case under his arm. He tore open the case, and gave one to Cox, too. "Thank you." "Yeah, no prob." Dallas said. "So what's the deal?"

Cox began telling Dallas about how rogue agent Skeets has been seen in several places in and around the Carib Basin, which is anywhere between Jamaica, south to Central America. "Last reported sighting that was confirmed was in Belize. Our Intelligence has him hooked up with the Mexican Cartels and he is selling them information and giving up the names of our agents down that way. However, here is where it involves YOU. Seems you have a younger brother, don't you?" "Yeah, and he is in school, Cox." "He's what, a graduate of U of Arizona, and in his second year of law school, NO?" "That's right," Dallas replied. "OK. Here's what we know about your little brother R.C. Streeter." Cox was now looking at a folder that Dallas hadn't seen because Cox was sitting on top of it. "Let's see, Randall Chance Streeter, D.O.B 12/18/61, Adrian, Michigan. Hey Streeter, how come you didn't bring him into the family business?" "Because it wasn't for him. I gave him a choice: A full ride to school only if he became what I should have, a lawyer, or join me and die young or all fucked up."

"What a choice. So you have had him insulated all this time. We didn't even know about him until two of his best friends disappeared and were found dead in the Mexican desert." "Cox, don't tell me that kid was fucked over for a thrill of a deal." "No, he wasn't. His friends were, though! As far as we know, R.C is still alive. We think Skeets is going to ransom him off to you! I'm here, Dallas, to make sure you don't get involved, and I mean at all! We have it covered; we know where he is and who's holding him. What's the date today?" "Hmm, the 7th of May, Cox." "We have a guy going in as you, a Special Op's guy. Even looks like you. If it's Skeets, and we think it is, we are gonna bring him in dead or alive." Dallas stood there in shock. The more he heard, the more he got sick. "I should have killed that son of a bitch when I had the chance. Now look what has happened. And I'm supposed to trust you guys with my little brother's life"? "LOOK, Cox put his finger in Dallas chest. YOU STAY OUT! That goes for your buddy Harvey, too." "OK," Dallas said, (he was lying as fast as he was thinking). "Yeah, OK Cox, you guys have all the resources, and the Intel, just tell me this – What Family has Skeets been selling his soul to?" "The Amada's. I know you know them," Cox said. "Oh yeah," Dallas said, "but I have only done one or two deals with them in ten years, and I'm retired now and they know it." (All lies). Dallas was working out a rescue plan as he lied in the face of a guy he couldn't trust to change the toilet paper roll in the bathroom. Off in the distance Dallas could hear the unmistakable sound of a Customs Blue Thunder Boat coming around the point. Cox looked at his watch "Well Dallas, that's my ride. I hope you heed my warning! We have it handled . . ." "OK Cox, don't fuck up, this is my brother were are talking about, and unless you want me to get out my old debt sheet from around the world, don't screw this one up!" "Cause you will, never mind!" Dallas stopped short of the threat.

Dallas loaded the beer and the smokes into the cart; his mind was spinning, Fucking Cox of all people, and what message? What was that all about? All the way back to the house he thought, what, or who, got R.C. into this shit? He had nothing to do with anything like he did, all his bills were paid, he had another year to go in law

school and was the first one in the family to have done everything
by the book. No drugs, no legal problems, not even a speeding
ticket. Nice women, nothing to prove to the family. A genuine
first-rate citizen. This was aimed at me! It wasn't the Ochoa's in
Colombia. "Hmm, that's a thought. Old Man Ochoa, he moves
ninety percent of his shit through Mexico now that I'm retired."
He wrestled with the thought of coming out of retirement to get
close to Old Man Ochoa. "Nah, that's exactly what Cox is waiting
for." In fact, Dallas was starting to think that the whole visit today
was more about getting him to make a move like that. He didn't
give a shit about my brother! "OK, that's one way of looking at it,"
Dallas thought. As he drove, he started to think clearly. "The next
move is to verify what Cox has told me." Who, he thought. Then it
came to him as he passed the Frogs mansions: HENRY! That's it,
er, whom! Henry has to be pissed off that they fucked him out of
his pension. Hell, he wasn't even an active agent when they asked
him to help bring out his ex-partner. Then what they call the chain
of evidence should have changed as soon as Skeets was in the
Blackhawk, meaning Henry was no longer responsible for Skeets
once in active government hands. Henry has got to have an axe to
grind, if for no other reason than to measure a man's worth after
twenty some years being the good soldier. Even when that included
covering the agency's ass when he knew it was lies, and innocent
people went to jail for it. Moreover, many did, and many more still
do. They call it "The Fix," or evidence tampering for the number of
closed cases. Morally wrong, but a fact in the DEA. In fact, Dallas
was sure that a guy like Henry kept a book - payoffs, rip-offs, when
information gained through Confidential Informants, and the C.I.
doesn't get his ten percent street value, or his what's called Motiay
rights, which is any and all property seized. When the outcome is
a conviction, and the supervising agents put it in their retirement
fund split in two.

So that's the starting point, that is after a visit to Carl Brewster in Jamaica to pick-up the Little Tiger! And ship it to Belize. Belize the only still English colony in the free world with English sterling as a currency, where Dallas could be able to access enough money to out-finance the DEA on short notice. Next problem. The Chief. "That I work on in the morning," he thought.

Here it was, May 7th, 1986. On the heels of the shuttle Challenger disaster, the whole government was in total chaos. They shut down the space program, and many satellites were now being used exclusively for military purposes. The cold war was still on. This opened windows of opportunity. Dallas knew that hundreds of drug flights resumed, and he was thinking about how to approach The Chief with the confidence needed to make the moves that were gonna be necessary to put together a rescue operation. Thank God for a ready cash flow. And a secret project that had arrived four months earlier while Janis was in the states closing down the assets left behind while they set-up home in a new country.

Chapter 2

T he Chief climbed the last two steps that took him up to street level. He stopped and looked down the street, first back towards his boat, and then in the direction he was going. Everything looked normal to the naked eye, but it wasn't seen but felt that put him on more of an edge than he usually had to go out just to the bait and tackle shop. As he walked down the shoreline street, the water was on the left with other charter boats, along with rows of shrimpers and conch boats. On the other side were the stores, shell shops and fresh fruit and vegetable stands, all painted bright colors with their wares out, and the smell mixed nicely with the fresh fish shops and stands.

Tall Banyan and Fichus trees grew along the street further up. The street had about a twenty-degree slope upwards towards the hills above, the Royal Poinciana trees were in bloom, ablaze in red and others with yellow. The Chief started to see what he felt. "Newbies," as they are called on the island. They were for the most part young guys. They milled about outside a clothing store that sells a lot of surf gear, sunglasses, and island style dress, which in other words means they sold shorts and sandals, and comfortable cotton shirts. He knew almost by instinct that they were in transit DEA recruits. It wasn't the haircuts, some had already begun to grow out their hair and first beards. The dead giveaway was their shoes, almost all had on the same style of new Reebok tennis shoes, shoes you can't buy on the island yet. A little bit further up the street he did see a face he had seen many times before. This guy was a known drug dealer and snitch. A guy that would sell a tourist a bunch of drugs and then turn them in back at their hotels. He was thirty-something and trying not to be noticed.

The Chief walked into his favorite bait and tackle shop, He bought a half dozen rigged Ballyhoo, and a ten-pound block of frozen chum, just as he would for any charter. He paid and told the kid to deliver it to his gate, and to wrap it good so it would not melt for at least an hour or so. As he stood inside the shop, he noticed the doper; his long blonde hair and island wear with very worn sandals walk by three or four times as the Chief wandered around the shop. He knew he was being followed now. He finished his business and left the store and walked up the street to a shop that he knew had a back door that led to an alley. He walked into this store that sold cold drinks, snack foods and fresh milk and cheese, he waved and said hello and walked straight through to the back door and out into the alley. He followed the curve back around behind the buildings.

The long hair was standing at the corner of the alley and the street. The Chief calmly walked up behind him and grabbed a handful of hair and pulled him backwards into the alley and grabbed his right-hand thumb and bent it back while putting him in a hammer lock. "OK, you nasty little philistine fuck! Who are ya? And why are you following me?" "Hey, hey Man what's with all the hostility? I'm just a messenger." "A Messenger? What do ya mean by that? Turd!" "I mean I was told to give you something." The Kid was wearing a tiger shark tooth around his neck on a leather braided strap. The Chief let go of his hair, swung him around, and grabbed his shark's tooth, held it between his fingers and put it to his neck. "What message?" "Hey man, I'm bleeding!" "Oh yeah, that's the shark's tooth! I'm gonna cut your head off with it, or maybe just this ear." And he moved it up over to his left ear. "No, no, need for all this, man really!"

The Chief patted him down for weapons, but all he found was two dollars and an unopened envelope. "Yeah, man, that's it, the message." "What, the letter?" "Yeah man, that's IT!" "Ok! Who gave it to you and why?" "Hey man why do people do anything?" "What! Don't get smart with me you scumbag," and with that, the Chief stepped on his big toe with his deck shoes on his sandal-clad foot. "Ouch, man that hurts!" "Yeah I bet. Now who sent you?" "Who do you think? The man." "What man?" The Chief demanded." "THE MAN", as in "D.E.A. MAN" ya know? All I was told is that you would know what to do with it. That is ALL, I ain't kidding, just give it to you and that you would give me ten bucks." The Chief broke out in laughter . . . "TEN BUCKS, shit, you're lucky I don't break you into little pieces and use this shark's tooth in a very creative way on you. Shit, TEN BUCKS! OK, riddle me this Batman!" The Chief said. "What's with all the Newbies in island?" "All are new DEA in transit, that's all I know about that." "Really, is there anything else I should know before either I hurt you a lot more, or I let you go?" "NO man I was told to give this to ya, and... ""Yeah, I know, Ten Bucks!" said the Chief. "Listen Jim, today's your lucky today. I'm just gonna turn you loose and keep this," holding up the envelope. "Let me give you a little advice Sonny Jim! You really suck at this line of work! So hit the bricks, and if I even see you again on my block again for weeks, I will make good on my promise to take this shark tooth to you in a most un-pleasant manor! READ ME?" as he stepped on his big toe harder. "Now go smoke your shit or whatever you do and get out of my sight. Got It?" "Oh ya, Mon I got it!" With that, the Chief pushed him out into the street and down on his knees and elbows. When the kid looked back, there was no one there. The Chief backtracked himself into the store he came through, said his good by and watched as the now dirty long hair passed by the windows and up the street. The Chief ducked out and was gone into the tourist-filled street. "TEN BUCKS! Ahahahaha, that's funny," he thought as he walked back to his boat. Hell, the best part of that guy ran down his mother's leg. Fucking Nimrod!

He cut a corner while headed down the steps to the main dock back at his boat and caught an edge of his left shoe on a full bloom Hibiscus bush root. His knee went out and down he went to all fours. All he could think of besides the random fuck, shit and goddamn it, was the old saying to stop and smell the flowers! Flowers my ass, His face was two inches from a half frozen ten-pound block of fish assholes, better known as Chum. Got a nice rigged Ballyhoo hook in the deal too. He picked himself up and struggled for his keys to get in his gate. Thank God the dock is wooden and not concrete as the tenants wanted a couple months back. He could just see himself in a cast or worse had it had been concrete. That's all he would have needed, a broken wrist or shattered kneecap.

He managed the gate and hefted the block of chum first, then grabbed-up the Ballyhoo and threw them both in the freezer side of one of the on deck electric refrigerators. He walked over to a salon couch and put his leg up. Sonata came up the stairs from the lower berths and laundry areas and asked "Martian, would you like a beer?" Then she asked, "What happened?" "I was attacked by sharks, honey, but I won. So hell yeah I'll have that beer darling." She went into the kitchen area and produced two beers. "One for now, and one for after," She said. "After what?" he asked. "After the first of course, silly." The Chief smiled and chuckled at the same time. "Of course!" He repeated. "I have a charter tomorrow. Do you want to go along? We are going to see Dallas . . ." Sonata, who had never met Dallas but had heard many stories of him, jumped at the invitation. "Oh yes, I must go and meet this man I have heard so much about!" "You mean the man that I have lied so much about, don't you Sonata?" She had a puzzled look about her. "Any friend of yours is a friend of mine Martian, you know this." "And that's why I love ya," the Chief replied.

As the Chief lay there on the couch, he closed his eyes. The

letter he held in his hand had typed letters on it, D. S. that was it.
The rest was blank, He held it up to the light and could see some sort
of handwritten page in it. He darkly looked at it. This means trouble!
He ran his fingers around the outside edges. Yeah! Trouble . . .
Thinking what that miscreant had said. "You'll know what to do
with it!" He sat up and propped a pillow behind his back, then he
took the letter and folded it into a paper airplane and launched it
into the kitchen area. "Oh DAL. What have you gotten into now?"

Dallas ran his little cart into the garage and screeched to a halt.
He sat a moment to get his composure back. Finally he got out,
grabbed the beer and cigarettes out and walked into the house,
pressing the garage door button as he went. Janis and Olivia were
in the kitchen working on the evening meal. Dallas walked up and
gave Janis a kiss on the forehead and walked out, not saying a word.
He walked around a corner to the left and headed past the game
room to a what seemed a coral rock wall. Before he did anything
else, he used a remote control to turn on the stereo, and then broke
a rack of pool balls on the table, sinking the Nine Ball. All this was
for the ladies' sake. He wanted them to think he was back in the
game room fooling around. It worked because the two ladies didn't
even break stride in the kitchen.

It was only then that he went to the coral rock wall and found
the hinged ring hidden behind a four by four-inch piece of coral and
gave the wall a push. The hidden coral door was perfectly balanced
on ball bearings. A one-inch stainless steel shaft ran the length of
the door on to the ball bearings enclosed in a circular race, one at
the top, another at the bottom. The door opened without a whisper
and he was in and closed it behind him. Janis knew about the old
boathouse, but thought the only way in was if one walked all the
way around the side of the house on an un-kept old wooden dock.
Plus, it had a pull down link gate that was painted to match the coral
rock cliff and a blue waterline. He always told her it was in too bad
a condition to be used and was better off left alone.

The smell of aviation gas was heavy. He flicked a switch and twin turbine exhaust fans slowly started to spin on the top of the cliff hidden amongst the sea grape trees. Two one-hundred-gallon fuel tanks lined the back wall, along with a built-in double-decked Snap-On toolbox. Also at the back was a wooden door. He flicked on that light and it revealed a large walk-in machine shop, carved out of solid coral rock. A recently installed four-foot wide walkway ran the perimeter of the room. On the walkway were boat cleats. He stepped on the aft one first, to check tension and scope to allow for tide shift. He repeated the same process all the way around, bending to loosen one on the starboard side.

After the fumes had been vented, it smelled like a new car show room. He walked back around to the port side and leaned over and undid two snap buckles, placing two fingers in a flush mounted latch he lifted the Plexiglas port side of a hatch. The rubber gaskets gave and the sound of a coffee can opening with a vacuum met his ears. "Ah, I love that sound," he thought to himself. The smell of new leather and electronics filled his nose. He reached up and ran his fingers down the leading edge of the port side wing. The newly invented micron mesh composite felt like fine grain sandpaper. It's actually a fine octagonal screen, only microns across. If bent, say into a half ball shape, it would look like a microscope sized geodesic dome. Its strength would have to be measured in the ten to the ten thousandth power at this size. Incredibly strong.

The Chief laid his head back and stared at the ceiling. Almost a clean get away! Jezz! He closed his eyes again and the last year rolled like a movie in his head. "C'mon Chief, just a couple days in beautiful Jamaica! OK, first it was Ramon Chavez, Dead! The guy that picked Dallas's locks at his condo and Janis, leaving, pulled the door open while Chavez was on his knees. She kneed him in the face. Massive head trauma caused by Janis's knee right between the eyes. Lenny Dead! Wayne killed him for making a phone call to the rogue DEA agent, Wayne Dead! Killed by that Rogue DEA agent the same night. Sydney, Marboy's nephew, Dead! Shot in the leg by the same rouge DEA agent during interrogation. Hit in the femoral artery, he bled out before he made it to the hospital in Mo-bay. Oh and the Topper! Ochoa and his pilot, whom I killed with a L.A.W. rocket down the tail pipe of Ochoa's helicopter . . . Officially died from catastrophic engine failure due to hydraulic failure. Least that's how the papers wrote it." The Chief could still smell and feel the sweat, along with the burning wreckage, a hundred yards away. Up-wind. His finger still feels funny when he thinks of it. And wishes it wouldn't. BUT it is just a couple DAZE in Jamaica Chief, C'mon..."

"Yeah," he thought, "just a couple days, chased and almost killed by that rouge agent on the boat that night in Great Inagua, Bahamas. Now This? Shit. And oh yeah! I completely forgot about Benny, the personal bodyguard of Ochoa's. Yeah, forgot him, Dallas in a kill or be killed over the money thing with the yellow Mercedes, yeah, Dal shot him while taking a piss. Hmm, never have figured that one out yet, man that was only a year ago, too."

He opened the other beer Sonata had brought him earlier, took a long tug on the bottle and looked at it through the light. Well, everything tells me this bottle is half-full, yet to some it's half empty. "Hey Sonata! Ya got everything we need for tomorrow ready?" "Yes, Martan (the Chief) I do, how long are we gonna be gone?" she asked innocently. Martin answered, slowly looking in the direction of the folded airplane letter sticking vertically out of the drain hole in the sink over his shoulder. "I really don't know baby. It doesn't matter, does it? We are on the boat, I don't have any charters, do I?"

"No, not until the last day in May, I think" she said, looking at a calendar. "Yup, the last day in May, I have it circled. It's a Russian guy and his wife." "Oh, great! A fucking Commie turned Capitalist. Is it circled in RED? Hahahah Fuck!"

Chapter 3

Sonata was in the forward V-berths turning the mattresses over so no mold would build up. The forward V-berth is the dampest end of the boat because of the chain locker storage compartment, and the two six by ten windows on each side over each bunk. That and the most forward eighteen by eighteen-inch tinted escape and vent hatch. She lifted the center cross board that connected the two V-berths into one large two-person bunk. She liked these quarters best, it had its own private shower stall and closet across from it, and with the door closed it afforded more privacy than anywhere else on the boat. The other two staterooms just down the passageway only had two windows that opened from the inside and the beds were queen sized. Only the forward V-berth had the skylight effect. A common shower was located in between the starboard staterooms, which the singles used, and a common closet was directly across the companionway for the guest to use.

Down from there was three steps up to the galley and lounge salon. The galley was large, with double sinks, granite counter tops, a Jenn air indoor gas grill and mid-sized Sub-Zero combo fridge and freezer unit. Plus all the normal kitchenware's that one would expect on a Hatteras Sport Fisherman of this size. While she worked, she felt the main generators start-up. She heard the electrical system start to hum also, somebody was starting the boat! Just after that thought the engines cranked over. She hustled up the steps and out on to the deck just behind the fighting chair. The hatches were raised to vent fumes, and she saw The Chief's legs in the air, as he was belly down with his head inside the engine compartment. He was checking the Racor fuel separators for water, and looking over the engines for leaks and or hisses that might suggest leaks in the hydraulic lines or cooling systems. She walked around the fighting chair and gently kicked the Chief in the ankle "Shit!" He yelled "What? That's my bruised ankle from this morning Sonata." "Sorry, but are we going somewhere?" She asked. "Yeah, go forward and handle the bowlines, will ya? Please." "MARTIN are we going somewhere?" She asked again. "YES! I already told you, yes we are." He picked himself up and closed the two engine hatches. Sonata, still standing there, asked "Where?" He looked at her - she had never seen the look he gave her before. "I thought we were leaving in the morning?" He didn't answer her. He went forward and undid the bowlines himself, then hustled back down the gunnel and cast off the stern lines too. He didn't say a word as he climbed the first of two fly-bridge ladders and kneeled on his captains' chair and took the Hatteras out of its slip; He turned to port and headed out the channel.

Sonata stood below looking at him, bewildered, as the boat headed out into the open ocean. Finally, the Chief looked down at her and said, "Look everybody else thinks we are leaving in the morning too." "Who is everybody?" She asked. He looked back at the channel, and then down at her. "Everybody!" Sonata looked around the deck. While getting her sea legs, she noticed that even the shore power line, while coiled neatly in the starboard corner, had still been done in a hurry - It hadn't been stored under the deck in its hatch. She went to the ladder that led up to the fly bridge and strode up it, skipping every other rung. At the top, the Chief was busy navigating the channel markers towards the open water beyond. "So? Do you want to tell me what is happening or am I supposed to guess?" "In a second love, I'll tell you everything that I know, but until then have a seat next to me while I get us out of here."

As soon as he cleared the last channel marker, he looked back at what was maybe the last look of a place he had grown to like very much. Sonata had never seen the Chief in this mind set. It scared her only in the way the unknown scares any thinking animal. All question marks and no substance to base the fear on. She certainly wasn't afraid of the man she had grown to love over the past year, because his presence inspired respect and confidence alone knowing that he would never let harm come to her. Obviously, there was a deeper reason than a flight of fancy to take to the water in what looked very much to a layperson as making a run from something. "No, that was not it," she thought. We were making a run to something, not from it. She didn't ask again about any of it. She knew he would tell her when he was ready, and she was ready to hear it.

It was almost three o'clock in the afternoon and miles from shore that he turned to her and began, "Sonata, you know I love you. I think I love you more than I have ever loved any one person in my life. And the truth is I have never been completely honest with you. Which isn't fair to you, and you deserve better." It was an over three-hour run to Dallas's island house. During that time, he talked about how he had landed on Trinidad in the first place. Then took her back even farther, to the days while on the run from the French, his time in Bolivia working as a security advisor for the drug lab and the horrible night and flight from a drug lord that probably would have never have let him leave after the killing of the Quanto natives. How Dallas pulled his ass out of the fire and put him back in into society. Gave him a job, albeit as a smuggler. But he was what he was, and that was a person that never forgot friends. He described how he had many high friends in low places, and of course the source of his money. He also described the same about low enemies in high places as well. The kind of enemies that they were avoiding at this very moment. People that could not leave well enough alone.

He looked at her. He thought how beautiful she looked, wearing only a tank top that gave away her figure, the figure of a thirty-something island girl. Her long brown hair was over her shoulders. He reached out and with a couple fingers held her chin up to look into her eyes. He was concerned that maybe he was going too far too fast. He looked for fear of him as he laid out his past in a clarity that would scare a lesser woman. What he found was no fear, no hesitation. Only acceptance of what she wanted to know for such a very long time now. Truth, and in that truth the comfort of a breakthrough to a higher place in his life. He asked; "Do you want to go back?" She looked forward, with a look he had never seen before in her. "I only have one question," she said. "And what is that, Sonata?" He answered. "How much longer do we have to go before we reached Dallas's Island House?" He smiled. "About an hour or so." He was a bit taken aback, because she never looked back to all she had ever known - she just looked ahead.

Dallas slid into the cockpit. Just to make sure, he leaned out to confirm the shore power was on. He visually traced the line from the plane back to the breaker box along the inside wall, six inches up off the floor of the walkway, satisfied that it was good and the power on, indicated by the red L.E.D lights that lit up the electrical system. A slight hum started as the planes electrical system sent a charge and the dashboard lights and panels came alive. A voice asked if power should be sent to the fuel system. He punched a button above the fuel system indicator and the voice said "Thank you." "Man! I just can't get over some of this shit!" He spoke aloud, and the voice asked please repeat the question. "No power to fuel system, negative." "Thank you" the voice answered. Dallas thought I better keep my mouth shut or this fucker will start the engines or something.

He reached up and activated the satellite telephone system, took out his wallet and pulled out a business card. Capt. Bob Richards, Day/Night charters, Tele# (305) 854-5500, Coconut Grove, Fla. 33133. Dallas checked the coaxial cable visually by tracing it from the hard line connector on the nose of the plane out over to the other side of the boat house wall, up the wall and out through the ventilation shaft to the unseen dish that sat between the two wind turbines on top of the ground at roof level with the house. "Jeeez, I hope that the sea grapes haven't over grown the dish." He dialed a phony number as a dry run. He could hear the sound of a signal beaming into space and bouncing off satellites. This is how it must sound calling the space station. Looking around the cockpit, Dallas found the voice activated systems switch and turned it off before actually placing the call. "Christ," he thought, "something I say might send the on board computer into putting me in space." Nope can't have that he thought. But he also thought about how in the event he was to get hurt or God forgive even shot, how handy it would be just to crawl into the pilot's seat and tell the plane what to do while he bled to death or something. OK, it works! I'd like to see those sons-o-bitches trace this call! He hadn't spoken to Capt. Bob since the day he paid him his $100,000 in cash and sent him home a year ago either. He hoped that he hadn't changed his number, Good old Bob, if he's not dead, he will help. For another big payday, that is. Some things never change.

Bob answered on the second ring. Dallas didn't go into many details, but he laid out a plan for Bob to be in Jamaica by the 12th of May. "That's five days, Bob, can you make it?" "Oh I think if the pay is good a good friend will be there," he said. While Dallas was laying out more details, he noticed a good-sized sport fisherman boat on the horizon line headed his way. It was almost sunset and all of a sudden, the boat turned on its spotlight. It blinked once, off, blinked again twice. "Why that old fucker, he remembers the visual runway signal!" Back when Dallas flew a lot of loads himself and the Chief was the ground crew coordinator, that was the signal that it was clean and green for approach. Thank God that the roll-up gate on the boathouse was linked and that one could see out better than see in, or he may have missed it. Dallas reached over and grabbed the handle for the plane's movable spotlight, aimed it at the sport fish and gave the same signal back. He closed out the call to Capt. Bob with a "Be there or be square," saying in code that it was a contract, and Capt. Bob replied "You bet buddy." That done, Dallas flipped on the voice-activated command again, and the voice toned ready. Dallas said "All systems to standby mode." The voice responded, "Standby mode activated, thank you. Have a nice day." Dallas shook his head and crawled out on to the walkway, turned and closed the cockpit.

Dallas could hear Janis calling for him as he reappeared back into the house. "Where have you been?" Janis asked with a cool eye. "Oh, I was out up on top fiddling with the TVs satellite dish love, how about you?" He threw back at her. "Looking for you." "Hmm, I guess we just missed each other, ya know I was one way, you another. Why? What's up?" "I think we are gonna have company Dal." "Yeah, I saw the big sport fish coming, when it signaled I knew who it is." "Well? Are ya going to tell me? Or ya gonna make me guess?" They walked out the lower level sliding glass doors at the pool and watched from on top as the sport fish got closer. "It is the Chief – he's early, like a day early." Janis looked at him with an "OK asshole, I caught you look." "Hey, don't look at me! I didn't know he was on his way today." He blurted. "Hmmm, going fishing?" She asked. "Well that was the plan." "I hope that's all yer planning on doing, you're retired, goddamn it. Or don't ya remember?" Dallas, without getting all defensive, cooled her off with a look, and a smile, she crossed her arms and turned around and went back in the house. "Fishing Huh? My ass." Was the last thing he heard as the doors shut behind her.

Actually Dallas was so friggin happy to see that boat early that he knew that she knew something was up. He had overheard her and Olivia talking before he went in the boathouse about he has not been the same since he got back from the beer run this early afternoon. They were on about how Janis was worried about him. And how it was just a feeling, but . . .

While the Chief slid his big sport fish up next to the tee head at the end of the dock, Sonata tucked her hair up and under a Detroit Tigers baseball hat and walked down the ladder from the fly bridge to the main deck. Dallas stood at the top of the stairs at pool level watching. He did not recognize this person. Who is that? He reached over to the electrical box that switches on and off the dock foot lights that run the length of the dock and around the tee head. He opened it with a key from his key ring – the person below was starting to throw the shore power line on to the dock as Dallas pulled out a fifteen shot Berretta that was neatly hung on inside. He closed the box and stuffed the gun in his back waistband. Still standing there he watched as this person ran the shore power line to the electrical box at the corner of the tee head.

Small for a guy he thought, but then again these islands are full of Orientals and native peoples that are small in stature. Then the hat fell off and he could see that He was a She. "Oh shit, I bet that's Sonata, the Chief's new squeeze." Dallas had never met her, but she fit his description from a year ago. Then out from under the canopy the Chief himself climbed down the ladder to the main deck. No mistake here, that red hair and mustache was a dead giveaway, even at this distance.

Dallas relaxed a bit and started walking down the stairs to the dock and then out to the tee head. The Chief was just finished tying off the bowline and placing fenders between the dock and the boat. He still hadn't seen Dallas walking out yet and jumped back in his boat, Sonata saw Dallas first, and smiled and pointed towards the cockpit, when a thunderous voice came out from the boat. "Ok! Sonatas kill him now!" Dallas stopped dead in his tracks and his hand went behind him and found the handle of the Beretta. "JUST

KIDDING! Sonata, give Dallas a big kiss for me! I'll be up in a second." "Hi, I'm Sonata," walking over and giving Dallas a peck on his cheek. "Well thank you. love." Dallas offered. He let go of the Beretta, and returned the kiss. Finally, the Chief came up over the side and gave Dallas a hug. He could feel the gun in Dallas waistband. "Do ya always greet old friends wearing a gun, Dal?" "No! I don't, I just wasn't expecting to see what looked like a small guy on board, but then I saw the hat fall, saw a she instead of a he, and deduced that it had to be you. But why are you early Chief?" "That's another story all together, and it involves you as a matter of fact." Dallas turned from looking over the Chief's sport fish walked over and looked him in the eye. "Yeah, some strange shit happening today, we'll have to talk about it. I am glad you are early though. So why don't you and Sonata come up to my new digs and that way she and Janis can get to know each other." Dallas pointed towards the two flights of stairs up to the house.

The Chief and Sonata started walking behind Dallas when the Chief noticed the 51' Morgan on the right. "Dallas, you really did like that boat didn't ya?" "Yeah, Chief, I love sailing this boat. I have it rigged just like the one we lost in Great Inagua on the rocks. So I went out and bought the best one around, and that was not easy, just finding one took the better part of a month. But look left, Chief." "Wow! Is that the same damn Scarab?" "Yupper Chief, remarkable what a new paint job and a few decals can do, huh?" "Ya Mon, even I wouldn't have guessed it except for the three 200 Ocean Runners on her." Dallas smiled when he said it. "I have a crew come in and clean them once a month." "What!" The Chief said, "you let strangers come out here?" "They ain't strangers, they are my live-in maid's sons. Do a damn nice job too." "Whoa! Live-in maid?" "Hell yeah, why not? It gives Janis someone to bitch at besides me all the time. Yeah, she gives them a laundry list of food and stuff, they are the step and fetch bunch! Least that's what I call them. I mean you could never use them for a real job, like a run, but they are good kids, don't steal and do what they are told, and paid to do so."

They reached the top of the stairs. Dallas unlocked the electrical box and put the Beretta back in its place, closed, and locked it. "Nice touch," said a winded Chief as they waited for Sonata to catch up. The Chief gazed around the pool area, taking in the waterfall, the river rock around the pool area. The last light of day was pushing through the sea grapes and casting long shadows. Sonata caught up and the three of them made their way around the pool and to the house. Sonata reached out and touched the Chiefs elbow. He looked at her and she was pointing at all the things like the waterfall. Things she had never seen before in a person's back yard, only in the wild. She pulled him down to ear level and like a giddy kid, asked if all Americans live like this. The Chief, embarrassed by the thought said, "No, very few Sonata, very few." Janis knocked on the window upstairs and waved at the Chief and Sonata to come up. Dallas waved back and shook his head yes, and opened the sliding glass door into the lower level.

The Chief stepped slowly inside, all the while looking around. He saw how the house was actually carved into the side of the cliffs. He really liked Dallas's eight-foot old-style mahogany pool table, and the bar built into a side wall with its refrigerator and freezer. He walked over to the desk at the opposite far end of the room and saw all the electronics. "Hell, if I didn't know better Dal, I'd say you were still in the bizz!" "Ah, that ain't nothing, why don't we take Sonata upstairs and introduce her to Janis, and we'll come on back down here and shoot a game and talk. Ya know trade some news . . . Wink, Wink." "Yeah, that's a great idea let's do that." Dallas led the way up the spiral staircase that to the Chief looked like it was carved out of one piece of solid wood "Nice," he said on the way up. "What's that?" Dallas asked. "These stairs." "Oh that. Yeah, if you're into stairs," he laughed. By the time they reached the upper level kitchen area, Janis already had cold dark Beck's in bottles out on the counter.

She saw the Chief and walked over and gave him a big hug, "Nice ta see ya, Chief, you're looking well, must be this womans doing I bet." "Yeah, this is Sonata. Janis, Sonata, Sonata, Janis." "Nice to meet you Sonata," Janis was obviously being Canadian, and very pleasant. "Please have a seat." Janis motioned to the bar stools that surrounded the wood-topped food preparation island. "Yeah why don't ya all get to know one another?" Dallas pulled Janis out of earshot for a second. "Listen honey, this chick don't know a lot about what or how we are here, so keep it on the down low, if ya know what I mean . . ." Janis looked at Sonata as she spoke. "Don't worry, with her living with the Chief I already figured as much, OK?" "Hey, Chief let's go shoot some pool and bullshit for a while, huh? How's that sound?" "Great, Dal." He grabbed the beers and they slid down the banister like a couple kids playing. Dallas, closely followed by the Chief, landed on the slate floor, laughing. The Chief walked over to the pool table and racked the balls, nine-ball style. Dallas walked quietly over to his desk and reached up to the media center, turned on the stereo, and flipped through a file of CD's.

Somewhere in the desert, headed south, trouble was on the road. And it was hot . . .

"Thirsty! Oh, I'm so THIRSTY!" He had been riding in the trunk of a car for what must be days now. All he could think about was how thirsty he was. His tongue was starting to swell in the back of his throat from lack of water, his lips were chapped and starting to crack. In the dark, Dallas's little brother had been chilled to the bone at night, and over-heated all three days and nights he was in the trunk of a car headed to, as far as he was concerned, nowhere. Just thirst was all that now occupied his mind now – He was drifting in and out of reality. One hour he felt no bumps in the road, only to be awakened by so many bumps his head hurt from hitting it on the lid of the trunk.

The three large bullet holes in the lid of the trunk were his only link with the outside world. His mind flashed back and forth between seeing his two friends killed while they sat next to him in the back seat of a rented Ford. Killed and dumped like so much trash on the side of a barren plain, a road with no landmarks. A road in the desert. A road with no name. It was all supposed to be so simple. Pool their money, drive across the border and to a farm. Party a while and take their pick of products. School was getting expensive. Once the product was picked and followed back to an underground tunnel system, and the just walk it back across the border to a safe house, split up and meet back up at school. All so simple! Big brother Dallas would be proud.

Something had, has, gone terribly wrong! He could hear Mexican radio stations on the car's radio. He could hear one fade out, and another fade in. His mind! He had to get control of his mind! As time passed, so did the incline at which the car traveled. He tried to move his hands – he pulled on his bindings behind his back and felt the tension pull his legs back. He was hog-tied, hands behind his back tied with leather straps and with another leather strap from his wrists to his ankles. Blackness was replacing the light that filtered in through the three bullet holes. Obviously, the holes were there for air and he could smell the smells that were carried by the rising humidity. Then finally, he heard in the thunder in the distance, and soon he felt the car sliding back and forth on a slippery road, as if the tires now followed a grooved track. The thunder clapped overhead and his thoughts were replaced by the sound of rain slapping the trunk and soon little torrents flowing in through the three open bullet holes. "Thirsty! Water!" He strained, lifting his head to capture a steady stream into his mouth. As the water replenished his body, his mind began to clear. "Not too much, not to fast!" His college education kicked in. Slowly, slowly he took it in. The smell of rainforest now permeated his tiny space. The car never slowed its steady pace as the driver worked the gutters the tires rode in as if he had done this many times before. They were on a steady incline for what were probably only minutes, but seemed like hours. As long as that water flowed in his holes, he could take more after the initial shock of wet wore off and his swollen tongue started to feel normal again.

As the Mexican radio stations faded, new ones, different ones began. These were mixed with English. "Where the fuck am I?" A large bump threw him into the air and he landed hard. Then it ended, and the bumps and ruts were gone. He was on a paved road again, and he felt the car pick up speed. Then he heard it! A radio station call sign, with it a strongly mangled British accent, and the time, "9:48 pm at KBLZ and don't forget the beaches people, they be nice dis' time of year!" At that, the radio went silent. That was the last thing he heard for the rest of the night.

Finally, the car stopped. He had no idea how long he had been asleep, but the heat from the trunk hood suggested that it was probably around 11:00 or 12:00 in the afternoon. Apparently, fatigue had set in and he was losing a sense of time. He faded in and out. As he awoke, Chance could smell the ocean, or was it a dream? No, that was the beach he could smell. More and more his mind raced after two and a half days of the blackness of a trunk. He heard a car door open – it was on the driver's side. As that door closed, a new one opened on the passenger side. He heard heavy footfalls coming down the side. The sound of the key in the lock and a shadow passed a bullet hole at the same time. It was almost dark and the shadows were long as the trunk opened fast. He smelled a cheap cologne, disgusting sweat and grease in general. A big paw of a hand rolled him over and Chance felt a sharp jab from a needle stick in his hip. "Hey, fuck you!" "No, fuck you," he heard distinctly in perfect Miami-accented English. The trunk slammed shut again.

"How much did you give him?" "I give him da same amount as

last time. Five minutes and he be back to sleep." "OK, I don't want him dead, asshole! Just out, OK?" That was all Chance heard as the nearly pure heroin began to allow the sweet arms of Morpheus to massage his Modula Oblongata. Chance was nodding out so fast now that all he heard was the trunk open again, as he tried to hang on. It was a battle he shortly lost. "Jeez! I swear I will fucking kill you if this kid overdoses, Pepe!" "My name is not Pepe!" It was at this point that Ernie Skeets looked at Fernando, and spit. "I don't much give a shit what your spic name is! Just hope this kid don't dose on your watch!" "Yeah OK! I hear you Mister Skeets – no harm will come, only a habit." "You hope!" Skeets shot back in a violent tone. "Now get him out of the trunk and into the house." Skeets hadn't noticed that his conversation was being carefully listened to by the owner of this 2700 sq. ft. beach house. The camera closely followed as Fernando hefted the now limp body out of the Ford. "And when you're done with him, clean this fucking car. It has blood all over the back seat." "Yeah, yeah, I know," Fernando struggled to say as one of Chance's limp arms smacked him in the side of the head. Ernie was caught off guard as one of the four garage doors swung up and open. Standing there in the dim light was Mr. Francisco Amada himself.

Ernie froze in place as Mr. Armada's glare caught his eyes. He was not alone. Out of the darkness stepped two extremely ugly bodyguards. They both carried Mac 10 machine pistols. "Help that man with that boy!" he snapped, without removing his glare on Skeets. "This better be good!" slammed Skeets in the ears. "Oh, um . . . It is a personal thing, Mr. Amada! Really." "I told you never come here unless I call you, Skeets!" Skeets reached behind his back as the bodyguard's guns came up at the same time. He slowly retrieved a wallet from his back pocket and handed it to one of the guards, who handed it to Amada. "I think this might help," he offered. Amada took the wallet and shook it in his face. "I will have nothing to do with your personal problems, I owe you nothing! You cannot bring your victim here to my home! You take me as a fool or you have no respect. I am not in the kidnapping business." He told one of his guards to turn on a light. The guard opened the door to the house as Amada opened the wallet. A shaft of light lit the room just enough for Amada to examine the wallet. The first thing Amada saw was the picture of a young man in his twenties. He carefully scanned the picture and finally his eyes fell on the name, Randall Chance Streeter. Amada quickly shut the wallet and threw it back at Ernie, hitting him in the forehead. "Put that boy in the maid's bedroom off the garage, and come upstairs!"

Amada turned and walked quickly back inside the main house as the guard and Fernando hefted Chance's limp body across the backside of the cars parked in the garage. Ernie followed, watching, telling Fernando, "Watch him, don't let that kid die! He's my insurance policy!" He barked. Ernie then was escorted into the main house. Amada stood at the top of a flight of stairs, looking down on Skeets as he wobbled with a limp up the stairs. "Time has not been kind to you Skeets! You look like you can hardly walk a flight of stairs. Are you well?" "Yeah I'm fine, just fine, thanks Frank." "That's Mr. Amada to you, Vato'." "Yeah, yeah, Frank you're lucky. Lucky that when I was a DEA agent that I never set my sights on you." "What was that, Vato'?" Amada asked. "Nothing, Mr. Amada. Nothing at all." "Good, I didn't think so. You will now go with Raul here," pointing at his guard, "and take a bath. You stink! I will not smell my home with you. Raul, take this Vato' to a bedroom and arrange for him, tu' savey?" "Si, Mr. Amada. You will follow me!" Raul took Skeets by a shoulder and turned him down a hallway. "Get yer damn hands off me, I can walk," Skeets managed to mumble. Ernie already thought it was strange how Amada changed his mind so quick. I'm glad I still think like a cop, Ernie thought to himself. "Be cool, jus be cool" he repeated over and over in his head, He knew he was in a lion's den. "Jus be cool."

Amada climbed the last flight of three stairs and stepped into his kitchen. His wife and the maid were setting the table for the evening meal. Amada was one of the last, great, great movers and shakers in the drug running business. He had strong feelings about this new way of making money, kidnapping for ransom. He believed that it brought bad things to a business that already was full of bad and quite insane people. Amada was raised in the old ways of doing business: Hold up your end of a deal and I will hold up my end. However, times were changing, not for the better. He wedged himself between his wife and the servant at the sink and washed his hands and face after touching the stinking Vato' ex-DEA agent. Of course, he excused himself first to his wife Lela and then to the servant. "We have company Lela, and fix a nice plate for, no, make that two plates for Fernando and a houseguest that will be staying in the extra maid's quarters for the next few days at least."

Amada turned to address the maid. "I want you to look in on that boy in room #2, take care of that boy, but do not let the Vato' Skeets see you. They are trying of make a heroin addict of him. What I tell you next is VERY important! I want you to get close to Fernando, steal his supply of heroin! I do not want that child an addict." Lela looked at the floor as she broke in. "Why my love do you care what the Vato' Skeets does with this boy? Who is he that you would take an interest in him, my love?" "That is between me and that boy! Enough now! Do what I tell you and do not speak of it again! Now get dinner finished, the Vato' DEA will be at our table tonight . . . Oh and Maria! I do not care if you have to sleep with Fernando, I want his drugs gone and brought to me by tomorrow or the next day! Now carry on with what you were doing, I'm sorry I disturbed you."

Amada walked out of a sliding glass door and sat on one of the hammocks gently swaying in the evening breeze of the Gulf of Mexico. "Randall Chance Streeter, that was the name on the drivers' card. That "escuria" Skeets!" In the garage, Amada had recognized the name at once. Swaying in the breeze, Frank Amada thought long and hard on how to what was taking place in his home. This could mean only one thing, and that was trouble. He thought, "I am tired of hiding this scum in my house, yet his secrets about the DEA had paid off. But I also have business with Dallas Streeter later this month, so I must talk with that boy downstairs, and I must talk soon." The sun burnt the thought of trouble brewing in his mind's eye. Ex-Agent Ernie Skeets, that Vato', was a person to be watched and could not be trusted. "What is the connection between him and Dallas Streeter? I've heard the rumors. Streeter has always performed his profession as a professional. Skeets? I jus don't know about him."

Chapter 4

Dallas needed to talk seriously with the Chief. He picked out some music that would cover any noises or conversations they were about to have. "C'mon Chief, I wanna show ya something! I think you'll get a kick out of it." Dallas, now that the music was playing, walked past the pool table and with his hand took the cue ball and slammed the nine-ball set up as hard as he could so Janis and Sonata could hear it upstairs. He looked back at the Chief, whose expression was one of total confusion and waved at him to follow him. Dallas quickly walked across the room over to the blank coral rock wall in front of him with the Chief in tow. Dallas pushed on a corner of a coral block in the wall, and to the Chiefs amazement, it flipped up and reveled a small ring. Dallas gently pushed with his other hand mid- way down the face. The coral rock wall opened almost 4 feet when Dallas caught it and held it open.

"Go in man! Quick!" The Chief sputtering a "what the fuck is this" and stepped inside with Dallas at his heels, closing the wall behind him. The Chief could smell aviation gas hanging heavy in the air. Dallas reached over and flipped on the exhaust fans. "There, that should clear the air." Dallas also hit the deck lights, which lit the room from lights installed in the walls. "Careful Chief, we only have four feet to walk on in here!" "I see that Dal. And I see trouble too! Is that a Goddamn airplane in your boathouse, Dallas?" "WELL YEAH, KINDA — SORTA! Well yeah Chief, it's

a DUCK actually!" "Does it quack to Dallas?" "Nah, but it hum's
very nice though . . ." "Oh, I bet," shot back the Chief. "I don't
want any part of this Dallas! You're at it again! You are aren't ya?"
"At what?" asked Dallas, with that tone that only the Chief knew
all too well. "IT! You know! "IT"!" "What, work? Oh that. Look
Chief, I am just tying up loose ends. We left the scene and still had
a few outstanding obligations. No? Like those Canuks that paid
for one hell of a nice Sportfish that you tool around in! Or have
you forgotten that? Remember? Chief we are not thieves, and we
didn't start last year. So like it or not, somebody has to make an
effort to right the boat, and not just write it off! Now that we have
been informed, that whomever, like "Skeets," has grabbed my little
brother doesn't give me many options, does it? So save the self-
righteous bullshit for someone else. I made you a rich man! And
I'm calling in that marker tonight!"

This whole time the Chief had spent walking around the little
seaplane, touching it here and there. Taking mental notes. By the
time the Chief got all the way around to the other side, he looked
across as Dallas finished his tirade, and said, a simple "You're right
Dallas. When do we leave?" "First, I think you better grab a beer
with me and let's take a walk down to the boats. Janis has probably
almost got our steaks done, so let's make an appearance, grab a
beer and tell them we'll back to eat in ten minutes. The plane and
how it got here is another story altogether. Let's go for a walk." Just
as Dallas predicted, Janis and Sonata had the dinner going strong
and were told as they walked through the kitchen, "OK boys, you
have fifteen minutes, and I mean fifteen, Dallas!" "OK, baby just
grabbing a beer and a look at the boats and we'll be right back,
honey. I hope Becks suits you Chief?" "Oh yeah, gotta love those
Becks," the Chief replied. "C'mon, you heard the lady! Fifteen
minutes." "Yup!" They hustled out before Janis could think of some
other thing to say.

They popped through the Sea Grape opening and down the

stairs. All the while, Dallas was setting the stage to pop the Chief with the biggie. They landed on the main dock and walked towards the Morgan 51' sailboat. Dallas paused. "OK, we are here." "Where?" the Chief asked with a grin. "Here," pointing at the Morgan. "Yeah, so? You know I've been in one just like it before." "Notice anything strange about this one Chief?" The Chief walked the length of it and back. "Nope, same as the one we gave up. Nice new paint job though. And it looks like it's ready to sail." "It is Chief; it is very soon. "Oh, are you going sailing?" "Well yeah, KINDA - SORTA!" "Oh, fuck no!" railed the Chief. You have to be kidding me." "No my friend, this boat spent three months in Port San Antonio in Jamaica. Our crew got her ready to go like it was a cookie cutter job of the last, without the prying eyes of that DEA agent Sands in Port Royal. Plus, it also has a beefed-up engine. Almost twice the speed of the old one. It will, with the roller-furling and twenty percent larger sails, will hold almost 17 knots with both doing their thing. And that's even to weather, how about that?" "Dal. You mean I'm standing looking at a fully loaded and ready to deliver boat?" "Is it ever! Ready to Rock and Roll! C'mon, more after dinner, I'll fill ya in with the plan. As you like to put it (as I remember) the who's, where's and why's. After all, you had to of figured out that I called you for a reason Chief. Let's eat!" "I ought ta kill you here and now Dallas!" "Save it for after dinner please, my last meal if you will?"

Capt. Bob Linden was one of Dallas's main captains from the golden age of Dinner Key Marina in Coconut Grove, Florida. The old docks there were once called, and still called, Seminole boat ramp by the few water buffalos that still live in the grove. At these docks Dallas embarked as a smuggler while still in his teens. He was a horse in the vernacular of the trade. It wasn't long before he was a driver and then and coordinator for the loads that slipped in and off-loaded tons of bales. It was at these very docks in the 1970's that while one boat was unloading, another was waiting on the back side of the spoil islands that surround the actual boat ramp with its small dock of only twenty-five or thirty feet. Everything from pick-ups to twenty-two foot trucks circled like vultures, each one waiting for a signal, each different from the next, to allow the truck in to meet its boat. Dallas, with radio in one hand and a hand held colored flashlight in the other, patrolled the area. Rip-offs were an on again, off again problem. When caught, they were dealt with in a very un-complementary way; being taken out of the lineup and then disappearing for the night. Same went for line jumpers. Caught the usually Spanish boat that was pushed away from the dock at gunpoint and told, come back at the end of the line or lose your load, because there was always an empty truck just waiting for this exact opportunity.

This was before the Mariel boat lift, and Americans controlled the dock, especially this dock! On one particular night Dallas counted no less than eight to ten different boats in the lineup. The vehicular traffic was so fast and furious that if it had not been for the legit boat traffic, there would have been headlines in the Miami Herald the next morning. It was after one or two, or he didn't remember, that Bob refused to unload there. The whole operation was moved south to Black Point Marina, or Jimbo's Marina on Virginia Key. Whatever Bob felt was dead on because Seminole Docks were busted within the month. After hundreds of loads (ours) it was a done deal. Time to learn how to fly. Dallas's crew was and had been a seagoing gang, but only a few had what it took to take to the air. Dallas was one of them; Jimmy (My Ways the Fly Ways) Kurtz was another. Capt. Bob still handled the airdrops at sea. In addition, he was responsible for deciding his point of entry. He was never busted. Bob was one that could be trusted. That's why he was now on his way to Jamaica. At first, the Haffler brothers started Dallas with short hops to the Bahamas, but soon Dallas scored his twin engine rating, and the is when the longer trips to Jamaica started. He quickly learned the payoff rates for airstrip owners and their crews. As expensive as it was, the size of the loads doubled and often tripled. And so did the money he made, it seemed at the time like a sea of cash. His teacher, oldest of the crew Kelso Simms, taught him radar evasion, a must!

"Damn! These are some big ass bugs Dal." Dallas smiled as he spoke about how they come from deeper water than our Florida cousins. "Please pass the salad." Two bottles of white wine, a 78 and 80 Chardonnay graced the table. Texas Garlic Toast and some exotic native bean salad, compliments of Sonata's talents also were present. Sonata was amazed at the various ways Americans eat. Dallas and Janis were the first Americans besides the Chief that she had broken bread with. Dallas ate with his fingers most of the time, stopping to pick up a fork to take something off a plate or eat the salad. Janis was a little more refined, her French side took over at the dinner table, and she dressed down Dallas for his obvious lack of grace. The Chief heard her say, ""Dal, you had better stop that!" more than once, referring to his proclivity for splashing everybody with lobster juice. He merely shrugged it off, saying "ya had better eat before it gets cold, Dear!"

Few words were spoken during dinner. That was until Dallas dropped the bombshell. It was at this point that the wine had loosened his tongue, and he raised a glass and stood up. From there he filled in the whole table with what had transpired over the last nine and a half hours. The sound of a jawbone hitting the tabletop stopped Dallas in mid-sentence. It was Janis. It wasn't that sound as much as the "Oh! No fucking way Dallas!" she spat that turned everyone's head at the table. Dallas slowly lowered his glass. He spoke in a tone of voice that was neithero angry or passive. "Janis," he addressed her, "When we were married a year ago, I distinctly remember the words for *better or worse*! No? We even wrote our own vows, remember? You have known me and what I have done and I always backed you, as well as taken care of your every want and or desire." Janis laid down her knife and fork and propped her blond head on both hands. "Look honey, this guy, this killer ex-DEA agent, has escaped and been on a crusade to kill me. No, kill us! He has and will use whatever means possible to get to me. That means you also! Three people at this table had a hand in setting him up, not to mention shooting him twice and drugging him. Three people at this table had a hand in turning him over to the DEA in the hopes that Wayne, Lenny, and Marboy's nephews' deaths would not go unpunished! But here we are. This guy has my little brother, fer Christ sake! Family, Janis, family. You don't really believe that I would take Assistant Director Cox's word that they have it handled? They are the ones that he so easily escaped from that night. Hell you, I, none of us can take that chance. You above all people should know this, love. So I give you a choice – You can "go" or "stay." I consider you a very valuable asset. And you would be missed, because I love you. But here it is if you go with me. This is what I expect. Or you can stay. If you do not go, I will not expect to see you here when I get back. And I will respect your choice, of course. I will make arrangements so you will always have money and never want for anything. But I have come to expect a little more from you than all the others. "Share my bed! Share my life!" That was in our vows. I think you "wrote" that line, yes?" "But Dallas," Janis tried to break in. "No dear, not now. I'm talking family!" By now the Chief and Sonata had poured more wine and began eating again, neither one spoke a word.

Janis slowly pushed away from the table and left the room. Dallas shouted after her. "Think about it if it were your sister or your brother. I would not even have to be asked!" With that Dallas sat back down. The Chief leaned over, "Boy, you sure can turn a phrase, son," he said in a whisper." "Pass me a steak please, and another lobster, Chief." "Some wine Dallas?" Sonata offered. "Yes, thank you Sonata," Dallas said as he was served another lobster and winked at Sonata. The Chief saw it and asked, "How the hell can you eat after all that?" Dallas looked at the Chief and winked again. Dallas just smiled as he looked at his plate and cracked open the lobster with his hands, pulling the tail out of the body. Out of the corner of his eye he saw Janis at the corner of the room.

Janis slowly walked back to her seat and sat down. "OK, I'm sorry, but I had to make sure that Olivia would be OK while we all left her alone for a few days." A great sigh of relief and smiles opened up. "OK, "Big Shot," "What is the plan?" Dallas leaned over and kissed Janis on her forehead and said "Oh, the plan?" "Yes." "I have a plan. But first let's finish our killer meal ya all fixed. Then we go to the planning department downstairs. But don't rush, this may be the last great meal we get for a while, unless ya all think that tacos and burritos are great eating. Of course we can fish . . . Er, you guys can fish, right?" "What do ya mean by "us," Dallas?" Janis asked with a smile. As Dallas put the final chunk of lobster in his mouth, savoring the sweet and succulent juices inadvertently running down his chin, he said, "Well that's all in the plan ya will hear in a bit. Now y'all stay up here and police up the mess, I have to set up the show. Be right back!" With that, Dallas pushed away from the table and kissed Janis again, this time on the lips.

Olivia had the night off; she spent her off hours watching satellite TV. With her out of the way in the far end of the house, Dallas felt safe as he set up a couple charts of the Caribbean Basin and a map of Jamaica. He also went over and opened the hidden door in the coral rock wall that led to the "abandoned" boat house. "Boy is Janis in for a shocker," he thought. The rest of his new crew cleaned up well, the Chief cleaned up another beer. "Hey! You! You're a big help. Can I get you another?" Sonata asked. "Nah, yeah, OK." The Chief returned with a smile while holding the bottle

up to the light, rolling the spit shot left back and forth. "Yeah!"
"Make yourself useful honey." "Screw you, Chief!" blared out of
Janis's mouth. "Get yer own damn beer, useless." "Now is that any
way to talk to Mon Capitan?" as the Chief downed the last drop.
"Captain, huh? Only thing you're Captain around here is taking
out the garbage! Take that!" "Oh, Janis, I'm glad you changed your
mind! You are always good for a laugh Blahh . . . and it is going to
be a pleasure sailing with you. NOT!" "Chief, you are so full of shit
when you drink, Sonata how do ya put up with it?" "Oh Him! I don't
know. I guess the same way you put up with Mr. Dallas."

The Chief pushed away from the table and grabbed the garbage
out of Janis's hand. "Which way, Janis darling?" "That way," Janis
exploded with laughter as she pointed to the trash chute on the wall
next to the dishwasher. "The what? Trash chute?" The Chief was
spinning in circles as Janis held his arm and led him to it. "Now
pull it open. Yeah, that's a good boy. Now put the bag down the
chute." "Jeez, to many moving parts around here. I bet this is really
your escape hatch." "You're drunk! Sonata, let's make espresso, I
think we are all gonna need it, and soon too," Janis suggested. "And
maybe some of this," holding out a coffee cake from the fridge.

"Hey! Are you all about done up there? C'mon let's go, it's ten
to ten." At ten o'clock, we all set our watches, so close it up and get
your collective asses down here . . . Please!" Dallas implored. Dallas
sat down in his desk chair as the now half in the bag crew made
their way down the spiral staircase. The Chief jumped up and took
a corner pocket spot on the pool table. He gently pulled Sonata, and
slid back to make room for her between his legs. Janis took over
Dallas's desk chair now that Dallas was on his feet standing in front
of two charts. "OK! Now that we are all here we can start. There
will plenty of time for questions later. First I'm gonna lay out the
whole operation."

Dallas walked around his desk to the first chart. "This is us."
He pointed to a speck on the map. "This is our island right here."

He used the tip of the pen against the chart. "This is Jamaica up here. That's where you guys are gonna pick up Capt. Bob." "And where are you gonna be Dallas?" Janis blurted out. "I said questions latter! Now please listen and learn, you have a lot of listening to do!"

"Now like I said, Capt. Bob will be waiting at Port San Antonio. That's on the north side of the island, so we should not run into a lot of people we know. You guys will call him on the radio, and he will get dropped off onto one of the boats, either the Chief's or the Morgan 51.' He will have all the "TOYS"" we need Chief, OK?" The Chief, with a lost child look on his face hesitated, "How's that, Dal?" "Cause I'm leaving tonight!" "Tonight Dallas?" "Yeah tonight for Jamaica. But I have ta make a stop first in St. Kitts and Nevis. I'm gonna need cash, a lot of cash, so I have to be at the banks when they open in the morning. From there I'm shooting straight over to Jamaica." "Oh yea?" Janis jumped in. "And how the hell are you do all this? On a magic carpet or some shit?" "Now listen, I'm not done," Dallas growled. "Chief, the way this works is Capt. Bob will be in Jamaica by the twelfth of May. You'll have to leave in the morning."" "The morning, Dal?" "Yup, no later than seven a.m. You're gonna make it look like you have the Morgan under tow. Of course the Morgan will be at full throttle, just throw a couple lines back to it and make the best speed possible." "Oh, OK that's solid, I'm starting to see where you're going with this now – I'm helping two ladies in distress thing. Cool!" "Yeah Chief, when we get where we are going, we are gonna need an "Operations Platform." That's your Sportfish!" Dallas smiled as he saw the lights finally come on in the Chief's head.

Dallas moved to the other map. "This is "Belize" and it is our final destination." Dallas had moved the map closer so everybody could see the details. "OK, at the west end and on the beach is a house. I think that's where my brother is being held. This house is no ordinary house. Mr. Francisco Amada owns this house. I know 'cause I've been there! Nice big beach house. OK ladies, in case you were wondering why I won't be on any of the boats, please walk this way." Dallas calmly walked towards the slightly opened coral rock wall. The Chief followed the ladies at a comfortable distance. "OK, here it is!" Dallas grabbed the ring from under its coral flap, and gave the wall a push. The wall made no sound as it opened into what was still darkness. Janis, the first one in, coughed from the smell of aviation gas. "What the hell is this?" she coughed. "Just a min, honey," as Dallas flipped the exhaust fans switches. "It will be better in a minute or two." He also brought up the lights that surrounded the base of the boathouse. As the lights came up there was a loud gasp. "Oh, Hell no Dallas! OH HELL NO" even louder this time. "SHUT UP, this is it! My way to be a lot of places in the shortest amount of time!" Dallas smiled as he winked at the Chief.

"Well just what in hell is this?" Janis asked. Dallas, walking around the plane said, "It's an airplane, of course." He reached up and ran his hand down the leading edge of tail fin. "Nice, huh? This plane will carry me and my luggage first to St. Kitts & Nevis. While there, I will go to the bank, refuel and fly to Port San Antonio in Jamaica. I already have Capt. Bob waiting there, or he will be by the twelfth of May. Marboy will also be there. With transportation." "Hey Dallas," the Chief broke in. "Maybe he will still have the Little Tiger!" "I wouldn't doubt it, Chief. Knowing Marboy, he's kept it in the shape we left it in, too. But anyway, from there I'm going ta see Carl Brewster. Any requests, Chief, if ya know what I mean?"

By now Janis and Sonata were both looking over the plane. They walked around it, touched it. When Dallas looked, Janis had already popped open the cockpit. "What the hell! This thing is made of plastic! Dallas are you outta your friggin mind? This thing won't fly!" Janis said, with a very French attitude. "What you are feeling, honey, is the most advanced material in airplanes today. I won't even try and explain it to you, you will just have to take my word that it not only flies, but it's 99% radar proof and it will land on land as well as water. I had it built in parts and brought here while you were in the States last year. You of all people should like it – It's French and it's a nasty little bugger that flies so well I can't believe it myself!"

"You mean you have actually flown this model airplane?" Janis was steaming in her boots, so to speak, as the rant began . . . "Yer fucking an idiot! A MORON. A guy with a DEATH WISH. Only you! And all this bullshit about being retired! CRAP! All CRAP!" Janis walked quickly over to the Chief. "Raise your arms, Harvey!" He did so, while at the same time asking "Why?" "Oh, ya wanna know why? I'm looking for your gun. I'm going to shoot him, that's why Chief! Where is it? All you fucks carry a gun. C'mon, hand it over!" Janis was feeling up the Chief, and he was starting to giggle. Finally, the Chief said "I don't carry a piece in your house, 'cause if I did you would get all pissed off, and we don't want that to happen, do we Janis?" "Listen Chief, don't patronize me! Asshole! I'm serious! And as for you Dallas, well never mind, but you are not going to fly this mouse trap anywhere, except maybe back to where it came from. How did it get to the island anyway?" "Look Janis, this is as safe or safer than any plane I have ever flown. It even has its own on-board computer with satellite navigation, its own satellite phone. Hell, it can even fly itself if I'm hurt or lost. So please let me finish the plan before you start shooting holes in it or somebody! OK?" Janis nodded.

"Right, where was I? Oh yeah, after I get done at the bank and fly to Jamaica and see Carl, Bob and I will fly out to where the Chief is anchored off shore. I'll land and Capt. Bob will take the Morgan into Belize City, supposedly for repairs. You, as in all of you, will now be aboard the Chief's sport fishing boat. From then on, ya all look like you are on a charter. The little seaplane will be tied up behind it. Depending on the seas, they'll dictate how far out you can anchor, Chief. Do ya all see a little plan so far?" Dallas asked as he looked around the boathouse. "When I fly in with Capt. Bob I will tell you more." "You mean you will have more plans made up, don't ya Dallas?" Janis growled. "Well now that you brought it up, yes that's exactly right. I need to see Capt. Bob and Carl first. I have a lot of shit to do and a short time to do it, so don't get all negative, Janis, you're scaring Sonata! When I land at the boats, I'm gonna have a lot of money and arms on board. Janis, you of all people know the "devil is in the details." This can't be any worse than what happened a year ago. I pulled that off. I'll pull this one off! And I don't give a shit about anything else right now. That asshole Skeets has crossed the line this time. If Chance is at the Amada beach house, I have a chance of getting him out in one piece."

Chapter 5

Dallas had come to the end of what plan he had. "Chief, I want to speak to you alone." Dallas had pulled him backwards as they all left the boathouse. "Look, as you probably noticed, I left out a couple things." "Oh like the fact that the Morgan 51 sitting out there is fully loaded? Or the fact that I will be towing it?" "Well yeah, "Kinda – Sorta," but I didn't leave much more, did I?" Dallas looked at the Chief, who was mock singing the lyrics to *White Rabbit* from the Jefferson Airplane:

"One pill makes you larger,
One pill makes you small…"

"Yeah OK, I get the point, Chief." The Chief, with his patented smirk, leaned in and asked, "What about the guns Dal?" "The guns, Chief? What about the guns?" The Chiefs glasses slid down his nose. "Dallas, the guns have to be two things." "And those are, Chief?" Dallas inquired, like he had never had a gun before "Un… Huh? Just two, Chief?" The Chief chuckled out a low "shit" and said "two things" – semi and full." Dallas looked at the Chief with a furrowed brow. "Semi and full?" "Yeah dumbshit, as in *a-u-t-o-m-a-t-i-c*. One 14X power sniper scope with range finder and laser pointer. Oh, and infrared. One of the .223 hypervelocity AR-15's we traded Carl ought to do nicely. I think he may even have one of our M-4's. If he does pick that up. Four, no make that six, Berettas .380 – 9mm. Oh, another thump gun .25mm and a brace of small Uzi's, plus a shit load of ammo, of course." "Oh Fucking A, of course Chief! Some Claymores?" "Sure why not." "Anything else, hero?" Dallas queried. "I only have so much room on this little flying boat, ya know!"

Dallas looked at his watch. "Ouch, it's almost one in the friggin' morning. I'm gonna grab some shut eye and I won't be here when you wake up. So you fully understand the program?" "Yeah, Dallas I got it down. I'll tow the Morgan out around seven a.m. with it under power, too. It's gonna take about twenty-seven or thirty hours to make our connection off Jamaica." "Just remember to be radio set," Dallas added. "By the time you get up there I'll have been to the bank and have seen Carl, too. I plan on being at the bank by the time it opens tomorrow, then I'll head your way. So if I don't see ya before I go fer anything, be careful and I will see you in a day or two at the given coordinates. Night Chief, and good luck!"

Chance Streeter was rolling around on his bed at Armada's, his ass hurt where they had been giving him the shots of heroin. But it seemed like hours since the last shot, and his clarity of mind was starting to come back. "Ah, Shit!" The thought of his two dead friends flashed in his mind. It all happened so fast! The last thing he remembered was them driving into the Mexican desert, the sun was starting to go down, when somebody lit a joint. The all-day drinking beer and shots of "Ta-Kill-Ya" had taken their toll, and Chance passed out. Next thing he knew he was running away from gunshots into the desert. He was tackled from behind and felt the first needle jab. From then on, the next two days were a trunk ride, with the car stopping every six hours, and another needle jab. It was only now that the serious shit started to meander into his mind.

"What the fuck did I get myself into?" Chance muttered as he tried to swing his legs off the bed. He could see the bathroom across the room. He sat on the edge of the bed for a minute or two. His legs were weak, and he almost fell twice as he reached from one thing to the next, pulling the chair along from the desk that sat next to the bed as he went like a walker. He reached out for the bathroom doorframe, dropped the chair and used the bathroom's doorknob and wall for support. Being so weak from a diet of no food, little water and heroin, he collapsed on to the toilet.

"What the fuck!" he thought as he saw the gold plated hardware, the faucets, the sinks, the shower heads, and there were six of each in the shower alone, a gold towel holder graced the opposing wall, and the whole shower was trimmed out in gold. He got up and turned to flush, and a gold handle awaited his push. "Jeez! Just where the fuck am I?" He washed his hands and face, pulled a towel off the gold rack and it felt good, a big, thick, good-smelling towel. He repeated the hands and face, this time catching his neck and forearms in the process. "Damn that felt good," as he took a handful of water in his hands and swished it around in his mouth, and spit it back into the sink before taking a swallow from the faucet itself. A gold trimmed mirror allowed him a look at himself. His elbows and knees were in bad shape, both bruised and the left elbow had been bleeding. He turned around and walked back towards the door. His heart leapt from his chest, as standing there was the Spanish guy who he was sure had killed his two friends.

"Come over here!" Fernando demanded. "Hey, what's going on?" came out of Chances half-tilted head. "Oh, feeling a little stronger, eh?" Fernando pulled his arm from behind him and pointed a rather large pistol at Chance. Chance could see the bullets in the gun's cylinder. Big fucking bullets too. "OK, OK, no need for that thing, I'll do what ya want. But put that fucking gun down!" "You will do whatever I want, and now bend over this chair." Fernando kicked the chair at Chance. "What, you want to fuck me?"

Chance blurted out. "No, asshole! This!" In Fernando's other hand he held up a syringe. What was in it was black, so black the light didn't come through it. "Oh Hell no! You ain't sticking me with that shit!" "Well you have a choice, Amigo!" Either this, Fernando held up the gun, or this, holding up the syringe. "You will find this one the better of the two, believe me." Chance undid his pants and leaned over the chair. "Cocksucker! That hurt like hell, asshole." Fernando just smiled, and said "If you're hungry later, or hungry now, there's good food on that tray over there HA HA, Amigo!" and Fernando walked out and locked the door behind him.

Chance walked over to the tray that had been set out for him. He knew he only had a few minutes before that shit injected in his ass would make him a slobbering idiot, so he tried to eat the nice chicken and rice. It smelled so good that he ate like an animal, having not eaten in almost three days. As he took his fifth or sixth bite he could feel those warm arms enclosing in on his brain. His face fell into the food, and he knew it was time to make it to the bed now or pass-out in his dinner. Even though it was only three steps, the bed seemed farther and farther away. Just as he was almost completely overcome, he felt the pillow hit the side of his face. "Ah, made it," was his last thought as he drifted farther and farther into the nether world. He was starting to like this feeling! It was like floating in a gentle stream. All down the stream and into his dream . . .

The table was set. Two servants hustled around it making sure that everything was in place and everything was in its place. Raul walked around the table looking over the night's fare. He snatched a dinner roll as he walked by as he headed towards the French doors that led out to the deck above the beach. This is where Raul would later eat. He laid his shoulder-strung Mac 10 on the railing and ate the roll, while watching the waves roll in as well.

Mr. and Mrs. Amada took their seats at the table at opposite ends. Amada was talking quietly to his wife when a bump and a thud caught his attention. Skeet's knee had given out on the stairs and his coat pocket caught a banister peg, sending him head first on to the dining room floor. "Ah, Shit!" he mumbled, as he grabbed his knee where the Chief had shot him almost a year ago. "You look drunk Skeets!" Amada hoarsely announced. "Some nerve you have to come to my table too drunk to stand. Get up this instant!" Amada ran his fingers through his hair and looked at his wife. "I said "Get up!" "I heard you," Skeets spoke back with a little vinegar on his tongue. "It's not what you think. I ain't drunk at all. Yet! My knee gave out where I was shot, and that stupid carpeting on the stairs didn't help," adding insult to injury. "You were shot Skeets?" Amada asked with a little less hostility and more curiosity. "Who shot you Skeets? And what for?" Skeets, now back on his feet and holding the back of a chair, replied, "The guy who works with that smuggling bastard Streeter shot me. Not only shot me but drugged me too. Hell, they shot me twice – once in each leg. It happened while I was trying to arrest them."

Skeets was flat-out lying like the carpet he stood on. He was thinking now's as good a time as any to put Streeter in a bad light. But then again he caught himself short, thinking "Jeeez! I better shut up. I'm standing in the dining room of one of the biggest smugglers." "Christ, I better have that drink now if you don't mind, Mr. Amada." "No, no have a drink. You look like you need one. But first have a seat, here, sit here." Amada pointed at a seat, one on the right side of the table. Amada had seated Skeets there on purpose. Skeets had his back to the view outside, with Raul standing guard in the blackness of the deck outside. From here Skeets had a great view of the kitchen door. Every time the maid came in or out of the kitchen, Skeets stared at her ass. Amada saw this and leaned over. "Hey Skeets, when was the last time you got laid? Oh, where are my manners? I am sorry dear," Amada said as he looked back towards his wife. He noticed that she had put her knife and fork down. Yes, I think that is a question better left for drinks after dinner out on the terrace, no?" "You are absolutely right dear, and I am sorry. Please keep eating." Amada noticed that Skeets still had on the same clothes as he wore when he had gotten there. He just looked him over – every time he reached for his wine glass he also poured a full glass, and slurped it down in between bites. The word "Boracho"(drunken pig) kept creeping into his head. Amada wondered if this pig even bathed after the almost three-day car ride? Probably not!

Amada looked back over at his wife, who was picking at her lobster and linguini. "Honey, please eat." "I'm sorry Frank, I can't eat tonight. Please excuse me," and she got up and left the table as Skeets poured another glass of wine, wiping the dribble off his chin. "Ok Skeets, let's have our drinks outside, and you can tell me all about how you got shot, and why." "Yeah that sounds like a good idea, Frank. You are gonna bring out some off that fine fifty-year old cognac? You know which I mean, don't you? I can almost taste it now." "Oh sure Skeets, I think I have a bit left, you put a dent in it last time you were here, but you had good information for me. What do you have this time, asides from a kid locked-up down stairs that you are slowly turning into a skag addict! Like what's that all about?" The two of them left the table. As Ernie got up he snatched the last open bottle of wine off the dinner table and followed Amada out through the doors leading to the terrace.

Amada walked over to the railing and stood there a moment. Raul was standing at the corner of the terrace, cradling his Mac-10. Ernie found the table, the one with the umbrella and four chairs around it, and he set up his stolen wine bottle and two glasses and began to pour. Amada walked down to Raul. "Raul," Amada asked, "Did you find any dope in their car or bedrooms?" Raul nodded yes. "Actually I found quite a bit, far more than I expected Hefé." "Like how much are we talking about, Raul?" Amada inquired. They both stood at the end of the deck watching the pig Skeets guzzle glass after glass of wine, as if no one was watching. "Well, Mr. Amada. I found almost a kilogram, black tar. Far more than they would need for just one kid." Amada stepped back. "What did you do with it?" "It disappeared Mr. Amada." "What about Fernando's room?" Amada asked. "I have not been there yet." "Raul make that your next stop. Understand?" "Yes Mr. Amada, I understand."

Chapter 6

At four-fifteen a.m. Dallas slipped out of bed. Janis barely moved. All the wine at dinner with her new friend Sonata had taken its toll. Still in his boxers, Dallas walked out of the bedroom and down the stairs. He made his way across the lower level and flipped up the cover on the wall. The wall, as quiet as ever, pushed in without a sound. Dallas felt his way over to the light switches and flipped the lower set on. As quietly as he could, he un-did the stern lines, which were Wincher snap stays and snapped directly on to the plane's tail loop fittings. Before he forgot, he ran back over to the swing door and pushed it shut as quietly as it had opened and locked it from the inside. At the foot of the wall Dallas found his duffle bag and fished out a pair of shorts and a shirt, and once dressed he popped open the cockpit doors. Both went up without a sound, only the hiss that a Jeep's rear hatch might make as it would lift.

Dallas pulled the cockpit windshields down, buckled himself in tight with the over the shoulder and waist harnesses. The roll-up boathouse gate kept it nice and calm inside. He reached up and pressed the power up switch, resulting in a verbal response from the onboard computer: "Pre-flight systems check now in process," the computer's sexy female voice stated. As Dallas sat there, he could see all the different systems and their lights blink on and off as they cycled through the automatic pre-flight computer program. "All systems are flight ready, engaging the fuel and hydraulics systems."

Dallas mumbled "OK, computer off." He reached over his head to the input board for the electric maneuvering fan. He pulled the red snap cover down and flipped the switch. In the cockpit Dallas heard a slow hum that was picking up speed. Out of his duffle bag he pulled the automatic boathouse door controller, which looked like an ordinary garage door opener. He pressed the button and the roll-up gate started its ascent. Dallas held the yolk firmly in both hands. From a button on the yolk he depressed the flaps adjustment, so the flaps were fully extended. The roll-up gate was almost at the top, and Dallas nudged the yolk forward ever so slightly. Slowly the plane moved silently out of the boathouse. The electric fan was little more than a hum as it pushed the plane out into the open water as he continued turning into the wind.

It was a calm night and the waves broke against the fuselages bow silently, only a slight rocking gave away the fact that the airplane was moving. Dallas reached over and activated the onboard computer again. He spoke slowly, "Deploy stowed wings sections to full." As Dallas spoke, the starboard three feet of wing tip slowly lifted from its stowed position. Dallas had been told by the guys who built this plane to make sure he heard the wing tip lock into place. As the wing settled into its place, completing the full wing, Dallas heard an unmistakable power-assisted lock snap. So it was also with the port wing. "OK, everything seems good," Dallas thought. Still under electric fan motor power, Dallas taxied a good distance from the house. The fan was pretty damn efficient for a twenty-two-inch fan, which for all intense and purposes looked like a common house fan on steroids – it had almost a 90-degree turning radius. Dallas kept it at half power for the sake of noise.

He had a logbook that was attached to the yolk, went through the final checklist and decided that, "OK, this baby is ready." Dallas pressed the computer's button; a light on the dash indicated that it was waiting for instructions. He could see in the moonlight the tip of the island come into view. He gently turned the plane around the tip of the island and took a look back. "OK computer, go for main engine start, disable electric fan and stow." A small hatch opened and Dallas watched over his shoulder as the fan disappeared into the main fuselage. Approximately ten seconds later the main engine starter motor engaged and the main propeller started to spin. When this happened the whole interior dash and navigation lights came on, startling him a bit. The computer asked "An assisted take-off? Press the yellow light for yes or press the red light for no." Dallas reached over and up and pressed the yellow button. "Ah, shit, why not let it? At least I'll find out now if all the French shit really works!" Dallas spoke out loud, talking to himself. Even though Dallas had his hands on the yolk, he could feel the computer take over. "Cool, really fuckin' cool!" By now the engine was roaring away and the boat was seconds away from being a plane. It picked up speed fast and it took twenty seconds by Dallas's watch and he was no longer a boat but a plane, gaining airspeed and altitude fast. The computer came back on line: "Please set G.P.S. coordinates on the LED panel located above you in red." Dallas looked at his log and entered the numbers and letters for the Island of Nevis. The computer then requested Dallas set cruising speed and altitude. Dallas again looked at his log – he had charted the course around the islands that might, or did, have mountains above the 500' level. After that, he set the forward-looking radar as well for a once every three minute, 360-degree sweep. Dallas thought, "Hmm, at 500', according to the Frenchie's, I should be almost invisible to radar. Well we shall see, won't we?" Little did Dallas know, but the whole time, at least from the time the plane left the boathouse, someone was watching. The Chief stood at the top of the cliffs watching as Dallas taxied out and headed towards the north end of the island. He watched as the wings un-folded and the electric fan disappeared in the moonlight. He moved quickly over the rocks to be able to see the plane's engines start and head away into the darkness. From then on, all he heard was the roar of the engine and the sound of the boat become a plane. He ambled back into the house and back to bed. He wondered what tomorrow would bring.

At 5:30 a.m. the Chief woke. "Jeeez, already?" he hummed. He slipped out of bed. Sonata was still fast asleep. He picked up his clothes he had laid out the prior evening and headed down the stairs and into the kitchen. While there he fixed coffee and set out a box of eggs, bagels, milk and a slab of bacon. He set the timer on the coffeemaker for 6:00 a.m., all the while getting dressed. He figured that the smell of fresh coffee would wake up the rest of the house, and so he headed out and down to his Sportfish boat. Along the way down the dock he looked over the Morgan 51'. From looking at it he sure couldn't tell that there were a thousand pounds of coke secreted into the hull – it looked just like a normal, very expensive sailboat. He continued on to his boat. He jumped from the dock to the top of the gunnel and stepped down onto the deck. Pulling out his keys, he opened the sliding glass doors that led into the salon.

First thing he did while inside was go to the kitchen and start his own coffeemaker. After that he walked down the stairs to the cabins, made sure that they looked nice and opened the hatches to air the place out. From there he backtracked up the stairs through the kitchen and lifted the stairs and locked them in the upright position. This exposed the access door to the main engine room. Just in case, he grabbed the fire extinguisher off the wall next to the stairs and went down into the engine room. He held his nose up in the air to see if he could smell any leaks from the fuel or toilet system; not smelling anything out of the ordinary, he proceeded over to the mains. The mains are the two panels next to each other that are the switches that turn on all the systems on the boat. He flipped the switches to their "up" positions and could hear the electricity course through the boats bowels. A nice "hum" and he heard the bilge pumps start. After turning on all the lights around the engine room, the Chief picked off the wall a clipboard with the checklist he had to go through every time he started the boat's systems. The Chief knew his boat inside and out, and so skipped a few of the items on the list. But things like fuel separators, fuel amount, oil, and about ten other things could not be ignored. Such as opening the water intakes, opening the fuel petcocks for the Westerbek generators, priming the fuel intakes, opening cooling water outflows... and that was just in the engine room!

Once done with all that, the Chief climbed back up into the salon control room and pilot navigation center. He thought to himself if the people he chartered had any idea just how complicated running this vessel was, every time he heard from some stumble fuck who had trouble starting his or her BMW in the morning about owning a boat, he would just laugh with them, saying "Oh yeah, you would love it," while thinking "Jeeez what a brain trust." He would just laugh and say "Yeah sure, if ya want one, I'm sure Sonata here can help you find one almost just like this!" (NOT). The Chief turned the two keys and pressed the red pushbuttons that said "Generators." After a couple of seconds, both generators were humming away, charging up the whole boat's systems. He sat there a few seconds going over the checklist in his mind. "OK, in half an hour, the main engines would be ready after the generators topped off the batteries." From there he went back out on deck and looked over the sides to visually check the water intakes and outlets. All looked good ta' go. "Now if I can get the women ready in an hour or so, we can be on our way."

Just before he left the boat, the Chief walked out past the Fighting Chair. At its foot, he snatched the two rings that lifted the rear hatches. In the bottom of the locker he found two 100' foot long, $1^1/_4$" inch dock lines. "Perfect, he thought, and if these aren't enough I'm sure Dallas has at least the same lines on the Morgan 51' sailboat. Plenty of line to make it look like we are towing the Morgan 51'." The Chief looked up at the house. The lights in the kitchen were on and he could see someone moving around. "Good they're up at least. Now let's go see what kind of mood we have going." The Chief walked back past the Morgan 51' and the 42' Scarab. "Hell, it would be nice to have that with us, but I can't see how, so oh well." He started back up the stairs. At the top he nearly stepped on Goliath's tail. "Goddamn lizard! Scared me ta' death, you little prick!" Goliath turned and looked back when he heard his name and stared at the Chief. To him, "Goddamn lizard" sounded like his name. After all, the maid Olivia called him that all the time. And Goliath was hungry, it was almost feeding time. The Chief walked into the lower house and could hear Sonata and Janis talking. As he stepped through the doors he could see five or six neatly packed duffle bags,

"Christ," the Chief thought, "They're taking this seriously. All packed and ready? Hmm, this is to good ta be true." He climbed the stairs, taking the steps two at a time until he was standing in the kitchen. He was met with a fresh cup of coffee and a bagel. "Well ladies, are we about ready to get this show on the road? Hmm, good bagel," the Chief spoke as he chewed. "Well as you can see, we are. How about the boats?" Janis asked, thinking, "No it will be a bit," "I have this to do" or "I have that to do yet." The Chief answered. "Hey I'm waiting on you guys, OK? Let's be loaded and outta here in fifteen minutes, ladies!" As he walked back down the stairs, he said, "That's fifteen minutes, not fifty! Right?"" The Chief heard an "Aye, Aye Captain," and he responded by saying "yeah, very funny, ha-ha. Yeah funny, everyone's a comedian. Now move your collective asses. I'll carry what I can, just grab the rest. Oh yeah, Janis? Do you have a key to the electric box at the top of the stairs?" "Yeah I do, here, catch," and she dropped her keys over the balcony to the Chief on the pool deck.

The Chief hurried down the steps, almost at a jog. He stepped, then leapt over the Morgan's two safety lines and put the first key into a small paddle lock on the companionway hatch, unlocked it and slid the top back and lifted the four teak boards out of their slots and placed them on the deck at his feet. With that done, he hopped over the companionway lip and down the six steps to the sole of the boat. He looked around. "Nice friggin' boat, Dal!" He quickly undid the latches that held the steps in place, removed them and opened the engine compartment. As he looked at the engine, it sure as hell looked ready ta' go. He checked the oil level and looked over the Racor fuel separators; they were clear of any standing water at the top, and he pushed the button at the bottom, which is spring loaded, and leaked a little diesel on to his fingertips. "Hmm smells OK, in fact, fresh," he thought. "Funny, old Dallas has been busy." A final check of the air intake and he closed it up. No leaks, no runs, no errors. Means no problems. He replaced the stairs and latched them back up.

"Roomy boat down here, lots of space, the two women should be fine, hell they be eating on my boat anyways, so let's go start this bad boy up." The Chief popped up and back into the cockpit. The center cockpit is a favorite among the yachting crowd. Nice big wheel finished off with small gauge rope with little knots all the way around. In front of that was the compass. He knelt back down and felt down around the inside of the salon wall – there he found the electrical switchboard and flipped the breakers to the "on" position. On the side of the compass standard was the engine key switch, along with a couple of weatherproof toggle switches for the running and spreader lights. He slipped the rubber-coated ignition key in, pulled the choke knob and turned the key. The boat was trying. He heard the starter motor throw the bendix gear into the flywheel. He pushed the choke knob back and forth a couple times and ran the throttle back and forth. He turned the key again, and when the starter motor did its thing this time it coughed and a blast of light blue smoke shot out of the flapped exhaust pipe. "Ya Mon! That-a-girl!" he spoke out loud, He pushed in the choke a bit and let the engine warm up like a spring morning. A little slow, but a sure bet.

By now the ladies were coming down the dock. The Chief hopped back over the side and gave them a big smile, but no help with their bags. "I'll be right back," he yelled at them as he hit the stairs. The Chief climbed the stairs and once at the top reached over the gate to the electrical box that turns on the dock lights. He used the last key on the ring and opened the box. There, right where he saw Dallas replace it, was the fifteen shot Beretta in its nylon black belt case. "Yeah, this will do nicely," as he put it in the small of his back and pulled his shirt down over it. He quickly closed and locked the box again. While there, he took the key off the ring and placed it on top of the box, just in case the Olivia needed to get in it, not thinking she might just already have a key of her own, being a live-in maid and all. At that he skipped a couple steps on the way back down and was back at the Morgan just in time to heave the last bag over to Janis. "And just what the hell was that?" She demanded. "What?" the Chief responded.

"Just cast us off at the bow line, I'm gonna take her out about a hundred yards and wait for you and yours to get that 'tub' you call a yacht away from the dock. From there you can throw me a towline. Oh yeah, make sure you give me a lot of scope at first, and I'll adjust it as needed." "Aye, Aye, Jeeez H. Christ, mon Captain!" The Chief bellowed back. "I'm on it, OK?" At that the Chief ambled over towards his boat, stopped, and turned back. "Hey! You do have everything, right? I mean eye shadow and all?" "Yeah, yeah Chief. Keep it up!" Sonata had never heard anyone talk to him that way, man or woman, and was pleasantly surprised the way Janis had complete control of everything on the boat. As Janis passed the Chief's Sportfish, the Chief yelled, "On the radio go to number 5 – 1. That's 51 for so much fun I'm sick already, OK Janis?" "OK Captain, that is 5 - 1." Janis chuckled back. Sonata sat back and just watched in amusement, thinking what a love-hate relationship these two had for each other.

"Janis?" Sonata asked, "Is there anything you want me to do, I have been living on the Chief's boat for almost a year, and know a little bit about the radio." "Hey perfect," Janis answered, "Yeah, please change the radio over to channel 51. And make sure it works, there's a switch on the wall, I think third from the top left. That will turn on the power to the radio, and cabin lights too." And "thank you," Janis added.

The Chief fired up his engine – rumble-rumble. After about two minutes, he pulled away from dock the at idle, and as the boat headed out, the Chief scrambled to pull in all the dock lines. He gave them a quick coil and jumped back into the lower captain's station and gave the boat a bit of speed to catch up with Janis, who was waiting a hundred yards to starboard. The Chief pulled up slowly next to the Morgan 51' and Sonata threw him a towline. He threw one back from his boat as well. Sonata let out line until Janis told her to stop. The Chief tied it off and took up the slack. Janis was now on the fore deck tying a Bowline knot, and cleated them both off on both sides of the bow. She waved the Chief off. The Chief slipped the Morgan's line through the stern line hole on the port side, and waved Janis off. The Chief went to the radio and dialed in channel 51 (for so much fun) and hailed Janis for the first time. "Hey Janis, ya there?" "Yeah I'm here, and all set, so what's the plan?" The Chief answered, "Look ladies, just make yourselves comfortable for a while. I've set the auto-pilot and I'm gonna have a beer. I suggest ya all do the same, and maybe get some sun, or sleep. I'll wake ya if or when we have any changes. So just relax. Talk to ya later."

Chapter 7

D allas loosened his shoulder straps a bit. "Well I'll be damned if this mother don't fly itself." After he had punched in the coordinates for Nevis Island he just sat back at the ready in case there was a problem. But no, all he felt was the plane throttle up and run about 100 yards, ascending at a good clip. He knew that he had about a four-hour ride. It was still dark and Dallas kept his eyes glued to the red-lit gauges that half surrounded him. He was really intrigued by the forward looking radar, which showed the smaller islands in a split screen. One was surface-to-air (or) profile, the other was a 180-degree sweep with a 360-degree sweep every 30 seconds. He saw a blip on the profile side, and using a toggle switch, he maneuvered a small circle on top of it. The profile of a ketch with its two masts showed in profile. "Hmm, this is so friggin cool!" He gently used the toggle and placed the circle back in the upper right hand corner, and when he did this, the radar resumed full screen. "Ah, another smuggler . . . Yeah, no running lights, just the stars to look at, and when you are on those waters the stars are so bright that you can see a silhouetted boat and or islands, that's how bright they are."

Seeing this boat, Dallas wondered if the Chief, Janis and Sonata had made a clean getaway and were headed north on schedule. "Well, good luck to ya partner, wherever ya are." Dallas looked at the clock on the instrument panel. "Hmm, I've got about almost two hours till sunrise, think I'll grab a few winks." Dallas pulled his log clipboard off the yolk. Holding a pen in his right hand and small flashlight in the left, he found the what's and how's to set the alarms for altitude and radar contacts. He pushed the buttons, after which the computer asked: "Music?" Dallas, in a normal voice, spoke into the headset mouthpiece "No thank you." And shook his head. "Friggin amazing, just ridiculous. Hahahh!" Between the drone of the engine and the race car-type seats, Dallas put his head back, and the smell of fresh leather lulled him out in about 30 seconds.

Dallas woke to the sound of an audio alarm; the computer was babbling away and Dallas calmly reached up and turned down the volume. He looked at his screens, then his altitude. "OK, I'm at 500' and this has got ta be the island of Dominica, which is my better than half-way point. Still 45 minutes till sunrise and the topography of this island matches Dominica." He released the autopilot setting and banked 45 degrees to starboard while climbing to a more comfortable 1200 feet, right at cloud level and right on past the mountains on his left. Dallas thought, "OK, another hour, + or -, and St. Kitts and Nevis will be in sight. That puts me somewhere on the water in Nevis in one hour, so I better not sleep anymore."

Dallas reached around behind himself and snatched his briefcase, opened it and checked out his stuff. "Yeah, my Croc money belt, three passports, four different types of sunglasses, a clean shirt, and a clean pair of linen kakis." Then under the whole mess he slid his hand. "Ah . . ." He felt the grips of his American Express Colt Mustang .380. He patted it and shuffled around and straightened up the hastily thrown-together Crocskin briefcase. Now he seriously started to think about where he was going to land. He had an 8-foot Zodiac with a 5hp Johnson motor in the back hatch folded neatly. "So I figure I can land in the anchorage and sorta slide into the city docks . . . Yeah, I'll land outside and motor in, anchor out and the motor into the docks in the Zodiac. That way I won't grab as much attention when I land. I know the anchorage, so . . ." He reached under his seat. Yeah, there it was . . . The flag of the Commonwealth of St. Kitts-Nevis. "I'll put this on the antenna. If nothing else, it will keep them guessing long enough for me to get in and out of the bank."

After twenty minutes or so, Dallas could make out the outline of the island of Barbuda. This put him only 20 minutes out. Dallas took over the controls again and flew almost due north, putting him on the outside of Barbuda and he dropped back to 500 feet to get a better look at what was coming in only minutes now. The sun was up over the horizon line, and Dallas, being on the east side of these islands, could see everything very clearly. As planned, he was gonna make a landing out of the rising sun. The wind in the morning usually always blows west to east, which will cover the sound of his little single engine plane like a blanket.

It was at this point that things could get dicey. Coming out of the sun his view was perfect. He could see the anchorage. But this anchorage is no ordinary anchorage. It's full of long-range cruisers, big Sport fishers, and 50' and over custom sailboats. The smaller boats, those less than 50 feet, were relegated to the end of the line, at the west end. This was where Dallas chose. Still heading into the sun, he did a 180 degree turn and headed down to about 100' feet above the water. He could not chance a flyover, so this was it. He picked a spot down the center of what looked like a channel. He reached up and flipped on the computer, engaged the autopilot for a straight-in water landing. It did its jobs – Dallas could hear the different systems shutting down and others powering up. The taxi fan hatch opened and the steering fan rose from its cradle. Dallas sat back, hands hardly on the yolk, just sort of feeling the planes control. "Ah, Hell, this is the deal right here, if I had had one of these ten years ago, wow man!"

As the plane touched down on the glass surface of the bay south of Nevis, Dallas popped the Cockpit windshields. He pushed the seat all the way back and drove with his feet on the yolk. He was looking for a place to anchor. He saw a bearded older guy, obviously in his 60's. Dallas waved at him and the guy waved back. He had a nice 45' Irwin Ketch. Dallas made a gesture to go to the radio, he yelled "16" at the guy and he waved back. Dallas stalled the fan down just enough to hold position, and then he heard a husky older voice on the box. Dallas spoke back slowly. He asked the guy if he could approach. The old guy took his time responding, then answered, "yeah, but stay downwind and hook up to my stern buoy." "Rodger that, Sir," Dallas answered. He was surprised that this guy would let the likes of him approach. But then again, he thought, "When was the last time this guy had ever had a look at this kind of seaplane, Dal," although he had his own trepidations about this scene, too. He slid his .380 out of the briefcase and tucked it in its holster in the small of his back. He hailed the old gentleman. "Hey, aboard the Irwin! Captain, permission to come aboard!" The old guy was pulling in his stern line and shorting the distance between the two vessels. "Ah just hold on a damn minute son!" Dallas answered. "Yes sir, no problem!" "Good. That's one thing we don't want is a damn problem, too early for problems, eh son?" "Yes sir," Dallas answered. When the older gentleman had pulled the plane closer, he took a long look at it. "Sheese, that's some damn contraption!" Dallas, now with in talking distance, said "Watch this!" He reached under the cockpit to the control panel above the windshield and flipped the "fold wing tips" switch. The old guy stood in awe as a third of the wing tips neatly folded up and down on to the top of the main wings. "Fucking spacecraft err something yer driving their boy?" Dallas laughed out loud. "Hahah! Well yeah, kinda – sorta, I guess." Still standing in the cockpit, Dallas asked again, "Mind if I come aboard, I have a deal fer ya, if you're interested." Dallas followed with "My name is Kline, Mr. David Kline, and like I said, I have an offer ta make ya!"

"Ok Mr. Kline, bring yer passport aboard with ya, and I'll listen. But if I don't like the offer, away with you and yer damn whatever it is OK?" "OK, give me a second, and I'll step on over." The ole Gent added "NO GODDAMN GUNS! Right?" "RIGHT" Dallas answered. "Weapons of any kind sir, would be bad manners." "OK Sonny, then yer welcome to come aboard. Just made coffee, too!" Dallas lashed the last line to the fuselage loop and went below to his briefcase and pulled out the Trinidad passport with the name Kline on it and headed up. He also slid the Colt .380 into the small of his back. "Ya never know," he thought. The old gent gave Dallas a hand up from the stairs that led down to the waterline from the Irwin. Dallas said "Coffee? You have fresh coffee going? Great! Man, I really could use a cup of strong coffee right about now." "Been flying long, son?" The old man queried. "Yeah, about 4 hours from Trinidad, straight through, too!"

The old man finally introduced himself. "You can call me Tucker. This is my boat and I been living here for about 6 years now. My wife died a few years back and I sorta just live out here, no one bothers me, and I don't bother them." "You must know the town pretty well," Dallas asked. "Oh yeah," Tucker responded. "If I can ask, what exactly brings you here, Mr. Kline?" "Well I have some business in town, shouldn't take me more than a couple hours at best," Dallas answered. Tucker stood up and looked back out the window. "Well ya can't take that thing into the city docks, that's fer sure!" "That's the reason I'm here Mr. Tucker, or Tuck if I may? I have an 8-foot zodiac on board with a 5hp engine, but that's gonna take me all damn day. I saw that you have a 12 footer hanging in the water with a 20 on it." Tucker looked at Dallas "Oh, that's the deal. You want to borrow my Zodiac, don't ya?"

Dallas stood up and reached in his pocket. He threw a wad of fifty-dollar bills down on the settee table. Tucker sat back down. "That's a lot of money son. You ain't a doper doing illegal shit, are ya?" "No, just the other way around, I have to get to my bank on Nevis and pull out a bunch of money to pay for the plane that sits outside. No, sir, I have nothing ta do with drugs of any kind, and you're welcome to go aboard my plane and have a look around, if ya don't believe me!" Tucker looked him back directly in the eyes. "No, I don't think that will be necessary Mr. Kline," as Tucker looked at Dallas's passport. "But that's a lot of money son, just to borrow a boat." Dallas said "Then take what ya feel is proper and we will call it that." "Well the boat's all gassed up. But the banks won't be open fer another hour or so. Wanna fish?" Dallas was taken a bit back at the offer, but said "sure." "Or we can play checkers . . . Which is it son?" "Well I'm kinda partial to checkers Tuck, do ya by chance have anything like Bailey's Irish Cream, or maybe even a little bourbon ta put in this great coffee? (Because Dallas really thought this guy can't make coffee to save his life). "Bourbon." Tuck reached over his shoulder and poured.

Tucker slipped one fifty off the table and pushed the rest back at Dallas. "This ought to cover gas and a few things I really need in town myself, so just consider me a taxi service if ya will. I needed to go in any way, so let's do it. The banks open in about 25 minutes and it's a 15-minute ride to the city docks." Dallas responded, "Roger that Captain, I'm ready." Dallas led the way out, up the stairs and into the center cockpit of the Irwin. "I have to get my briefcase off my plane, so hang loose for a second or two."

Dallas hoped the three feet back onto the fuselage nonskid foot pads. These pads were laid out so a person knows where to walk without harming or denting the front end of the plane while hooking it up via the two oblong rings to another boat and or dock. "OK Tuck, just let me grab this bag." At the same time, he slipped the .380 pistol out of small of his back and threw it in the back seat. He placed a tee shirt over it as he changed into the clothes he had laid out to wear to the bank. He emerged from the plane and Tucker gave him the wolf whistle. "Oh boy, ain't we going ta town!" "Yeah, yeah," Dallas muttered. Tucker had brought the Zodiac closer. Dallas got in and said "Let's Go!" "Well son, ain't you forgetting something? Like closing up your rig?" At that point, Dallas held up a key ring with a rounded black fob on it and pressed the button. The port cockpit windscreen and entrance at the bottom lowered, and then raised into place as they both heard the locks engage. "You were saying?" "I ain't saying nothing again, that's fer sure," Tucker assured Dallas.

"Hey!" Tucker yelled above the whine of the engine. "Ya know I didn't even hear you land this morning." Dallas yelled back. "That's because I landed about a quarter-mile out and used the electric motorized fan that you saw below the main prop. I was hoping that I wouldn't have to use it all the way in. I really appreciate this lift, and to find a person so nice as you is a real stroke of luck." (Dallas was laying it on thick, but he really did get lucky finding this guy!)

The rest of the way in they mostly talked about island politics. In fact, he learned a lot about what's been happening there. The talk of the town was that the de-facto government was going to, or was in, negotiation with the U.S. to open the banks up to the feds to audit accounts that were large cash deposits. In exchange, the U.S. would supply new patrol boats and the manpower to train the locals, i.e. D.E.A. plants, in the local police force. The D.E.A. always used this tactic to get a foothold, and actually never turned over the goods to the locals. They always put what they call "observers" in the mix, and in that mix the observers controlled the routine of the boats. The D.E.A. lies a lot, and then before the locals know it, anybody that travels the lanes between here south are usually the first to get investigated. But the locals on Nevis are hip to this so-called "arrangement." Tucker affirmed this when Dallas just mentioned that he had come to Nevis to get away from the places like the Bahamas, Turks & Caicos and a half dozen other "Spice Islands." Tucker said, "Yep, pretty soon half the island is pointing their finger at one another, and there goes the neighborhood. When really, it's the U.S stirring the pot, so ta speak." Then Dallas said, "So you keep up with what's going on?" "Oh Hell ya I do! Right now the powers that be are keeping the idea of open banks "closed," but every few months these assholes come down and sweeten the deal. But at the moment privacy is the rule. If you're a good neighbor then nobody cares what or where your money came from. Hell, even the so-called shady ones contribute to the upkeep of the island. Personally I think, and so does most of the island, we don't want the damn U.S. hanging around all the time. They make us all feel like we are all under investigation. The hell with that!" Dallas obviously had opened a can of worms. He thought old Tuck would have talked his ear off if Dallas hadn't changed the subject.

"So Mr. Tucker, ya say you lost your wife some time ago?" "Yeah, it will be almost six years in August." "Did ya all get hit with any storms last year?" Dallas inquired. "Nope, they usually head north; we have been real lucky the last few years. And call me Tuck, just Tuck, OK?" "Sure Tuck, anything ya want," Dallas answered. "And just call me Mr. K, least while on the island, OK Tuck?" "Sure, anything ya want Mr. K.," Tuck answered, parrot style, and they both had a little laugh. "Well we're almost in, the anchorage is really calm this morning, almost nine o'clock. Your bank ought to be almost open. Ya know, island time and all." Dallas responded with a "Ya mon, island time, eh! So yeah, Tuck, think I can catch a ride back with ya when ya go? I mean I really don't have anything planned, so if you want ta hang out fer a bit and grab a couple beers, it's cool with me. Of course, I'll be buying! Hell maybe we will even get lucky!" Wink, Wink.

Mr. Tucker sort of scratched his head and took a long look at Mr. K (Dallas). "Well, I do know a bar, and it caters to our sort." "And just what kinda sort are we there, Tuck? Hmm?" "C'mon, Mr. K, our sort and you know damn well what I'm talking about, too!" Dallas responded, "Hmm, our sort . . . OK, ya got to promise me one thing though, when I get done at the bank, we don't bring that up while drinking, you're just showing an old friend around." Dallas looked at the clothes he was wearing, then looked at Tucks. "Hmm, I better hit a surf shop and change back into some shorts and a tee shirt. What ya think? Especially if we are going to a locals-type bar, huh?" "Yeah, maybe some sandals too." Tuck added. "OK, my bank is two blocks from here. Where ya wanna meet back up?" Tuck looked at his watch. "I'm only going to the pharmacy and the grocery store, so let hook back up . . . See that Tiki hut down the street there?" Tuck pointed at a thatched roof about two blocks down the street. "Ya can't miss it, somebody will be playing checkers er something." "OK Tuck! I'll meet ya there in an hour or so, er whatever."

Dallas lingered around that area along the boats until Tucker was out of sight. As soon as he was out of sight Dallas headed straight to the nearest tourist shop. He walked in and quickly picked out a pair of cargo shorts and a flowered collared shirt and some cheap sandals. Along with that, he also picked up a medium-sized backpack. He managed a smile at a very pretty girl and paid with a fifty-dollar bill. "Oh Sir, I don't have change for this," the clerk said, holding it up to the light. Dallas asked, "Well what would the change be honey?" The little blonde rang up the amount and replied, "your change would be seventeen-ninety-six." "Is that all?" Dallas laughed. "Well today's gonna be a good day then. Why don't y'all just keep that change and we'll call it even, OK?" Dallas snatched the bag off the counter and wasted no time getting out of the door. He headed east two blocks and took a left. The bank was on the corner. True to island time, it was late and just opening.

Wearing the backpack with his change of clothes, and wearing his Ralph Lauren white button-down and dress khaki pants, he walked directly to the safe deposit box desk. Still carrying his briefcase, he placed it up on the counter and asked the large black lady behind the window and bars, "Good morning, I would like to get into my box this morning." "OK Sir, I need two pieces of I.D. and your key. A passport would do nicely along with a current driver's license."

"Well here's the key and my passport, but we have a little

problem. I don't have a valid driver's license, how about a valid pilot's license? I'm now living in Trinidad and haven't gotten a driver's license yet, but if you will have a good look at my pilot's license, it has my picture and signature and all the valid stamps." The large black lady took all the I.D., which Dallas hated, and walked away with it. He checked his briefcase to make double sure that he had given her all the same I.D s with same names on them. He peeked inside the case while the lady had her back turned. "Woo, OK, I did." Since Janis had set this box up at this bank he had to use his real name. In fact, Dallas had never even been in this safety deposit box. He really had no idea what he would find in it. Finally, after the broad finished with her supervisor, she reappeared. Dallas let out a silent breath of relief when the lady said, "Well sir, usually we would not do this, but my supervisor remembered your wife." "Oh really, that's great." About the same time, he heard the locks on the gates to the back room unlock. He was in! He walked around the end of the counter and through from appearances what appeared to be a pretty sturdy gate. Dallas and the rather larger-than-he-first-thought black lady entered the box room. "OK, number 714, number 714," she mumbled twice before finding it. "Ah yes, here it tis." She slowly glided it out. Dallas had to back up and slid down along the center table to accommodate both the box and the attendant. He heard her under-slip rip, or split down the center, when she backed the box out of the second from the bottom space. He felt embarrassed for her when she finally got the box up on to the table. "Will you be wanting a private room, mister?" She was so out of breath Dallas thought she was going to have a stroke right there and then. "Oh heavens no, love! Dat be jus fine right there, and thank you ever so much for your help, Mum."

Dallas heard the door lock behind the attendant. He quickly opened the box. On top of all the money were two things: a letter from Janis, and her little 5-shot, brushed stainless Colt .380 Mustang, the one he had given to her on their second anniversary.

Dallas picked it up and checked the clip – it was full and even had one in the chamber. He opened the letter. The letter from Janis read *"Dallas, honey, I thought you might find this handy, since you wouldn't be able to carry one into the bank. And if you're reading this it means something is happening, so in this box is almost four hundred-thousand dollars. We must be in trouble for you to open this box. Take the gun Dallas! I imagine you will be walking out with a lot of what's in this box."* Dallas stepped back and looked at all the money. While this was only one of four other safety deposit boxes, she had given him this key to this box and only this box. Dallas stepped back up to the box and started filling the backpack he had brought. It was all in hundreds and Dallas stuffed, according to his loose count, two hundred and fifty thousand in the backpack. He quickly stuffed the .380 pistol in the small of his back and his shirt hid it nicely. He went over to the intercom and summoned the attendant. She arrived in seconds.

"Ok Mum, I'm done in here, let's close it up till next time, OK?" "Yes mister, I hope you found the papers you wanted." "Oh yeah, everything's just fine, thank you so very much for your troubles and I soon come back to see you. So be good, and if you can't be good, be good at it, OK?" "Yes mister, and you be careful after you leave, ya hear?" "Yes Mum, always." Dallas cruised out the sturdy gate and out through the lobby. Once out the front door, Dallas looked from the top step of the bank for the place he was to meet his new friend Tuck. "Ah, there it is, about two blocks down just where he said it was." Dallas hustled towards the outdoor thatched hut roofed structure. There sitting in the shade was Tuck with a couple bags of groceries.

"Hey Mr. Tuck!" Dallas sorta low-voiced as he approached, taking a seat next to him on his left. Tuck looked at Dallas for a short minute. Then he asked, "Why didn't you tell me who you really were?" Tuck had glazed eyes, and his disposition had changed to one to that of a man deceived. Dallas was caught flat-footed, to say the least. Dallas's demeanor changed too. "Why? Who got to ya, Tucker?" "Well let's just say that someone at the bank alerted somebody else." "Well, are you ready ta go?" Tucker asked. "Yeah, let's go. You can tell me about it on the way back to my plane. And maybe I can answer some of your questions in return. Sound like a deal? OK then let's get the funk outta here, NOW!"

They hustled back down along the docks the way they came. Dallas was ever on the lookout for a tail, but didn't see one. He didn't even feel one. It was as if he was getting a pass. "Go collect $250,000. Pass Go and pick up a "Get Outta Jail Free Card" on top of it all." For whatever reason, they made it to the boat, hopped in and were gone. Dallas checked his watch, thinking, "Ya Mon, ahead of schedule." It was only ten forty-five a.m. Dallas clung on to the small backpack with it over one shoulder, feeling the little Colt Mustang .380 with the other hand. He had no idea what old Tucker may be up to. So Dallas broached the subject. "What's on your mind Tucker? Ya caught me plain-out flat-footed at the docks!" Tucker took a long hard look at Dallas before saying anything. Finally, he broke the silence. "Well Mr. Kline, or what the fuck ever. . . Dallas! It is Dallas, right? As in Dallas Streeter?" "Yeah you got me! Now what ya gonna do with me, Mr. Tucker? And who ID'd me in town? I haven't been to that island in over a year and a half at least. So while I was gone at the bank, what happened?"

"It didn't happen at the place where we met back up. I was in a store just doing some shopping, and this black fellow walked right up to me. Said "So you're the one sailing Dallas Streeter around the islands these days? Doing a bit of shopping I see. Make sure you get some fresh conch, Dallas loves it!" I said, "I'm sorry mister, but the guy I'm with is named Kline! It ain't Streeter or whatever you think it is." Right about then this guy pulls out a D.E.A. badge. "Did you read it, Mr. Tucker?" "Yeah I did. It had the name "SANDS" on it."

"Ah," Dallas breathed a bit easier. It was the young agent who had helped him in Port Royal Jamaica last year. "So Tuck, what did he have to say?" "Just that he was surprised to see you on the island,

and that besides Kline not being your name, that for my information if I didn't know it that you are some kind of super smuggler! And that I should be careful when with you." Dallas shot back in reply, "Do you believe him? Have I given you any reason to not trust me?" Tuck responded, "No, but the day ain't over yet!"

Chapter 8

Dallas slowly eased away from Mr. Tucker's sailboat. He paddled over to his plane as Tuck eased out slack so he could pull his dinghy back. He turned his back on Tuck to open the cockpit. Dallas felt it, and Mr. Tucker surely saw as Dallas's little 380. pistol hit the wooden floorboard of the dinghy. "Ah Shit!" Dallas sighed as he bent down to pick it up. He looked back at Tuck and saw a 12-gauge riot pump coming up in his hands. "Ah, hey," Mr. Tucker spoke in a serious tone. "I think I'll have my dinghy back now and it's time for you to leave, "Mr. Kline!"" Dallas slowly put his pistol and bags into the now-open cockpit." "I think you're right, Tuck. Won't be but a min . . ." Dallas tried to say, but was interrupted mid-sentence, "NO! I think it will be less than that, Mr. Kline!" "Yup, you're right – I'm going, going, gone!" Dallas really felt the need for speed at this time and buttoned-up as fast as he could go while cranking the engine on the small plane at the same time. Just so he didn't get shot like a duck while taking off, Dallas turned on a hard spray, a monsoon of water on old Tuck, just enough to blind the old guy for a few precious seconds, just long enough to get the hell outta Dodge!

Dallas roared out, away from the idea of a shotgun tearing a hole in him or his plane. As he reached air speed, he pulled hard back on the yoke and disappeared like fly shit on a windshield to the safety of the air. He let out a deep breath. "That was my fault, I told that old guy no guns, but ah well, I must be getting old, fat or stupid. That would have never happened a year ago," he thought to himself in disgust. As he reached a thousand feet, he looked over his gauges. He gently tapped the fuel gauge, then thought how stupid that was, it was a digital readout. "Goddam computers!" All of a sudden music filled the cockpit. "What the hell did I touch this time?" He spoke aloud as the Stones blasted *"I Can't Get No"* out of the speakers as he searched for the volume button. Finding it, he just smiled and said, "Neither can I Mick, neither can I." Again he checked the fuel gauge, and it read sixty-one percent fuel used. Dallas grabbed his flight plan and tried to figure what that meant in flying time left, but gave up and pressed the range button on the console. "Hmmm, just a little over four hundred miles left." "Well," he thought, "I hope Capt. Bob is south of Cuba by now cause even with the thirty-gallon bladder fuel tank untouched, I'm still gonna need fuel when I get to Jamaica." He looked at his map on his lap and used his middle knuckle of his right hand index finger as a measure of one inch against the map's distance legend. "Yep, I think the computer is right," laughed out loud and turned the music back up, leaving today's shaky business in his wake and hoped old Tuck had dried off.

He sat back, listening to the Stone's *"Satisfaction"* disc. He thought that these new so-called compact disc deals were cool, now he wouldn't have to search a pile of tapes, he could search though a pile of stackable discs. "I wonder how long it will be before a lot of musicians used this new format? A new young South Texas guitar player named Stevie Ray something or another had his first new work on them, so I bet a lot will follow, cause this guy was hot shit. Hell, here this kid is playing "Voodoo Chile" like a madman and was a big hit in the states already." The plane caught a piece of bad air and woke Dallas out of his musical dream. He quickly compensated and checked his bearings. "OK, another few hours and he would reach Port San Antonio just about eleven p.m." Capt.

Bob had left a day and a half ago in his Scarab, and even loaded with extra fuel his boat could and had (even with a full load of weed) carried his ass at a very pleasant seventy-mph. As well it should, with three two hundred horsepower Merc cruisers screaming down the shipping lanes. But with just extra fuel, he can easily hit eighty mph on a calm sea. "So he'll be there in time to meet up with Marboy (the Jamaican) on the beach where we moved several loads of J's finest in 1981, just before Dallas had finished his own landing strip up in the mountains above MoBay. "Jeez, I remember that first month the strip was open and I had to pay off what seemed like the whole Parish up there. Man that sucked, but it was the only way, the best way, if ya did every flight in and out was looked forward to by the farmers; nobody knew where the cops and Jamaican Defense force was better than the locals." It also raised the quality of life all around. Hell Dallas even bought some of their local "Lamb's Bread," the best pot money could buy back then. There was not a lot, but Dallas took every bale he could get, making everybody (Ire Mon) all smiles. Dallas laid his head back again and thought, "Man those were days when life seemed simple. Now I have ta deal with fucking kidnappers? How fucked up this is with it being my own family? I don't care if the D.E.A. is helping me again, I will kill this prick Skeets this time! This time he crossed the line between being professional and being a scumbag killer. At least pros have a moral compass, whereas now he is just a soulless ghoul . . . And he will pay, fucking D.E.A. or not! And that prick Assistant Director of Operations Agent Cox better not get in the way!"

Now, as in the past, Dallas had never been able to be as close to his family as he wanted, instead he formed up the closest thing to it. His dreams were snatched away by his mother's need to be happy first, and more to the point she paid outta guilt for everything a young Dallas Streeter wanted, or what she thought he wanted. That was cool, he had his own apartment before he was out of high school. What he really wanted was a good education, but to his amazement there wasn't money for "that,"" his mother told him as she bought him a twelve-thousand-dollar boat at graduation. He hated that boat. His friends loved it. It made him a chick magnet. That made, of all people, his mother happy, so Dallas showed a happy face when she said, "Isn't this better than a year at some college?" "Sure it is Mom; sure it is . . ." He smiled.

In Port San Antonio, Marboy rolled out the Little Tiger from its carport. "Mon, dis is one fine paint job," he said aloud to himself, arms folded across a blown-out chest. There sat a Subaru four-wheel drive wagon. What was once a custom sunburst orange, ah hem, was now a badly camouflage-painted mess. But Marboy was proud as he loaded groceries, water, his bag of clothes and a twelve-gauge Mossberg riot pump shotgun. "Oh boy, Dallas gonna be so happy when he sees dis car and me with the same gun he give ta me years ago." He clapped his hands and opened the door, jumped in and was gone to his meeting with Capt. Bob and dey Boss Dallas . . . He had just gotten to the road at the bottom of his driveway when a goat dashed out from his neighbor's farm. "What dat was?" But the goat brought memories still fresh of his younger nephew, killed while cleaning a goat that they had hit driving to meet a plane at Dallas's landing strip, the day after a really ugly American D.E.A. agent showed up after Dallas had paid them at the MoBay Yacht Club picnic tables, and because Sydney was a quiet boy not used to being questioned and refused this agents advances on his person for answers about where Dallas was and with whom, he shot the boy in the thigh and Sydney died. He bled out from a shot to the femoral artery, in one of Dallas's jeeps on the way to the hospital. This memory saddened and shifted Marboy's good mood to somber and rage.

Capt. Bob gained speed from a north wind and a following

sea. He was making eighty miles per hour when he first spotted the far off spot on the horizon. It brought a clean smile to a dirty face awash in sea spray. "Ah man, only four hours and I can crash the hell out." He was starting to talk to himself after two days and two nights on the water. "Just keep it together a wee bit longer Bob," he thought.

Marboy dusted up the road, the Tiger hauling ass nicely. "Nutting much happening around des days, I wonder what the old man Brewster is doin des days?" He was thinking of Carl Brewster, the long-gone, over-the-hill Vietnam vet who came to Jamaica after Nam and never left. "Ya Mon, I knows we gonna be seeing him soon, soon as Dallas get here. Ya mon I thinks some ting big be up wit Dallas coming in and all." So Marboy just kept driving. Port San Antonio was on the eastern side of the island, about six hours of modest jungle canopy roads far and away from his modest house in Negril on the west side. He would be passing the pretty hidden entrance of Carl Brewster's property. He had heard rumors that Carl had been having problems, as it seems a lot of folks were with a thug posse of thieves, but he hadn't heard any news lately and he just assumed Carl, being a Vietnam vet would be all right. One thing Marboy knew though was that if Dallas was gonna hit the island he would be seeing Carl.

Capt. Bob turned off his running lights so he was able to see his new gadget. It was called G.P.S. "Wow, this is some shit!" he thought as he looked at the numbers change every few minutes. Now if it can only find the hole in the reef where he had to turn in to the beach drop spot he'd used so many times before. He'd done all the chart work and checked the tide table even though his Scarab only drew two and a half feet at the water line. As it got darker he could see some of the ports lighted waterfront. "Ok, where is that cut?" "Oh yeah baby, here she is," as it all came back seeing the tree line in silhouette. Bob could smell the beach, the smell of seaweed and the slightly fishy smell the sand gives off at the water line. He squinted hard, the half-moon was just giving off enough light so he could now make out the split in the trees above the mangroves, "Oh I got it." He trimmed the engines up and backed off the throttle. His depth sounder was pinging as he gave it one last bump, just enough to push the Scarab's bow up onto the little beach. Bob killed all the power and lights, and sat quietly and listened to the breezes and rustling of the trees. It seemed all he could hear was the lapping of small beach-breaking waves. Capt. Bob grabbed up his beach kit, and looking it over saw that everything was there – a small camp stove, assorted ropes, his hammock, two small battery-powered lanterns, three or four old sea ration dinners, and a crazy mix of suntan, mosquito netting and lotions. Of course, he reached under the console and placed his Berretta 9mm and hand-held Motorola three-channel radio in his waistband. "OK, where the hell is Marboy?" Looking down at his watch, he mumbled, "Hmm, I'm early. Or is he late?"

He grabbed the bowlines and jumped off onto beach. Bob fell flat on his face, and the urge to laugh and swear overcame him as he crawled back up to his knees. "Ah, shit! I've been on the water too long," he whispered hoarsely to no one. "My ass hurts from sitting and my legs are numb from all the bouncing for the last sixteen hours. I have to get my land legs back!" Struggling to his feet, he pulled the bowlines tight around a coconut palm on both sides of the bow. It was slack tide so he knew that the boat was going to rise and fall over the next twelve hours or so, and gave the Scarab enough scope to allow it to rise and fall with the tide changes. "OK, let's set up camp," again talking to himself. Bob had been in the military and had a lean-to and a small fire going in just twenty short minutes. Finally, he strung his hammock up and laid down. "Man, what a freaking day and night and day and night," he thought. He was counting the hours on his fingers when the drone of a revving car engine caught his ear. He rolled out of the hammock, pulling his

Berretta 9mm down with him on the side, away from the oncoming noise, leaving the hammock swinging wildly in the breeze.

- Marboy, after having made a half dozen stops since he had left, didn't think anything of just whipping it into four-wheel high and crashing into the bushes that now covered the fire trail that once was a road so well-traveled that he was driving more on muscle memory than actually thinking about it. "Man, I wonders if Capt. Bob will make it OK safe in here tonight?" Capt. Bob could hear the engine getting very close now. He belly-crawled backwards a couple more feet. "Damn! Whoever it is, they're going to come over that berm, go airborne and land right the hell on me!" Marboy started singing some obscure Rasta song when he hit the berm. "OH Shit!" slipped out as his front tires left the ground, almost flipping the Tiger. When the front wheels came down, Bob jumped up, gun in hand, and screaming like a madman rushed the strange looking camo-painted car. One very scared Rasta mon was in the front seat. Marboy saw Capt. Bob, Capt. Bob saw Marboy, and the laugh riot began . . . "What ya doin mon? Why ya in da middle of da freaking road!" "Well I was just waiting for this Jamaican to drop by and I didn't want him to miss me!" Bob shouted back, as he slowly put his gun back in his waistband and climbed back into his hammock, only to roll out and hit the ground with a thud. "Man, ya don't need me to runs ya down, you can't even stay put laying in yer own bed without hurting yerself!" Marboy slammed the Tiger's door and walked over to the little fire that Bob had going. "So Capt., when the big boss coming in?" Bob, getting up from the sandy ground, looked up at Marboy. "Hmm, I think he'll be due in about an hour, that's how I have it timed. Yeah just about an hour," looking up from his watch.

Marboy asked, "Ok Capt., what's the real story? Why I has to come out of my comfy house in the dead of night, eh? Dallas back in business again? Are we going back to work? Ya knows things aint the way they used to be . . . We have trouble all over the Island nowdays. It aint like we can just run wild anymore!" "OK, I'll tell you what I know," Bob said, walking over to the fire and throwing another branch or two on it. "All I know is that scumbag D.E.A. agent we left on that Morgan boat up in Great Inagua, Bahamas has somehow done a bad thing with Dallas's little brother, and that this time it's personal! I also know that the Chief and his boats are on the case too, so we have a full team and it may get ugly, real ugly before it's over. When Big "D" gets here, I'm sure he'll tell us more." "Well, Capt., if Dallas need me I be here fer the man." Marboy squatted down in front of the fire, poking it with a little stick. "I wonder if we gonna go see ole Carl Brewster? I think dat why Dallas had us come to dis here beach, it's a short drive up to his house, but I hear ole Carl has taken a beating or two from dem mountain boys - they calling themselves a "Pussy" or a "Posse." What's that mean Capt.? A Posse? What's that?"

Bob looked over at Marboy and shook his head. "A Posse, huh? Well it can't be good, that's what I would say. No damn good! Well hell, where's the fucking beer Marboy? Don't you even tell me that you didn't bring any beer! I aint having none of it!" "Of what, Capt.?" "I aint having you tell me that you came all this way and didn't bring any beers. I aint having any lies, I know that you never go anyplace without a case of Red Stripe." "Oh, be my beer dat yer after Capt.? Why don't ya just ask a man for a beer, I have beer-a-plenty mon, nice an cold too! Jeez, you damn white boys! Always be playing around," Marboy sang as he got up and walked over to the back of the Little Tiger. He grabbed a cooler and walked over to the edge of the small camp, parked the cooler and opened it, threw Bob one, grabbed two for himself, "Jus so I's don't have to get up twice. You be getting yer own after dis one."

"So Marboy!" Capt. Bob yelled after his fifth Red Stripe. "You know Dallas is gonna kick your little black ass when he sees his "Little Tiger" all painted up like a fucking tank, you do know this? And by the way, what in God's name possessed you to do such a thing anyway? I mean what the fuck were you thinkin? Look at it! Shit, do you think you could have done a little bit more to fuck it up proper? Ya know maybe shoot some holes in it too? I mean hell, why not?" Marboy sat quietly, listening to Capt. Bob's rant. He sat drinking his beer and turning a stick in the fire . . . He looked at Bob and said, "Ya know Capt., you don't live on dey damn island no more! Mon, I'll tell you what, you move back here and drive a nice car, in two weeks everybody on dis island know who you is, they knows where you lives, dey know every ting bout you, in two weeks" . . . "In three weeks you be robbed, raped, and probably burned out of yer damn house! I paint dat car so Dallas have a car when he need one, and one dat looks enough like "Trouble" to "Keep Your Ass out of Trouble." You getting it, boy?" Marboy took the stick out of the fire and lit a big spliff with it. "I's hopes you is." "Just the same Marboy, I wanna see ole Dallas's face when he sees that," pointing at what was once a sunburst, burnt orange, four-wheel drive, four-door hatchback Subaru tough-looking little car. Not the para-military transformed in paint only, with the chrome bumpers now painted flat black and the rest covered by the best cans of green and black spray paint a Jamaican dollar can buy. "Oh boy I can't wait, can you Marboy?" Capt. Bob said under his breath as he grabbed another beer and headed back to his hammock.

Chapter 9

Dallas had been in the air over six hours. "Man I need fuel, or I'm gonna be a boat in about forty-five minutes," he grumbled, reaching over the seat searching for his handheld radio. "Ah ha, here it be!" He ran his hand in the glow of his instrument panel over the length of the radio, feeling for the antenna. "Ok it's seems OK." Flying with his knees, he turned the firm Motorola knobs, the light on top glowed red, he keyed the mic and it glowed green. "All righty then!" Even though Dallas could not yet see the island, his new G.P.S. thingy said he was within radio range. He keyed the mic again, and with a deep voice he spoke into it. "This is inbound traffic on Channel 2, I'm looking for a friendly voice, repeat this is inbound traffic on channel 2 and I'm looking for a friendly voice! C'mon guys, how about that channel 2?" Dallas switched fuel tanks. "OK, one more time! This is inbound traffic on channel 2. Getting pissed!" Dallas yelled. "Hey wake the fuck up, Marboy . . . Bob!" All of sudden there was a distant crackle. "You have a friendly voice on channel 2, come back! We can barely read you! Can you boost power?" "Ah, shit, I'm still twenty miles out," Dallas figured, using his watch. "Yeah, stay on 2, back in five mins - ten the most, over." He lowered the radio and started his descent to about three hundred feet, and ten percent of that every 3 mins, til the warning light which comes on at fifty-feet goes off with the crash warning.

"Yeah I know," he thought. "There aint going to be any crashes this time in Jamaica, I'm over those, really . . ."

Back on the beach, Marboy and Capt. Bob started cleaning up the beer bottles and shit off the beach. "OK Marboy, he was about fifteen miles out, I can tell because his radio was still crackling. Anyway I think he'll do a fly over, like always. He's in a seaplane, how big it is I don't know, hell it can't be very big, that's for sure. So have a seat and watch the car, if he needs help, I'll go and get him in the Scarab. But I think if he is flying alone he won't need me. He'll probably pull right up to the beach. At least that's what I'm hoping. Hell I don't want ta go swimming tonight, ya know?" Marboy shrugged his shoulders in a yes or whatever way. But he didn't say word one. He just stared at the sky. Shortly thereafter they both heard a small airplane engine coming in off the beach breeze. It grew closer, and finally was flying directly over them. They both looked up, and then at each other, as it passed over and then out of sight. "Jezz!" Bob said, "That's one of the smallest damn airplanes I've ever seen! Eh Marboy?" "Ya mon, what the hell is he flying? Sounds like a mosquito strapped to his back. Man dey boss gots a new toy. But it goes like hell though." "Yeah, it sure does go like hell. Where did he go?" They both searched the limited amount of sky above them and listened for the sound again. "Nothing!" Bob said. "I don't hear a damn thing, do you?" "No, not a damn thing here Capt. Where he go?"

The wind was picking up slowly and Dallas circled back around to the south and decided that he'd put down a couple hundred yards from where the campsite was set up on the beach before the wind became more of a problem. He banked in, and while he had an onshore breeze, managed to head upwind a bit, hit his flaps, reduced his air speed to about forty miles per hour, and just before he touched down goosed the engine and lifted the nose just perfectly. At that moment, he was no longer a plane, but a boat! He ran the main engine until he could see the dim campfire glow, then cut it off. He leaned over and above his head flipped the toggle switch for the electric fan motor. It hummed up out of its compartment and Dallas switched over to it on the console control panel so he could steer the plane into the beach. Dallas saw the fire better now, and lined up the nose of the plane with it. He knew it got shallow fast in here, so he also flipped the switches that automatically started the wings to self-fold up. He gave a little blast on the horn, to let the now in-shock crew know that he was coming in.

Bob was the first one in the knee-deep water; he had already grabbed the nose ring on the plane and was guiding it into the mangrove slip that had been prepared before Marboy showed up. Marboy wasn't far behind - He went directly to the tail section and was getting all wet from the electric fan motor, which Dallas cut off a second or so too late. With that all done, Dallas popped the pilot's side hatch. It sounded like a fresh can of coffee being opened, a real vacuum sound. "Schwoop" it went. The pressure escaped, and Dallas called out "HEY SO WHAT BRINGS YOU GUYS OUT ON A NIGHT LIKE THIS ? Can't be pussy, can't be beer, and it CAN'T BE A GOOD TIME!" The two of them, Marboy and Capt. Bob, stood there looking at Dallas with like "What the Fuck?" looks on their faces. "Well just don't just stand there with those "what the fuck looks! Hey, wake up and get me a beer please! We don't have a lot of time, OK? Guys? A beer, please? I'm parched." Dallas hopped out into the ankle-deep water and headed towards the little fire. Marboy was already in the cooler and bringing a beer "Ahh, that's better," Dallas said as he took a long draw on the Red Stripe. "Man, do you know how long I have been thinking about this? Yup, sometimes it's the little things that are the best . . . Hey Bob! There's some cargo netting in the box behind the seats, can you and Marboy please spread it out over the plane? It'll hide her from prying eyes, as long as those eyes don't get too close. I don't know yet, but one of ya all may have to stay here and watch things . . ." His voice dropped off into a horse whisper as he pointed at the car. "What the Fuck is THAT? Is that my "Tiger?"" Without even looking at Marboy, Dallas was on his feet walking towards it. "Oh my Fucking God, what in the Hell did you do to my car, Marboy? Jeez, you're kidding me, right? This is a joke, right?" His hands now on the car, looking down, he said, "You are so dead Marboy, after this, you are so dead. I can't believe this! OK, never mind the small shit, c'mon over here and have a seat. I want you two to know what you are getting into, or at least know what I know before we go. Because we are going, that's a fact!" Both Capt. Bob and Marboy took a piece of ground around the small fire. Bob lit a Marlboro Red and gave a deep sigh. "How come I get this feeling, Dallas, that this aint any regular party on the water?" "Well Bob, cause it aint. It's ugly and it's personal this time. People are going to get hurt most likely, and that's why we are having this pre-movement talk. But never mind that now."

"OK, this is the deal. You both know that I'm pretty much done as far as our business goes, right? Right. Well I've settled in on my little island pretty quietly over the last year or so. Oh, sure, I have just done a few things, maybe, but nothing I can call big. I'm sure ya all have heard rumors, but I swear whatever I'm doing is not like it used to be. Are we agreed on that?" Both Bob and Marboy shook their heads, Bob shook his "yes" and Marboy shook his "no." Dallas saw this and just cocked his head and sort of laughed to himself. "Well," half-laughing, "then I know that at least you are listening." "C'mon Dallas," Bob spoke up "Would you just tell us what the fuck is going on, we don't care what you are or aren't doing, just tell us what the HELL is going on, and how we can help. Look you have had us, or some of us, come a thousand miles!" Dallas stood up and put his hands up. "OK, here is where we are. It looks like, no it is . . . remember that scumbag D.E.A. agent, Ernie Skeets? Remember how I had put him in his own trick bag on that last deal? Well I don't know how, but he managed to escape from his asshole fellow D.E.A. buddies who promised me that he would never see the light of day for killing Wayne out by the airport that week in

Miami, when we borrowed that plane and I crashed it and so on, and I gave them him exchange for you and you, Jimmy Kurtz, Janis and I and our money. Well that prick is back in my life, and not only that, he has grabbed my little brother Chance. We, gentlemen, are going to get the kid back. I got this info from Asst. Director Cox, remember him? Yea, he says to stay out of it. Of course. But I can't, you all know me to well for that."

"Asst. Dir Cox came to my island, and told me all this crap. About how they think Skeets is, and has been, helping Francisco Amada up in Belize. I don't know, maybe he is. But I know Frank Amada, and if he has my brother Chance at his place, Frank won't want any part of this shit. Frank is a stand-up guy, and if I was still in the biz, that's who I'd be doing it with. Read me guys? Yeah, OK, I have been doing this one little thing with Amada." Dallas was now in a "confession to friends" mood. "Anyway, I know where and how to get Chance back, I just need your help. Yours and Carl Brewster's. So who's going to stay here with the plane while I go see Carl? I think that Marboy, you should go, Carl knows you better. He might not remember you Bob, he's getting older now, and with all the shit that has been going on up in the mountain it's better that I take Marboy. You get it, don't ya Bob?" "Oh yeah I get it, I'll just stay here and hold down the fort. In fact, I have a nice hammock and a little fire, some beans and franks, and I'll gas up the Mosquito while you're gone. I'll be just fine; you guys go deal with ole Carl." "OK then, saddle-up Marboy!"

Dallas once again looked at his Tiger, and winced as he walked over to it. "Really? Fucking Cameo? Marboy you are gonna pay to have this re-painted, I hope you know that!" "I's gonna have it as nice as the day you left it with me next time you see her boss, I promise." "You better or Carl will, I'm sure he is gonna have something to say about it too. You can bank on that, my little Rasta buddy. OK, do we have everything?" Dallas looked over the inside of the car. "What is that smell, Marboy? What the hell stinks so bad in here?" "Oh, I thinks dat be dat goat." "What goat?" Dallas shook his head. "Goat?" "Ya mon! Remember when we killed dat goat last time you came in and crashed your plane all to hell boss?" "No, you killed a goat before I came in and smashed my "borrowed" plane all to hell. Yes, I do. So what?" "After dat bad agent man, SKEETS shot my nephew Sydney, I put the goat in da Tiger, so we could take Sydney to the hospital. And, and . . ." "OK, OK," Dallas sighed. "Never mind. Just forget about it, OK?" "Yes sir." Marboy ended that story there. "Fucking Goat! That figures. OK Marboy, get me to Carl's, OK?" "Ya Mon, we going to Carl's the back way, he been having a problem with dem mountain boys up der." "That's what you were saying," Dallas said, quietly. "When was the last time you saw Carl, Marboy?" "Oh it been about six months at least. Dallas. He don't look right." "What is that supposed to mean?" "Well it looked to me that he was digging or burying something, boss." "Really? Why, was he all dirty or what?" "Well I don't know from dirty, but he was looking like he hadn't been sleeping too well, and nows dat I's thinks it, he had a tool in his hand, maybe it was a weapon, but I think a tool, yup." "Why can't we go the normal way?" Dallas asked, in a curious tone. "Oh Hell, he shut down the main road. It's all wired with cameras, and I hear booby traps. So we gonna go the new trail. It's the only way in or out, as far as I know . . ." "Well," Dallas asked, "and how fast is this "new way," Marboy?" "Oh it is quicker than the old way from here. We be der in about twenty-mins. It's through the bush, you'll see." "OK! Let's just get there and find that ole hermit, I have a deadline to meet. I hope he is in a good mood." They drove in silence the rest of the way to the entrance of Carl's property. The only noise was the night birds and the sound of shifting gears on the Little Tiger.

"Opps! Der it was!" Marboy hit the brakes and the Tiger created a cloud of dust that came in the windows. "Damn-it Marboy," Dallas choked, "we missed it?" "Yea boss we missed da turn." "I didn't see any turn or driveway, or anything. Are you sure Marboy?"

"Ya mon, I's sure it be right back here," Marboy said, now driving in reverse. "It's der! Right der Dallas," Marboy said, pointing at a black hole in the wall of jungle on Dallas's right. "That's it? I don't even see any tire tracks, or even a path. Are you sure?" Without a word, Marboy had backed up and shot through the darkness, dragging vines and branches along the side mirrors. All of a sudden, it opened into a semi-worn goat path with two trails for tires to ride in. The Moon shone the way and the two followed the lines in front of them. "Hey Marboy, I know where Carl's house is, and we going uphill." "Ya Mon! We coming out on top his house, we gonna park and walk down."

"The hell we are! Take that path to the right, it will take us down onto the driveway. I'm not walking up on Carl! Hell no! He'll shoot us dead before we get fifty-yards from the house. No, we are going to drive right up to the front door. I'm not sneaking up on him. I'm his friend, and friends don't sneak around in the dark outside another man's house! What's wrong with you Marboy?" "But boss, Carl is different nowadays." "I don't give a shit, we are not walking down!" "OK, but you see, you see Boss. Da man aint right no more." "Well good, then I may have gotten here in time to get him right!" Dallas put his arm out and braced himself as the Tiger downshifted on the little hill it was going down. The Tiger crunched its way onto the driveway, just at the beginning of the circular driveway. Marboy gunned it around the circle and came to a stop in front of Carl's house.

"Holy Shit! What the hell happened here?" Dallas stared out at a familiar but strangely dark and unkempt house that used to be all lit up; a house that once had orchids and Birds of Paradise flowers, as well many other plants, all in a natural landscaped front yard. "Man, Marboy, you weren't kidding, this place looks like it's abandoned." "Well boss, he's here. I's knows it." Dallas laid on the horn and gave it the standard S.O.S. blast. "This should bring him out," he thought, and he should know who it is, too. That is if he has any mind left. "I can't or don't believe that Carl's gone south on us, but from the looks of his house . . ." Dallas got out slowly and surveyed the house. Bullet holes were everywhere, like somebody just drove up and shredded the place. The fountain in the center of the drive way was all shot to shit, no water, nothing but weeds growing around what was once a centerpiece of the front yard. Dallas called out, "Carl! Hey Carl, it's Dallas. C'mon out. I'm with Marboy. We are alone, it's Dallas Streeter! Carl!" Dallas heard what sounded like a large rat under the front porch. "Yeah Carl! It's Dallas. C'mon out man . . . It's OK. It's Dallas!"

With an almost silent whisper, Dallas could hear and see what looked like a trap door open on the left side of the top of the porch. Dallas felt a cool breeze down the back of his neck, as what was left of his friend popped out with a very large .50 caliber automatic rifle pointed in his direction. "Hold on now Carl," Dallas yelled. "It's me man, Dallas." "It is, huh?" a voice in a low tone spoke. "Carl! Put that goddamn gun down! It's me, fer Christ sakes." "And Marboy," Marboy said, in a rather shaky voice. Carl came up another two steps out of his hole. "So it is, so it is!" Carl laughed. "Oh boy I had you, son! I thought you were going to shit yer pants." Carl broke out laughing "Of course it's you. Who the hell else would be so stupid as to drive right up into a kill zone, except you? That took balls, son. Well what are ya waiting for? C'mon and give your ole Uncle Carl a hug! But drop any guns you may have first!" "What? Carl, you know I don't give up my gun to nobody!" Dallas spoke in a defiant voice. "That's what I wanted to hear son. I don't see real well in the dark, but your voice just confirmed what I already thought! Now come on up, Dallas, nice to see ya again, it's been too damn long." "Well, we'll get into that Carl, but first your gonna tell me what the fuck happened here."

"OK, but first put "MY" Tiger on the side of the house, under that canopy. And who the or what the fuck did you do to "MY" car?" "Yeah about the car . . . Ahh, we'll get back to that, but right now we have to talk Carl. Why are you in a hole under your porch? I see that you aren't living "in" your house, and so why is the next question." Carl reached back and took out the rubber band holding his hair back in a ponytail, and shook his head like a wet dog would to dry itself after a bath. "Well son, you just get yer ass up here and follow me down, I'll tell you why." Slowly Marboy backed the Tiger into the canopied garage. Then Dallas and Marboy slowly navigated the stairs up to the top of the front porch and walked towards the open trap door that Carl had sprung out of. Dallas noticed a poor lone orchid on the wall of the house. It was the only live plant anywhere within fifty feet. "Well I see you have saved your old friend here at least," pointing to the orchid. This orchid was one that Carl had a long-term relationship with, and Dallas had never known Carl to not have this same plant always next to the front door. Carl called it by name and everything, but Dallas had forgotten the name. Some woman's name, he remembered that. "Oh yeah, she and I go way back," Carl mumbled as he showed Dallas the first steps that led down into somewhere. "Jeez Carl, where the hell are you taking us, down?" "Just follow me and be careful, don't touch anything, and I mean anything." "You bet Carl. Did you hear that Marboy? Don't touch anything." "Well can I's walk on da floor?" "Shut-up Marboy," Carl growled. "Just follow me and Dallas, put your damn hands in your pockets, how about that?" "OK Mr. Carl, hands in my pockets." Carl broke out laughing at Marboy's answer. "Jeez Dallas, I see you're still running with nothing but the best!" "OK Carl, now it's your turn to shut-up," Dallas joked back. "Can't ya see your scaring him?"

Carl and Dallas, with Marboy behind, descended down the stairs, which was more like stairwell since it turned to the left every six or eight steps. "Damn Carl, we must be like twenty-feet down." The smell was a musty, earthen smell. It reminded Dallas of when he was just a kid in Michigan digging for worms on the bank of the small creek that ran behind his house. Roots from the large Gumbo

Limbo's and Strangler Figs fought for the rights to the moist air in the stairwell. They finally hit bottom. Carl reached over and threw a switch, and Dallas finally could see where he was. "Christ Carl! You're fuckin' kidding me!" Dallas spoke from the entrance of what he was seeing. The lights lit up all along a neatly dug and compacted tunnel. The floor was all interlocking pavers, the kind you find on driveways, the lights were flush mounted in the walls every ten or fifteen feet. Carl looked back at Dallas and smiled. "You ain't seen nothing yet son!" "Lead on Carl, lead on!" Carl spoke back at Marboy, "You still have your hands in your pockets, son?" "Yes I's do Mr. Carl," "Well why Marboy? That seems like a foolish thing to do, a grown man with his hands in his pockets." A laugh followed. "You can take them out now, just don't touch anything, OK?" "Yes sir, I won't." "OK Carl, lead on," Dallas said. "This is a hell of a place ya got going here. But why, Carl?" "Oh, let's just get to the kitchen and we can have a seat, I don't have much in the way of company these days, at least friendly company anyway."

Grabbing a chair from around a small table that did double duty as a butcher's block, Dallas and Marboy sat, as Carl turned away and opened a small refrigerator. "Beer?" Carl asked. "What?" Dallas said. "Do you want a beer?" Carl repeated. "Oh yeah, sure, thanks Carl, got one for Marboy?" Carl grabbed a third one and begrudgingly sat it down in front of Marboy. He handed Dallas his opened, and then opened his own and took a chair himself. Dallas started off. "Now you wanna tell me just what in the fuck has happened here? I mean the whole f-ing upstairs is shot to shit! I mean Carl, there must be two hundred to two hundred-fifty holes in the place, and they look like AK-47's too. Your Mac-10's leave bigger holes, even though I think I saw those too. So shit. What happened Carl?" Carl sat back in his chair and took a huge tug off his Red Stripe beer, then he reached across the table and took a Camel straight out of a pack half-gone, reached deep down in his pocket and took out a Zippo lighter. It had a shield on one side. On the top was a yellow horse's head, in the middle was a diagonal yellow stripe, below that the number 101st in yellow also. He held it up to the light, rolled it between his fingers, and flicked and fire was born.

"Well Dallas, as you can see, there have been a few changes since the last time you were here. After you split on your boat with all that trouble on board, ya know what I'm talking about, you left a hell of a mess behind, son. With you shooting that scumbag Ochoa's helicopter down, and leaving a half a ton of "Puro-yeh-o" here at my house, hell I had every fucking gang snooping around up here for months. Oh, and the fucking "Don't Expect Anything crews." "The who, Carl?" "The fucking D.E.A. Dallas! Jeez son, where the hell have you been? That's what they are called now! the "Don't Expect Anything" gang. They are just as bad as the rest. Except that at least they don't drive up shooting AK-47's at the house. No, they just get out and start snooping. While two are asking me questions about you, or the gangs, or trying to get me to work for them . . ." "WAIT! Just hold you cock there for a second, Carl. Get you to work for them? Is that the truth, Carl?" "It is, I swear to God, Dallas. More than once, too." Carl flicked his cigarette butt into an open Maxwell House coffee can on the floor six feet away. It hit with a resounding "Ting" and a "Thud" as it hit the bottom. "So that accounts for all the bullet holes, and broken windows, yer bombed-out planting shed, and so on, right?" Carl looked down, and then up and around at Dallas and then Marboy. He had already lit another smoke. This one he took a long drag on and passed it towards Marboy. "Hmmm," Marboy smiled as he followed Carl's lead. "Ire Mon dis be da Lamb's Bread, Dallas, have a go Dallas!" Dallas eyeballed the blunt, and looked at Carl. Carl just shrugged his shoulders and nodded. "Sure why not," Dallas spoke in a low tone. "But we can't get all fucked-up either, Marboy, we have biz' to take care of too. Remember, Marboy."

Carl broke in loudly. "Yeah, I heard that Skeets has your brother, Dallas!" Dallas, caught off guard, shot Carl a look. Carl continued,

"That's why you're here. Right Dallas? More than just a social call, huh son? Ya know son, I live up here, alone, as I always have. After Viet Nam, it was different. I couldn't stay stateside – I just didn't fit in. I know the hippies had an agenda, and I agreed with most of it. But I could not pick a side, man. Black Panthers, White Panthers, S.D.S., "Turn on, Tune in, Drop out . . ." Bullshit! I had to get away from all that shit, man. I had to clear my own head. So I came here. It was cool here man, almost like a quiet piece of Nam, only none of the hustle and bustle cons that plagued that place. No guns here, maybe a walking stick, but the smell, yeah the smell of this place put the hook in me. Now look at me! Dallas, shit, I'm in shock! They came again a month ago. Just rolled up in their fucking jeeps and started shooting again. It's lucky I had started on this down here about four months ago." Dallas felt like saying something, but he really couldn't even get the words out. Carl keep going about how he had only worked at night and had help from one of his nearest neighbor's son. The ones he could trust, that he had known the family for 20+ years. With this young man the two of them had dug, cleared and even put down a lot of the concrete together. "Wow!" Dallas jumped to his feet. "Do you need anything Carl? I mean can I help you? I will, but right now I say we do a little bartering. You're right Carl, aside from coming all this way to check up on ya, yes I do need your help." Dallas sat back down after making his point and changing the subject all at the same time. Carl's face seemed a bit more focused than it did a few minutes before, that's for sure. "OK, Sonny Jim, what ya have in mind?" Dallas pulled out a small notebook out of his cargo pants pocket. "Hmm, let me see . . . Carl, remember the Chief?" "Yea, of course I do. He traded me some fancy L.A.W. rockets for some Claymore mines, of course I remember him." "Ahh . . . yeah Carl, about those, do you still have them, or did you . . ." "No Dallas, I still have 'em. Why? Ya need them?" "Carl where I'm going I need whatever you may have on hand that you might not need, at least till I come back down here

and help you get right with these punks. After all, it is "Kinda-
Sorta" my fault that everyone from the mountain posse's to the
D.E.A. boys are up here hassling ya!" "OK Dallas, if you promise to
come back soon, you're welcome to whatever I have down there . . ."
"Down where?" Marboy finally spoke up from his chair next to
the refrigerator. Carl looked at Dallas and chuckled a bit like Bella
Lugosi and pointed into the darkness with a slightly arthritic finger.
"Down there," he motioned to Marboy. Marboy's eyes got wide.
"What mean there's a down there, down there, Carl?" "Oh yes,"
Carl spoke back in a spooky voice. "C'mon Marboy," and grabbed
Marboy's wrist. "Oh hell no, Dallas I's gonna stay right here," and
planted a foot. Dallas broke out laughing,, "OK, OK, you just stay
right here in the kitchen, Marboy. You don't have to go! Jeeez, Carl,
now ya scared the shit outta him. That wasn't cool, Carl, now I gotta
carry all that shit myself." "Nah" Carl said. "I'll help ya."

The two of them walked out of the lit room of the kitchen. All
Dallas could really see was the frame of the kitchen door, beyond
that was darkness. Carl led the way as the two of them walked into
the darkness and back onto the packed clay floor in the hall. "Hey
Carl, you have lights in the tunnel, don't ya?" Dallas asked in a low
tone. "If I can find the switch we do," Carl chuckled, as he reached
up and found the switch box. "Jeez, Carl, I guess you do have lights."
The tunnel was lighted with inset ceiling lights, and all along the
way were electric cables, every now and again there was a caged light
at about shoulder height. These lights were placed near the openings
to tunnels under construction, or to rooms already built-out. Some
had a pantry of dry goods, other were empty. Along the way Carl
stopped, took out his pocketknife and trimmed some roots that
were growing down from the ceiling. One was wrapped around one
of the caged lights; as he trimmed it the smell of Jasmine filled the
tunnel. "Goddamn Jasmine trees, they're the worst, fucking grow
down instead of up, I swear!" The tunnel kept its downhill grade
for about two hundred feet and then leveled out. Dallas noticed

that along the way there were square holes with little steel doors on them. "Hey Carl, what's up with the boxes?" Dallas had tried to open one in passing – all had a safe-like dial lock. "Oh those, never mind those," Carl shot back. "Things." "What?" Dallas asked. "Just things?" Carl looked over his shoulder. "I said never mind the boxes. You hard of hearing, boy?" "Oh, no, just curious, Carl, just curious," Dallas answered as the walkway got a bit narrower in the tunnel. Carl stopped and reached up to a kind of switch, and all of a sudden a large room opened. This was not a tunnel room; this was a vault! "What the fuck, Ca..." Dallas couldn't even get the rest out.

The door on the outside, when closed, was finished to match the tunnel hallways, so if the door was closed you would think you had hit a dead end. But when opened, the four-inch steel door frame, and six three-inch rotary deadbolts, sank into the walls another four inches. Inside was a glass-backed door showing the workings of the mind that had built it. "Hey Carl, nice touch. Just where the fuck did you, never mind "where," how the hell did you get this fucker down and hung without anyone noticing a fucking bank vault being installed in yer basement?" "Ah, shit Dallas, you know better than to ask stupid questions. Didn't I teach you anything, Son?" "Yeah, but Carl . . . It's a fucking Bank Vault Door!" "OK, enough with the fucking door already." "All I was saying," as Dallas swung the door to and fro, "is that I have a hidden door too, and I see you have this one balanced just as perfectly as I do mine." "Yeah son?" And what do you keep behind yours? Your fucking shoes and socks? Shit, hidden door, what the fuck do you know about it?" "Well, asshole, I know enough to keep my fuckin PLANE in it, Mr. "I live in a hole under my fucking house!"" Dallas said, in a quick blast of fresh "piss-off" attitude. They both looked at each other for a second, and broke out laughing. "Good one son, I guess maybe I haven't wasted my time on you after all . . ." "Hey man, this is all fun and shit 'till someone loses an eye. I have lost that eye Carl. I'm not playing around with this screwhead Skeets any longer. He has something of mine and I'm going after him." Carl just stepped inside the door, turned, and looked at Dallas. "You're reminding me of a guy I used ta know, before he bought a private island, and bought into the "party life" with "Rock n' Rollers" and forgot who he was . . . Son if you're serious, you know I will do for ya. Count on it. Now get yer ass in here and let's see what the ole man has left." Dallas followed him in, and with all the drama of a movie, Carl turned up the rheostat until the whole room was lit.

Dallas stood there, looking, trying to take it all in. His left hand had come to rest on something next to the door. He glanced down. It was a square bale of *Fifty and One Hundred dollar bills*. "What the fuck is this?" he asked, picking off a stack from the top and blowing the dust off it. "Why you ole fuck! You never spent any of the money I gave you?" "What, you actually think I need your money, boy?" Carl looked bemused. "Nope, not one dollar!" "But shit Carl, there has to be at least *Seven Hundred and Fifty large here!*" "So what's your damn point?" Carl chuckled. Dallas dropped it back on top of the bale, and just shook his head. "Why, do you need money son? If ya do, help yourself, it's yours anyway." Carl spoke in a concerned tone "But I don't think money is your problem." Dallas continued to scan the room, bales of cocaine here, bales of cocaine there. "Carl, is this the coke I had Marboy drop off from the Port San Antonio move? This is why all those hoodlums as well as the D.E.A boys are always poking around, do you know that? Why the hell haven't ya just gotten rid of it? Man Carl, c'mon." Dallas looked down at a pistol on a small table. "I mean you're living under your house because of me." "Oh, Christ Dallas, you know how I am. For either of your reasons am I living under my house! I'm getting old man. I still am having Vietnam flashbacks, and they are getting worse. I'm down here cause I have to feel safe from the world. You will never understand, and I don't expect ya to. It's just what has happened. It's what happens to an old vet living alone in a jungle."

"Well when I finish what I have ta do, Carl, I'm coming back for ya, and I'm getting ya out of here. You can come and stay at my place on the island, it will be good for ya." "I aint going nowhere, son, read me?" Dallas looked at his old friend. He knew he was talking to a wall at this point. Carl is right, *he aint going nowhere.* "OK old man, let's see what ya got!" Carl moved some crates aside as he walked towards what looked like another blank wall. He reached behind a rock that stuck out from the wall and gave something unseen a hard tug. Dallas stood in awe as what looked like a small garage door opened up from the bottom. "You gotta be shitting me!" Dallas stood in front of a hell of a lot of guns, all on racks, in rows. "Carl!" Carl spoke up. "Yeah go ahead and help yourself. Mi Casa, Su Casa." "Where in the hell, did all these come from?" Dallas walked over to a rack of .380 cal. Uzis with shoulder straps and fold-open shoulder stocks. He wrung the 30-round clip out, lifted the ejector flap and blew down the barrel . . . "What, no Mac 10's -11's?" Carl tilted his head in a "why?" way. "There, over there in that trunk with the rest of the garbage" and pointed at it. "It was a joke, Carl." "Fuck I hope so. Since when did you go ghetto on me?" Carl snarled as he picked up a chromed AK-47 and was fiddling around with the semi-full auto switch. Dallas looked over the collection and again asked, "Where?" Carl looked back, oblivious "Where what?" "Where the fuck did you get a hold of all this?" "Oh, that. Yeah I told you I have had a lot of visitors. Now I have a lot less visitors." Dallas set down the Uzi. "Visitors with guns, and now a lot less visitors stopping by? Wow!"

"I really like these over here Dal, these I picked up from a few Colombian visitors. How the hell they get a hold of the latest hardware from our, your, government, I'll never know." Carl held out a new model of an M-16 that Dallas had never seen before. "Man that looks light," and taking it from Carl, Dallas looked at the shortened version with the ribbed fore-stock and pull-out shoulder stock. "Oh I like these, and especially this." It was a scope only about six inches long. "Yeah I thought you would. And it has what we used to call back in the old days *"starlight capabilities."* Yeah man, a new AAA battery and you're peeping in the dark . . ." "Holy shit Carl, you just lightened my load by a hundred and fifty pounds." "What ya mean, lighten yer load? Are you flying again? Remember what happened last time you flew in here, didn't have a real good landing if I remember correctly, now did ya?" "Bullshit, Carl, anyone I can walk away from is a good one." "Yeah, ya know people are still asking how some American guy's plane got all tangled up in the bush up on your property." Carl now in full smug laughter, walked over to Dallas. "I was told by the guys that stole what was left of your engines on that Queen Air to "shake the hand" of that pilot if I ever were to run into him again. That poor son of a bitch came down from Miami when the defense force called him and told him that "they had found his airplane," and that it was waiting for him to come and collect it. In fact, it was the owner who told me to "shake your hand." He had been trying ta sell that bitch for a year, and that you did him a favor. He said the insurance was paying him almost twice what he was asking!" "Son of a Bitch." Dallas and Carl were now sitting on a dozen metal ammo boxes, laughing so hard that it wasn't until they heard over the intercom on the wall the sound of trucks pulling up topside . . . Marboy was pushing the intercom button so hard they could hear his fingernails on the plastic of the intercom box in the kitchen. "Well boy, we have *"visitors."* Marboy suddenly appeared at the vault door. "Yes we do sir, what do we do, dey gonna tek our life!"

"Now just slow down, Marboy, how many?" Carl asked. Marboy, still in panic mode, babbled out, "two, maybe tree trucks. What do they want, Mr. Carl?" "Well I'd say . . ." then Marboy saw what was in the room with him "Oh, dat's bad . . . dat der is real bad . . ." He was pointing to the guns and then he saw the money and all else. "Oh Shit. If dey find us, dey tek our life for sure, Shit! Oh, jah, please!" Dallas stepped back into the vault. "OK, here's the deal Carl – Two trucks, four guys, they look like Defence forces, except they have no patches on their greens, so I think they are just the scumbags that come and go. They probably saw us drive up this way, and when we didn't come back, you know, put two and two together, and that's probably it. What ya think?"

"OK, here's the deal, Carl said. "Those assholes have been here before, hell they even stole the fuckin' copper pipes from my outdoor shower! If they do get in, here" – Carl threw Dallas one of the little Uzi's. "Kill any mother fucker that comes through that door! I'll be right back." And Carl ran out into the darkness of the tunnel. "Fucking a, yeah, sure, kill any mother fucker that comes through the door . . . Jeeez! Yeah right, CARL, you asshole!" "Marboy! Swing that door in." "Ya close de fucker, Boss." Dallas stood at the vault's door, cracked just enough so he could hear any movement or see any shadows coming down the tunnel. He checked his Uzi and clip. "OK, you heard the man, here." Dallas handed Marboy the pistol that had been lying on the table next to the bale of money. "If I give the word, you just fucking start shooting, OK? But for Christ sakes don't shoot me!" "I's got yas, Dallas," Marboy shook his head "no" in typical Jamaican body language. Dallas saw it and just shook his own head in a "yeah, whatever," and rolled his eyes.

Carl had disappeared into the tunnel. Dallas could hear muffled laughter, and then two short burst of automatic AK-47 fire. The laughter stopped. "Oh shit, now what?" Not a sound could be heard after that. Carl strolled back into the vault. "What happened up there, Carl?" "Oh, I surprised those fellas. I popped up through a trap door. Those assholes were in my upstairs kitchen in the fucking refrigerator, no less. They had already opened some beers I had up there, I think they wanted ta stay. So I "killed my fridge" in front of them. Bitches, they were so scared they ran out the back, they didn't even take their trucks! They ran into the bush . . . I suppose they will be back for them. I don't think they saw the Little Tiger inside the grown-over garage. Maybe that paint job you did Marboy was a good thing after all. It might have saved our ass from getting into a real dark place." "Thanks Marboy, but repaint that car. I want it back the way I gave it to you!" Marboy stood staring at Carl. "Ye, repaint soon, Carl."

Carl turned back to Dallas. "Look I don't know how long those guys will be till they come back for the trucks. Let's go have a look in them." "Ya think, Carl?" "Hell yeah! Let's go son, move your ass." Dallas stuck the small Uzi in the back of his shorts. Carl led the way. They took another tunnel to the left and up stairs carved out of clay. Dallas felt the temperature and humidity rise on his skin. He could smell the Jamaican jungle, fresh air carried the scent of mangos on it. They popped out a trap door behind the house. It was almost dawn. Dallas was on the clock and knew it. He thought about contacting Capt. Bob back at the plane and his Scarab boat, but he had left his radio in the Little Tiger. They walked around the house, and there they were, two small canvas-covered trucks. Carl wasted no time. He was in the back of one throwing something out. Dallas stood guard as Carl looted the trucks – A few cases of "Vacuum Dried Meals" and some automatic weapons. "Fucking scavengers! Why the hell don't learn their lesson an and leave me *alone?*"

"Ah, hey Carl, this has been great, but I am on a mission, so can I please help you take that shit down and then pick out a couple pieces I might feel will come in handy?" "Of course son, it's almost dawn. We don't want ta be caught out in the open. Let's go back down." Dallas ran the few yards to the Little Tiger. He reached in and grabbed his radio, turned it on and helped Carl out with his *"visitors"* booty. At the top of the trap door, Dallas turned on his radio as Carl disappeared down his hole. Dallas pressed the mic button. "Echo, Lima, Foxtrot . . . Echo, Lima, Foxtrot . . . Come in, Capt. You on?" In a flash, he heard Bob's voice. "Roger, Foxtrot. Standing by. "OK Foxtrot, will be coming in *Hot*, repeat, I say *Hot*, you read?" "Rodger that Foxtrot. E.T.A?" "Ah, yeah Foxtrot, will be in *six-zero+ -* minutes." "Rodger that, will be a "moveable feast"

in s*ix* -*zero* minutes. Out." Dallas ran down the steps and back to
the vault. Marboy was standing in the middle of the room. Carl
was stacking automatic rifles, the nice new M-16 models, into his
arms. "This is what ya came for, right son?" Marboy turned, with
a concerned look over his shoulder. "Yeah Carl, that's fine, is that
a L.A.W. rocket in the corner? "Why yes, yes it is. Help yourself."
Dallas grabbed it up and slung it over his shoulder. "Oh, here! Have
a few of these, they make a real mess and go "Boom" really, really
well." Carl reached into a box filled with straw. "Ah, here!" Carl
walked over and handed Dallas four shiny new grenades. "Just pull
the pin and throw, seven second fuses, really killer Dal. Ya can't
miss with these."

Dallas hefted the canvas bag Carl gave him into the car. Marboy
was already sitting in the car when Carl popped out of nowhere.
"Goddammit, Carl, I wish ya would stop that! Shit, ya scared the shit
out of me!" "Well I thought you might be able, if you want, to try to
buy yer man back instead of hunting Skeets, and let his own greed
kill him . . . Skeets is that way, they all are! So here." Carl pushed
another bag on to Marboy's lap. "Like I said, it's yours anyway. By
my quick count, there's about Two-Hundred Fifty large in that bag.
Oh, and hey son, be careful, I know where you're going. Nice place
that Frank Amada has up there in Belize, Dallas, I looked it up!"
"What the fuck? How the hell do you know? Never mind. Thanx
old man! I'll be back for ya!"

Marboy fired up the Little Tiger, and with a four-wheel jump
it was out and climbing the hill path it had come in on. Dallas
organized the weapons in the back seat. The grenades rolled loose
back and forth. "Goddamn! I'm sure the fuck glad that is over, ya
know Marboy, that could have gotten real ugly real fast." Marboy
reached into his pocket and pulled out a rather large blunt. "Ya
Mon! I's tellin yas right now boss, dat I's knows ya loves dat crazy
ole fuck back der, but he I's think is over da hill and round da bend
crazy now. Mon, he got ta get out from under his house! He gone

batty . . ." "I know, Marboy. I gonna come back and try ta get the man out. But right now, I have a pretty full plate. I have to get to Chance. I know Frank Amada is involved, somehow. I've known Frank eleven years, that has to count for something, and when I took out his competition Ochoa last year, Frank knows he owes me! I only hope Skeets hasn't jammed up Chance before now."

Capt. Bob, having got the message from Dallas, was packing up camp. While they were gone, he had refueled the Mosquito per Dallas's instructions. He waded over to his Scarab, threw in all the crap he had dragged out the afternoon before back in and was about to get back off the boat when the sound of a rhino busting through a hedge row stopped him in his tracks. He pulled out his 9 mm and waited. Yes, he was expecting Dallas, but in Jamaica, "Who the fuck knows what's coming through the bush at any given time . . ." So he ducked down below the gunnel, with just enough eyeball to get a look on the source of the noise. "Whack! Thump!" The Tiger broke through the canopy. He stood up as they pulled as close as they could get to the little beach. Dallas was the first one out. Marboy wasn't far behind. "Hey Bob, just stay on the boat, I have a few things for ya!" Dallas caught his foot on a vine and dropped an armful of loaded and un-loaded automatic rifles. "AWW, shit!" as he went face-first into the pile of butt stocks. "Goddamn it! Now look what ya did, Marboy!" Dallas said, picking himself up and as many of the guns he could. Capt. Bob was laughing his skinny ass off when Dallas picked up a dark green tube with a woven canvas strap. "Yeah Fuckin funny, huh? How about I just use this "Fuk"" on y'ass?" Capt. Bob stopped laughing and jumped down to help his boss. "OK, just because we may look like the Three Stooges, we aren't, so get this shit, or at least most of it, on yer boat please . . . and don't make me say "please" again. OK?" "Right Dal, it's done, what goes where and how much?" "OK, I'll carry what I pick up, you and Marboy gather up the rest and Bob you take that on the boat to this G.P.S. location. That's where we hook up with the Chief and the other boat. Dallas took out a small notebook and ripped the page out and handed it over.

Bob looked at Dallas. "No shit, you have the Chief sitting at these?" "Yeah, and Janis and Sonata too." "Wow we have a regular navy going," he said with a chuckle. "OK, let's do this!" Dallas grabbed up the small Uzi and one of the new model M-16's and started to walk towards the plane, now sitting just below high tide. "Oh, Bob, throw me that green tube." Capt. Bob reached down and picked it up. "No fuckin way! I ain't seen one of these since Nam!" Handing it over, Bob said, "Light Armor Weapon, fuckin L.A.W.'s. Jeez Dallas! I wouldn't want ta be on the receiving end of this fucker." "Well keep yer head down and maybe you won't be!" A big smile crossed Dallas's face, then a light chuckle as he waded out to his plane. The water was warm, and it felt good after being in those cool dank tunnels of Carl's. All he really wanted to do was lie down in it, soak it up, recharge his batteries . . . But no. He popped the port side hatch and started loading. From behind him could hear Capt. Bob doing the same, telling Marboy, "No, jeeez that goes in the forward lazarett man, and pack them pointed to the front and the stocks to the back. Yeah, that's right, this way when I break waves they won't bounce around as much." Marboy was loading the last M-16 when Capt. Bob's eye caught a glimpse of an open bolt on the piece. "Hold it!" Marboy looked up. "What?" Bob walked along the gunnel, he looked down and pointed. "Hey, look!" Marboy then caught the mistake. "Yeah Bob, I'm sorry, I didn't notice that. Shit!" "Marboy, that's one of the "hot ones" from Carl, see the open bolt? Do ya see all those shiny brass things in there? At the bottom of the slide?" "Yeah Capt., those be the bullets huh?" "Yeah, those be the bullets, with an open slide, meaning that if I hit a wave right that slide is gonna start to cycle, then you know what happens?" "Ahh, you have bullets shooting holes in dey boat mon?" "Right Marboy, bullet holes in the boat! We don't want that do we?" "Nah mon, dat would be a bad ting . . . Mon!" "No shit, now close that bolt, and pack it right, OK?" Bob looked over at Dallas who was watching this circus. "Ya all right there, Bob?" Dallas asked, shaking his head and looking down with a smile.

Bob looked up at the sky. "Now all we need is a hurricane, and that would just about make my day, he thought. "Ok," Marboy said as he jumped up on the gunnel and walked back to the stern of the Scarab. Dallas waded back to shore, still wanting to just fall down into the surf and let it wash over him. "Now Marboy, come here, man." Dallas reached behind him and pulled out three stacks of hundred-dollar bills. "Look, Marboy, here is *ten-grand*. You get that fuckin car re-painted before I see you again! Also, you will check in on Carl at least once a week, you read me?" "But Boss, I's thought I was coming. Ya gonna need me!" "Not this time buddy. You take care of the island, and Carl. In fact, I want you to go up to my old strip on my property up on the mountain, make sure no one sees you, and have a look around. If it needs it, clean it up. I might need about seven hundred feet. You do understand what that means Marboy, right?" "Yes, I understand Dallas. It mean you mightin' be needing ta use dat strip." Dallas with a big smile looked over at Bob. "See, only the best and the brightest!" Wink! Wink! Bob almost fell off the boat laughing. "I see, only the best and brightest! Hmm, hmm . . ." "Eh Mon, who da fuck ya laughin at, Mon?" "No, no, Marboy, please just do as I asked and take care that for me, OK? Please . . ." Dallas half-pleaded, covering for Bob's bad joke. "Ya mon! I's do all dat, an goin tek care of Carl, too." "Ok, great. Help push Bob off first, then wade me out too, please!" Bob's engines came to life with a roar. Marboy pushed him out about twenty-feet as Bob swung the Scarab around, facing an open ocean.

Dallas waved him off, holding up two fingers, and then four more. Bob nodded and mouthed the words that could not be heard above the roar of his engines. "Twenty-four" and dropped the throttle. The Scarab jumped out of the water and was on full plane in seconds. "OK, now me, Marboy." Dallas was strapping in and sealing himself into the small French Sea Hawk again. He could feel Marboy pushing him out into the soft surf, the sun was at the horizon, the clouds above, white, crisp, high . . . Marboy turned the plane into the onshore breeze as Dallas cranked his main engine. Once, no luck. Twice, no joy. "OK," Dallas said to himself. "The third time's the charm," and with all the glory of the Jamaican sunrise the engine bit hard into the wind. Marboy jumped up. "Ya Mon!" giving Dallas two thumbs up. Dallas waved him off and went throttle up. The small seaplane taxied out about a hundred feet. Dallas sat a second, waiting for the right wave set. He saw his opening and let off the flaps and the Sea Hawk was no longer a boat, it was a plane, and it was climbing!

Dallas didn't catch-up with Capt. Bob for almost fifteen-minutes. "Shit!" Dallas muttered, that fucker must be moving eighty-miles an hour as he descended behind Bob. Bob hadn't noticed Dallas until he was just overhead. He looked up as Dallas past over him and dipped a wing. Both Bob and Dallas knew it was on. No turning back now, Dallas, he knew what lay ahead. Bob? Well Bob didn't have a clue, all he knew were the numbers on a little piece of paper that was handed him and that he had already put into his G.P.S.

Carl waited just long enough for Dallas to get out of sight. He picked up a shovel and turned back towards the house. He had some unfinished business. Just as he turned the corner on the side of the house, he caught the glow of a cigarette in the still dark canopy of green. A voice slowly spoke as a shadow moved out of the dark. "Well, Mr. Brewster, I see that you had visitors." Carl knew the voice. It was the voice of the D.E.A. "What the fuck do you want, Asst. Director Cox?" Carl's voice was ice cold, and the shovel came off his shoulder. "Where's he going Carl? I can call you Carl, can't I?" "Fuck no, you can't call me Carl! You sleazy fucker!" "Well then Mr. Brewster, I want to know where Streeter is going . . . and I want to know now, Carl." "Hey get the fuck off my property Cox!" Asst. Director Cox looked at Carl as he walked by, shovel in hand. Cox politely said, "I have to know Carl, I'm trying to help." "OH, Shit! You are trying to help!" Carl quipped, and turned around quickly. "Look, if it wasn't because of your dumb ass he wouldn't even be here! Dallas would still be playin' guitar down island, and living peacefully. NO! You Motherfuckers can't hold on to a guy, a guy that was one of your own, went bad and killed a shitload of people. And Dallas, he helped your ass! Dallas Streeter delivered him into your hands! You want to help? Like I said – Get the fuck off my property! NOW!"

"OK, OK, Mr. Brewster, I'll go, but I have to get to Dallas Streeter before he gets to Skeets, or there's going to be a lot more dead bodies than the two you killed this morning. Oh yeah, I know, I saw you. I saw it all from right over there." Cox pointed at the low-hung tree line. "Oh, yeah. Either you tell me, and I go away nice, or I do this." Cox held up a small walkie-talkie. "Agent Sands, you are standing by, aren't you?" A voice came in loud and clear. "Yes Sir, standing by." "If I do this, MR. Carl, a small fucking army is going to come over that hill. Then I guess you can figure out the rest, can't you Mr. Brewster?" Carl lowered the shovel to the ground and looked at it. He lifted his head. "OK Cox, you first tell me how you are going to help. If I think what you say isn't worth going to jail for, yeah, I might point you in a good direction . . . How 'bout that, Asst. Director?" Cox lifted up the radio. "Agent Sands, you still there?" "Yes Sir" came back in the same clear voice. "Agent Sands, I want you to leave my truck and go back to the airport. Await my arrival." "Sir? Did you say go back to the airport?" Cox lifted the radio again. "Agent Sands, I gave you a directive. Stand down and meet me at the airport. Do you understand?" "Yes Sir. Clear the area, report back to flight. Rodger." The voice trailed off. "Well Mr. Brewster, is that proof that I really do want to help?" "Yeah, that was pretty convincing, Cox. Now what?" "Look Carl, I don't care about those slimy fucks in the back. I saw what happened, you were just protecting your property, that's all I saw. Look "Mr. Brewster,

I want ta help, really Carl . . . Ya see, I want Skeets a lot more than Dallas. You heard me call off the dogs, now tell me where Dallas is. I am not playing Carl."

Raul knocked on Chance's door politely. "Mr. Chance, I won't bother you long but "El Hefe" wants to see you upstairs. "Who?" "Mr. Amada. He wants you upstairs." "Oh. Yeah. Why?" "I don't know sir; he just wants you upstairs." Raul never lifted his gun or even took it out. Chance saw this in a whole different light. "OK, I'll come. Is Dallas here yet?" "I really don't know, you will come with me now, Mr. Chance." Raul patted his 9mm and summoned Chance with a wave of his hand. "Yeah, yeah, I'm coming, I'm coming." Chance muttered "fuck you" and stood up. He walked the hallway to the stairs. "Not fucking again," he protested. "I feel like shit, Raul. I want my shit, man." Raul gave Chance a gentle push forward. "I'll see to your needs after you see Mr. Amada."

Mr. Amada was sitting in his woven canvas and wood deck chair. "Well, Mr. Chance, nice to see you are enjoying my "protection." I have a question for you. How well do you know your brother?" "What? I'm sorry, Mr. Amada, but ya know, go fuck yer self . . . and not for nothing too!" "Oh Shit, you are a Streeter! Ha, ha! You know you remind me of him when he was your age. Just the same, a Gringo, wisecracking ass. Ya know I admire your brother. He's a man of his word. You have to admire that quality in a man. I think, maybe, just maybe, we can be, well, if not be "friends," we can see a way out of your, your "situation" so to speak. You have to realize by now I am a man who, let's say, likes to keep my friends close. But here, I also like to keep my enemies "closer," for reasons that don't concern you.

Mr. Skeets, you know him as Agent Skeets . . . "No! I know him as a fuckin' piece of shit that killed my two friends in that desert back there, four days ago. That's all. I know him as the guy that fucking kept me in the trunk of the car, only stopping to dope me more, that's what I know!" "My boy, life is so complicated, it gets all, how do you say . . . "Twisted." Like a mop that you clean the floor with, it's a dirty, dirty, thing, this life we have. Look around, Chance, may I call you by your name?" Chance had taking a seat to Amada's left. "Yeah, that's all right I guess." "Look around you. I did not get here, in this chair, by being stupid. My boy, it was not by "Chance!" Amada got up and cracked his cane against the wall. "No! I got here . . . "Please, please!" "I'm sorry." Chance was covering his head with his hands. "I'm sorry. I just have problems that at your young age, you would not possibly know. For this I'm truly sorry. But as to why I had you come up here . . . This is what we are going to do. I'm going to put your "fate" in your own hands so to speak. Your name!"

Chance looked at Amada. "What the fuck are you going on about?" "I want to hear your name out of your mouth!" Amada took a large step towards Chance. "It's Chance! Chance Streeter, ya old fuck! What now?" "That's my boy. OK, we are going to play a game of "chance." Amada reached in his pocket. "Let's see. Oh, yes. These will do." Amada held up two American Quarters. "Raul, come here." Raul, standing back against the wall, walked over to both of them. "Raul, I want that black marker I gave you this morning. Yes, yes, the one I gave you, give it to me. OK, here, we will see if you are a "Streeter."" Amada took both quarters, and, one at a time, he colored in the front of one, and the back of the other. Amada held out to Chance his hand. "Take them. We play now," he said softly. "In my religion we have Saints - the "Saints of Santeria." We believe that if a man is destined to die, it is already known. It merely comes down to how. Very simple. You will take these two American quarters, you will "flip" them, as you say. If they both come up the same, or both different, I will "flip" the same . . ." "OH, Hell no!" Chance said. "What the Fuck?" "No, no, my boy. Trust your fate!" Amada again offered the coins to Chance a second time. Chance reached out, very slowly, taking the two coins out of Amada's hand. Amada stepped back. "OK, now we play for "Life," rather than "Death." This is a serious game, Mr. Chance. May the God Chango be with you, my son."

The wind bit hard at Chances cheeks, it took his hair up and down. Chance looked down the beach. Little dust devils kicked up and the sea air smelled the musty, salty, lingering smell of an outgoing tide. "Oh, Fuck, give me those." Chance snatched the coins out of Amadas hand "So, ah, yeah, you want me to toss a fucking coin to determine my life?" Chance had a trick he had practiced many a night in college with two of the same quarters. "Hmmm," he rolled the coins over his fingers, the black and silver sides, taking the sun and shining it in Amada's eyes. "You mean if I flip these, and they come up the same, I am "in"? And if I flip anything less, you flip, and if they both come up different, I won't have a choice in my fate? And if we tie? Who's the "tie breaker," Raul over there with his 9mm?"

Amada looked at Chance. "That's the deal. If you are a Streeter, we already know, don't we?" Chance cupped the coins. A smile crept over his face, a smile only his friends knew made its way across his lips. With a twist of his wrist and a "snap," both coins split in two and hung still in the air, spinning. One bounced left, the other broke right. They rolled in a circle towards each other and passed each other on the floor, did a "figure eight" and stopped cold and split again. They fell like an open clamshell against the deck. Two black. One heads. One tails. A shout broke the stillness. Amada shouted "Couno! Raul, see thhhat? I knew it! The boy, the boy is . . . See I told you!" Raul smiled. "Chango must be very happy indeed . . ."

Amada grabbed the young Streeter. "Come, we have to talk." Chance just smiled. He knew that "Chances" were in his favor in that game. Man, he had no idea what just happened, or how close he was to dying. But he even thanked what the fuck ever "Chango" was and kept walking, looking at Raul and saying, "Now can I have my *"Shit?"*

Chapter 10

Chief Harvey looked down at his console mounted G.P.S., put the big sport fish in neutral and walked to the fly bridge ladder. He stood looking behind as the Morgan 51' and its tow rope went slack. Reaching in his back pocket, he yanked out the small hand-held radio and keyed the mic. "Is anyone back there awake?" He lit a cig, and repeated, "Hey Ladies! Is anyone awake over there?" The Chief looked down at his watch, "Hmm, 7:05 am, shit . . . Taking one more drag on his smoke, he reached back over his head. His hand found the air horn chain. Taking the mic in his right hand, he held it up over the edge of the flying bridge canopy. Two of the horns faced forward, the third faced back. (This is set up is to let other boats behind know that a fish is online) when the Chief was actually "fishing." "OK, I asked. Now it's wakie, wakie, ladies."

The Chief gave a good hard pull on the chain. A resounding blast of "wake the fuck up" must have got somebody's attention. Even without the radio the Chief could hear faint screams – the screams of drunk, hung-over, angry women! Back on the radio, the Chief politely said, "Good morning ladies!" From his vantage point the Chief watched a wine bottle fly out of the cockpit of the Morgan and into the ocean. Soon his radio was vibrating from all the "God damn-its," "you assholes," and "go fuck yourselves" that could be squeezed out in a continuous stream of obscenities so bad that the Chief just turned down the volume level to a manageable low and let them get it all out . . . When he felt, and heard, a different tone, he turned it back up to normal. "Ok, ah Janis, would you please raft-up with me here, copy?" "Yeah I fuckin COPY you! Raft-up? Why now why would I want to do that Chief?" The Chief, not used to being asked "why" a whole lot, came back with a small attitude. "Janis, look, we don't have the time for this non-sence! Janis please just bring the Morgan and raft-up with me, please?" "Oh, and on my starboard side please. Just start the engine and motor on up, OK? OK?" The Chief could now hear his wife Sonata in the back ground, saying "C'mon Janis, please, no problems today, OK?" The mic went muffled as a short conversation took place. "Yeah, OK, starboard side. Sonata is starting the engine as we speak. Gimme five mins . . . Out!" The radio went dead.

The Chief went down to the deck from the flying bridge, grabbed two lengths of extra spring-lines and his boat hook and waited as the Morgan came to life. Sonata was on the bow coiling up the tow line, attached in a "V" to both bow cleats. The Chief waved and smiled at her, and even gave her a thumbs-up for the good job she was doing. She smiled back, and even gave him a little air kiss. The Chief reached out with the boat hook, Sonata placed in under a forward stanchion so the Chief was able to walk the Morgan's bow along the length of his bigger Hatteras. Sonata was ready with a couple "fenders" as was Janis at the stern, having now turned the Morgan's engine off. Janis used her boat hook and pulled the Morgan's stern towards the stern of the big Hatteras.

"Ah, not bad!" The Chief genially said to Janis as he helped her and Sonata off from one yacht and onto the other. "Not bad at all. Thank you both. I'm sorry about the wake-up call but I had to do it. We are here!" Janis climbed the fly bridge ladder. She stood looking around. "Hey Chief? And just where in the fuck is "here," anyway?" "Right where we should be, Luv . . ." "Yeah, right!" Janis snapped back.

"Well OK, c'mon down into the salon and I'll be happy to go

over our charts, OK?" Janis looked down at Sonata and the Chief, now in an embrace. "Look you guys . . . save that, or go get a room!" "What ya think baby? Wanna get a room? Oh, that's right – We have a room! In fact, we have this whole damn boat, Janis!" Sonata stepped in. "Now Martin, she's right. We can wait. Why don't we all go on down into the galley and Janis and I will make us all breakfast. What cha think?" The Chief said, "That's a great idea, No?" Janis just looked at both of them, and said, "Well I didn't bring Olivia (her live-in cook/maid) with me in my pocket, but as long as we can go over the charts and G.P.S. crap while we are eating, yeah, I guess we could have something to eat. But I want a Bloody Mary with my eggs and toast! Is that OK, Mon Capitan?" The Chief just shook his head no, but yes left his lips. "Anything your little heart desires, Janis… Now Sonata will show you where everything is. It's her kitchen, so have at it!" "OK, Sonata, where's the Bloody Mary mix?" Sonata pointed to the small wet bar. "Over there . . ." "Right!" Janis snorted. The Chief looked at his wife, and then the ceiling, all the while shaking his head and mumbling something. "How does he do it?" They both knew he was talking about Dallas, and how he "copes" with her. They both broke out in a smile, and laughed to themselves.

"OK, when you ladies are done eating and doing whatever you guys "do" in the morning, we are at the G.P.S. place that Dallas has given me. So we will be here a while. How long I'm not exactly sure, but I don't think we should be here a long time. So my darlings, we are going to get the boats back in shape!" Sonata kept eating, Janis dropped her fork into her eggs and gave the Chief one of those "Well have fun" looks. Having almost finished, she fished out a pack of Marlboro Lights, got one out and lit it at the table "Clean the boats, huh?" "If ya all would be so kind as to help me, that is." Janis sat and looked at Sonata, who was still eating. She took another drag, and blew a smoke ring up into the air. She picked up a toothpick and placed it in the corner of her mouth. "Sure Chief.

Let Sonata get done eating, and we have to go back to the Morgan anyway, so we'll clean your boat, Sonata and I, and you work on the Morgan. Deal?" The Chief looked at his watch. It was 8:11 am. "OK, OK, what, or how, bad is it over there? Sonata! Look at me!" The Chief spoke to his wife. Sonata slowly looked up. "Well baby, it's a mess!" "OK, fuck it! OK! You guys clean this boat up a little bit. Sonata you know how we like it, OK?" "Oh, yes, don't worry Martin. We have this place "ship-shape" when you come back." Janis looked at the Chief. "Oh, we'll have this place all cleaned up, I promise." The Chief looked around and thought, "Christ, there is nothing to do over here. Jeez, did I just get screwed or what?"

"First Janis, c'mon over here and let me show ya where we are, and what the deal is from here on out. Any problems with that?" "Nope, let's do it!" The chief already had his charts and paperwork out on a smaller setting table. There lay his hand held G.P.S., the small two-way radio, charts of the western end of Cuba, and a smaller chart the he had used to get up here from the Trinidad & Tobago area off the coast of South America. Janis could see another chart underneath the others. All she could make out was Gulf of Belize. "Hey Chief, what's that one?" She started to pull at it, when the Chief gently pushed it back under the pile of the others. "Ya don't need to see that one till Dallas gets here, OK?" "Yeah, OK," she said. "When is he going to fly in anyway?" "Soon, very soon. So here is where we are, this is how we got here. When Dal gets here, he'll tell us where we go from here. OK, that's all I got, Janis. So if you will excuse me, I have a sailboat to put back together." "Oh it's not that bad, Chief, really it's not." "Janis, sweetheart, two women have been living on that boat for almost *four-days!* I know what I'll find. So save it. Or come and help me." Janis sat back down and lit another cigarette. The Chief just looked at her and shook his head "That's what I figured." Sonata came out of the bathroom where she had been hiding out. "OK, what do you want done first?" The Chief just turned away and headed up the stairs and out on to the main deck. Sonata and Janis looked at one another and started to smile. The Chief bounded over the gunnel on his boat, and half-leapt onto the walkway of the Morgan, which sat about three and a half feet below.

The first thing he did was tidy up the fore deck. The Harken roller that the jib sail was hooked up to was too loose, so he turned the drum at the bottom to tighten up the half rolled-up jib. While walking back along the starboard side, he untangled the jib sheets, the lines that held the jib sail and allowed the sail to be let out or taken in. It was about halfway to the cockpit that he smelled it. "Jeez, what the fuck is that?" Two or three more steps and he saw it. "Oh, fer the love of Christ," he said, talking out loud. In the cockpit, which is about 8' feet across and two levels deep, including the lazarettes that double as seating in an oval shape, was a partially open, large Igloo cooler.

"Now what in the Hell!" poured out of his mouth as he kicked the lid off. "Oh, man, that is some foul smelling shit!" The sunlight poured in and the smell wafted out. He quickly reached down and replaced the top. "Man, I'll deal with that on the "off the boat" trip. It's too damn early fer that shit!" He stood up. It was damp everywhere. The dew rolled freely off the top of the cabin and the towels that the girls had been using on deck were wet and they were starting to smell like mildew, too. He peered down the companionway into the dark interior. "This is the same boat, the same boat that D.E.A. special agent Skeets had tried to kill him in, to kill him and Dallas! The flashbacks hit him, one after another . . . The muzzle flashes, the sound of splintering wood, the "Whomp! Whomp! Whomp!" of the Blackhawk chopper as it hung overhead.

The Chief shook his head, as if trying shake out himself out of a bad dream. It was the smells and closed-in feeling that triggered him into the daydream. He popped his head up out of the forward hatch. He stepped up on the v-berth so he could get his head and shoulders out. He stretched his arms out, and lifted his feet off the v-berths and held himself up by his arms and shoulders. This made him breath deeper, as he cleared his head. After a few deep breaths he lowered himself back in. "Jeez, I smell stale wine, too. No!" The Chief spoke aloud. Next to the bathroom/shower stall was a small closet. The Chief was holding court, speaking to himself out loud now . . . "What in the hell is all this?" He stood amazed, dumbfounded and speechless. Where the extra rope and rope sheets for sail lines, along with the other "Sailboat" stuff was supposed to be, had been very neatly turned into a floating wine cellar. Starting at the top, the Chief started a count, pulling out an odd bottle here and there, until he got into the 1963 and 1965 Lafite Rothschild's. "No Shit!" he said as he put two of these bottles down his pants. "Now I know this boat is "loaded," but I had no idea how loaded. It looks like while we were sleeping, and I was seeing Dallas off the night before we left, Janis was one very busy little girl, indeed . . . Ha, Ha, jeez, a Streeter is a Streeter is a Streeter!"

"This is all fine and good, but where the hell is the stuff that is supposed to be in here? We need that stuff! Let's see if she put it up in the v-berths." He took the bottles out, placed them on a salon cushion, and walked up to the v-berths. He lifted off the cushions and opened the starboard v-berth. "OK!" The lines, along with the extra anchor lines he actually had wanted, were there. He did the same thing with the port side. "Yup!" Everything was there. This little minor miracle was enough to lighten the Chief's mood. While still up foreword, he stuck his head up through the hatch again. The bow of the Morgan was about twenty-five feet less than his Hatteras' bow. He stood in the hatch listening for the sound of work, or at least the shuffling of maybe a pot or a pan in the galley. Nothing other than the faint sound of giggling, a brief moment of low talk, and then more low laughter. "Hmm, sounds like a lot is getting done over there." He lowered himself back down and walked towards the companionway stairs, grabbing the two bottles of wine on his way out. One he shoved in the front of his pants, the other in the rear, pulled his shirt over them, and was up and over the rails and back on his boat in seconds.

He looked around and didn't see either of the women. Feeling sneaky, he opened the sliding glass door into his salon. Still no one in sight, but the sound of laughter was louder. He took out the bottles and put them in the fridge, then walked over to the bow windows. All he could see was two pair of feet at the edge of a blanket, one pair of the feet decidedly darker than the other. He pulled open a drawer in the galley. There he reached all the way to the back and slid out a small semi-automatic pistol, Sonata's little .32 cal., stuck it in his shorts and pulled his shirt over it. Now he could hear the laughter getting louder, and the telltale sound of wine bottles clicking on glasses. "Ah, OK, if it's a party they want, it's a party they'll get. Just like women, they forgot that this is a business trip!" The Chief went out the sliding glass doors and quietly worked his way along the rail towards the laughter. Now even a boom box was playing. "Really living it up, hmmm? Not fer long." As the Chief rounded the corner on the starboard side, Sonata was the first one to see him. She was in the middle of pouring a glass of wine. Janis had her head turned and didn't see the Chief bend down and snatch the bottle out of her hand. "Hey, what the FUCK?" was the next sounds that the Chief heard. The Chief looked down at Janis. "What the FUCK? Here's What the Fuck!" The Chief tossed the bottle over the rail into the water. "That was a *six-hundred-dollar bottle* that you just tossed!" Janis, in a drunk, hoarse yell shouted at the Chief. "Oh, yeah?" the Chief chuckled. "Then you're really going to love this!" He pulled out the little pistol and sank it on the second shot. "There! So much for that *six-hundred bucks,* Ha, hah."

"Oh, that was hilarious, asshole! You just wait until my husband. . ." The Chief cut her off short. "Listen up, sweetheart! I can't wait for Dallas to get here!" The Chief was still waving the pistol around, when Sonata got up and gently held out her hand. The Chief popped the clip out and handed it over to her without a word. He went on with Janis. "Look this is NOT a vacation! This is a MISSION! A mission to save Chance's ass! I don't give a fuck that you turned that loaded with coke Morgan right there into a floating wine cellar. I don't care what the fuck you tell Dallas! I don't care if you tell him I took a shot at ya. Ya know why I don't care? Because he's gonna ask me why I missed! And I am gonna have to tell him that I was shooting at a *six-hundred-dollar* bottle of wine! That's why! Now you were saying something about how you can't wait until your husband gets here? No, *I* can't wait! Now clean this shit up and get both your asses over on that boat!" The Chief pointed to the Morgan with his thumb. "And finish cleaning it! That means I want the deck hosed down and that bucket of puke, too!" Janis, still plenty buzzed on about eighteen–hundred bucks of France's best vintages, looked at the Chief and said, with a slight wobble in her voice, "OK, we're going! But you didn't have to get all pissy about it! A simple "Please" would have worked."

The Chief just turned around and walked back into his salon, pulled a chilled bottle of 1964 Lafite Rothschild out of his fridge, pulled the cork screw off the wall over the sink, found a nice, stemmed glass, and poured. "Ah . . . Yeah, I can't wait for Dallas to get here . . ." From the sink he made his way over to his chart table, sat down and set about plotting the next leg of this trip on paper. On a side tablet he jotted down his present G.P.S. location, pulled the Coastal Waters of Belize chart out from under the others and first looked at the publication date. It was the newest one he was able to get his hands on while in town the day before he had left for Dallas's island house. He thought back to the little encounter he had with the little crack head in the alley, behind the stores. "Who was that kid working for, following me around like that, all over town? Hmm." He just shook his head and got back to the Belize chart.

Sonata walked into the salon. "Hi baby," she said. The Chief looked up and didn't see Janis. "Hi sweetheart! How's it going over there?" Sonata smiled. "Oh, just fine. We're almost done, and so is she!" "What?" The Chief looked up again. "Ya mean she's running outta gas? Man, I was beginning to wonder about her. That's why Dallas probably fell for her." "Why's that Martin?" Sonata asked. "I have wondered about why a guy like him would be attracted to her, I mean besides the fact that she is beautiful." The Chief sat back in his chair. "Nah, guys like Dallas aren't into the looks part as much as the brain part. Oh don't get me wrong, I mean he is a guy, and somewhere the "looks" do come into play, but you see how she is – a smart ass, a typical know it all – they just *fit*. I can't explain it. But for everything we see, Dallas sees something else. Like the fact that she would take a bullet for him. And him for her! That kind of thing you just can't put in to words, ya know?" "I think I do, but I would step in front of a bullet for you, too!" "I know baby, I know, now go check on her, and bring up a few more bottles of wine when you guys are done, OK?" Sonata walked over and gave him a light kiss on his forehead. "OK, I do this." Sonata walked out the sliding glass door, and the Chief watched as her little butt bounced down the stairs to the deck below.

No sooner than the door shut behind her, the Chief was up and at the stack of single side band radios. He pulled out his wallet and put on his reading glasses. "OK. OK. Yeah, OK, got it!" He slid out one of his business cards, flipped it over and punched in the set of radio frequency numbers into the top receiver. He flipped on a signal enhancer, then a signal scrambler/descrambler in the middle and finally the bottom unit, which just looked like a plain black box with a row of small lights. In the middle was a microphone jack and a microphone which was hooked on the side cover. "Shit! I hope this all works still!" He mumbled out of the corner of his mouth. "It better!" All he heard was static, but he knew it was working. Looking at his watch, he thought, "All we do now is wait." Sitting down, he got back into figuring out in his log his next movement for the boats, and his current fuel situation. The front port fresh water tank he had converted to an extra fuel tank with a liner system that some French guy sold him a year ago. It held high-octane gasoline that he had planned to sell to the little out island gas pump fuel docks. Now he wondered if Capt. Bob would need some and was glad he had it along. His mind drifted off as he enjoyed his own *"six-hundred dollar"* bottle of wine. He sat back and closed his eyes. "Ah, a little peace and quiet." After almost three and a half days of his own engines droning in his ears, he was ready for a break.

Chapter 11

Dallas was already finished eating some freeze-dried beef stew from the pouch he had mixed with water and shook up some time earlier, when he decided to check out just exactly where the fuck he was. He had been in the air just an hour and a half, and his onboard G.P.S. hadn't made a sound. He had been flying northwest at a hundred and thirty knots, so he knew just from doing the math in his head "about" where he was. He thought, "Oh yeah, I can try the radio, and I still have a ton of daylight left. So OK, let's see if anybody is listening." A thought crossed his mind as he looked out his port pilot seat. He had just come around from the east side of the island, and today the higher slopes still had fog on them. He looked for any familiar landmarks. He looked down at the waterline, where he finally found a boatyard that hadn't changed very much. Working his eyes up the hills, he spotted an old wooden three story hotel, one he had stayed at many, many times before . . . Mostly while his own property was having the little airstrip installed. Dallas opened the window a bit. He wanted to smell that "smell" of his jungle. His little piece of jungle! But he never did, as he passed over it. Ten miles to the North and west, he saw that several new buildings were going up along the road that his property fronted on. "Oh Hell! Fucking progress . . . I bet when I get back home on the island that there will probably be an offer on the property. Yeah, Carl told me this was coming. Everybody that was in the *"Biz"* has now waited long enough to spread a bit around and come out looking like a local hero. So all in all, that was a great investment, it has paid itself off several times over and was a load of laughs and a half . . . Including the last flight in! "Jeez, Dallas!" He was now smiling through his teeth. "I walked away, and so did Jimmy Kurtz and the Chief. Woo-Hoo, how close was that one? Too damn close! That whole trip was "F.U.B.A.R." out the ass."

Dallas gave the throttle a goose and got back into his mindset of the biz at hand. He went back to the radio, back to thoughts of Skeets. Back to the hope that Frank Amada had Chance safe and was taking care of him, away from that psychopath and his little buddy Fernando. Back to thoughts about what the plan was and/or would be, or how the plan would shape up if once all the facts and intel would allow a plan at all, without the goddamn "Don't-Expect-Anything" boyz getting in the damn way. Dallas mumbled to himself, aloud. "Fucking Assistant Director Cox! Who the fuck knows what he is thinking? Them and the "Fee-Bees" (FBI). Jeeez, they never cooperate with each other! They always are screwing up one or the other's "In-tell" sources." And money? Jeeez, some of these "snitches" get paid more than what they would have made just doing the deal for their bosses, and sometimes they got nothing but an ass-load of buck-shot or a Colombian neck-tie. Most of these informants were either so strung-out, or wiped-out poor with 15 kids and nothing of a life left, that they were easy to lie to, string along, and partial pay, while the field agents would just out-and-out steal poor Pepe's vig or payments. A pure case of these fucking guys telling them *"Oh, Mano! Mas dinero! (more money) Para yo! Mon ya na! (tomorrow)."* Pure un- adulterated horseshit! It flowed just like piss at the local bar's bathroom from all the watered downed beer that poured so freely out of the D.E.A.'s bars, and paid off the owners of them. They knew that once they had a guy turning in his boss, there was no going back. Only to a certain death and or the death of their whole family. This set Dallas off. He knew, these were the guys that weren't even the bad ones. But fucking Skeet's . . .

Dallas turned all his attention to the plane, to where the Chief was now sitting, and how far behind Capt. Bob was. He was getting more and more pissed as he just sat and flew. He reached back behind him into one of his packs. Steering with his knees and on autopilot, he fished out a few Percocet 10 mg tablets, and a cool coke out of the mini–fridge. Ever since the last crash, his back has been screwing with him. He never even mentioned it to any of his friends, but having a doctor on the island a few doors down had helped him keep up appearances, and work on his "project boats" within a limited capacity. Right now, after dealing with Carl and Marboy, lifting all the shit he had out of Carl's tunnels, and wrestling with Capt. Bob and so on, he hurt. Dallas undid his seat belt harness, sat back and waited for the Perc's to do their thing. He took a long tug on the cool soda. Out of the corner of his eye, Dallas caught a row of L.E.D. lights, and they were jumping. Hmmm! He looked at his watch. "Early! I always liked that about the Chief." The mic was just a short arms-length away, and Dallas was happy that it was. Dallas shouted to himself, "OK! Now we are on! Damn, and right on time! Damn! Damn! Damn! OK!"

The Chief, having just opened a second bottle of (as he put it), "really, really expensive juice," had just had sat back in his chair. He wasn't really even trying to make contact – in fact he had just turned on the system. He knew he had entered the contact numbers, but never figured he was going to "hit" as soon as he did it. His eyes lit up and he turned up the volume and tried to dial it in just a bit better.

"Dallas! This is On-Line . . . Repeat . . . This is On-Line . . . Looking for A Duck . . . That's a Flying Duck with a Capitol D!"

"Why, Chief . . . Nice to hear a friendly voice . . . From a friendly place . . . Repeat! Over! On-Line, I need a G.P.S. fix on your current position. Over!"

"Roger that, Flying Duck! Now transmitting fresh numbers on the secure channel."

"Roger that, On-Line. Setting secure receiver. Receiving G.P.S. now. Sending back Current G.P.S. local to you, On-Line . . . Please hold while I do the numbers and set intercept course."

"Rodger that, D, see you soon . . . It's good to hear your voice!"

"Ah, that it is, Chief!"

Dallas's voice was now coming out of a single speaker, mounted on the middle shelf in the back of a stack of digital receivers, including the custom-built unit that scrambles and unscrambles the signals coming in and going out. Dallas was already talking a mile a minute while the Chief was working the units. "Hey Man!" The Chief yelled into the mic. "Slow the hell down, man, I'm just getting caught up with the new rig here . . . OK? Give me a sec." "Oh sure Chief, I had forgot. I have been so alone up here . . . It seems like days, man!" "OK, all set, Dallas . . . you were saying?" "No, just that it seems that I have been alone for days, even though I stopped in "J" and saw Marboy and Carl . . . It was just weird. I, I'll talk to ya when I see ya. Chief do you have yer charts out? And can you get a proper fix on me? Please, buddy . . ." "Oh, hell, I'm already workin on ya, Dal . . . Shoot me your G.P.S. position and I'll bring ya right in. How's the fuel? You good or what?" "Rodger, Chief. I have about twenty-seven gallons at the moment." "And what is your air speed?" "Roger that, Chief. I'm cruising at five-zero feet at fifteen knots . . . OK, Chief, here comes my G.P.S. position . . ." The Chief heard the signal from Dallas digital transmitter going through the scrambler and watched as they locked into his and un-scrambled on the readout in front of him. "Ah, yeah Dallas, you are two-one miles southeast, sending course correction now. I'll have a visual on you in about eight to ten mins . . ." "OK, Roger that. Adjusting course and am going to maintain at fifteen knots for five mins, and start a visual approach." "OK, Roger that. You should have good visual in five mins. Wind from the northwest at seven, seas are a light chop. You're good for water at this time. I'll be on deck, with help. Aft approach recommended, and is open! Just nose right on up!" Dallas heard the Chief on the Hatteras PA system. "Ladies, we have company . . . Please report to the stern of the On-Line . . . WE have company, Repeat! WE have COMPANY! Please tighten all loose lines and break out all spare fenders and line the areas along the transom with the fenders. Dallas Streeter will be joining us shortly. Please stand by the rail for "ass-pection." That means you, Janis!" A loud laugh followed out of the speaker. Janis turned and looked at the Chief. "Hey, Chief, stick that mic up your ass, OK?" The Chief looked up just in time to see Dallas splash his little plane about seven hundred feet behind the On-Line, with perfect waves breaking evenly off the bow of the little plane.

Dallas used his main engine to get within the last couple of hundred feet, then cut that off and as his crew watched. He deployed the electric navigational motor, which swung up and into position, making a *click-click* sound and locking into place. He popped the gull-wing hatches and heard a small cheer and some clapping. As he stood up on the seat of the little seaplane, Dallas felt a wave of emotions well up in his cheeks and into his eyes. He was steering with his feet and his right knee. He reached down and pulled back on the knob that controlled the electric fans speed. He wiped away his happy tears and slid back into his pilot's seat. He could hear the Chief shouting out "*75 feet . . . 50 feet . . . 25 feet . . . OK!*" Dallas cut off the fan, and the momentum carried him right up and onto the On-Lines dive platform.

Dallas popped back up. "OK, here, lock these on to the eye loops on both sides, and threw two pre-clasped lines out "Hi, Baby," he said to Janis as he threw one to her, "Ya been a good girl while I have been gone, huh?" He gently tossed Sonata the other and asked her, "Sonata, luv? Has she?" Sonata just smiled and said "Oh, Mr. Dallas, I'm so happy you are safe and here and with us!" "Whaaa . . . Sonata? Oh, OK. Yeah, I'm fine, just fine . . .. How was the trip?" Right as he was about to get an answer, the Chief came down the stairs from the upper deck cabin. He had in hand a couple 6-packs of beers in a small cooler and flopped down into one of On-Lines twin Billfish fighting chairs. "Here, Man! I figure you are overdue for one of these babies!" The Chief placed the cooler between the deck-mounted chairs. They bumped heads as they both went for an iced-down cold one, and came up laughing. "Jeeez, I live through Carl, Marboy and Capt. Bob, and you're going at kill me with a head–butt! Fer Christ's sake, man! Chief, I just wanna sit the fuck down, have a cold beer and relax. Janis, that goes fer you too, Baby . . ." As he gently gave her the shove-off push from where she had sat down on the left armrest of the fighting chair. "I really have a lot to talk about with the Chief here, and now Capt. Bob is only like four or five hours behind me. He knows what we're doing, more or less, but Baby, let me bring Martin up to speed OK? You know the Chief, he's getting old and don't hear so well!" Dallas ducked, just as a rather nasty sounding backhand whooshed past is head. "See, Baby! Ya got him all pissed-off again. Please let us talk for a few minutes. It's important. And so are you! I'll be right in, I promise. Really!"

"Yeah, just keep laughing!" She looked at the Chief, too. "Yeah! Both of ya!" "No!" the Chief said. "Damn it . . . Janis, this is serious shit . . . And you know that! Blow! And let your husband and I talk!" Janis spat back. "And just who the fuck are you again? Asshole! DALLAS!" Janis screamed in his ear. At this point Dallas got up from his fighting chair and gently took his wife's arm. "OK . . . OK . . . That's enough . . . I'll be right back," he said to no one in particular. He slid open the salon's lower sliding glass doors, walked past Sonata and, still pulling his wife in tow, marched her downstairs to the first door on the left, and slammed it shut behind them.

Sonata walked out and saw her husband alone, drinking a beer. "What happened, Martin? Are they fighting already?" The Chief looked up and smiled. "Nah . . . Why would you say that?" "Oh, I see them, and no talking. Just down the stairs and slam the door. Are you sure no fighting?" "Oh, Baby . . . I'm sure. No fighting . . . *Almost fighting* . . . But no fighting now . . . OK?" Sonata smiled. "OK then," and turned around and went back in to start dinner. The Chief just smiled, and finished his beer. "Fucking women" trailed off into the distance from somewhere . . .

Sonata was setting the salon table, when she heard the lower bedroom cabin door open and close. Dallas walked up the stairs, pulling his shirt over his head. He looked at Sonata and smiled. "How you doin? You all right? The Chief been treating you right?" She looked over Dallas. She had never known Dallas well enough to make small talk, and this was a first . . . "Oh Me? Yes, Dallas, Martin is a good man to me. A very good man . . ." "Good," Dallas said back. "The day he isn't, you tell me, OK? Where is he anyway? I'm sorry we were interrupted like that, but a man has got to do what a man has to do what a man has to do," and let out a little laugh. "Now, where is the Chief, darling? I think he's with Capt. Bob . . . on his boat . . . "Oh Shit! Is Bob here? I didn't even hear him pull in! By the way Sonata, what's for dinner anyway . . . I'm starved. I haven't eaten in about three days, so I hope you and Janis have put on some chow. I know Bob is hungry, too." "Oh, of course Mr. Dallas! We have lots of lobster and steamed fish, rice and beans, a salad . . . Don't worry about eating!" Dallas's smile got wider and he winked at her as he walked out the door. "Thanks Sonata." Dallas turned around towards the sliding glass door, when another voice caught up with him. "What? I don't get a thank you?" Janis was standing at the top of the stairs. "Of course you do, love! Thanx Baby! As always, you're the best! Just what in the world would I do without ya?" "Yeah, I was thinking the same thing Dallas!" "OK then, ladies, the men folk have things to talk about. So we'll see ya in a while, OK?" "OK, Mister Dallas," Sonata sang out. Janis picked up a knife off the counter. "Yes, we will see you "guys" in a while then." "Oh hell yeah! And don't call "Mister," Sonata. Jeeez. OK Sweetie? It's just "Mister" to Janis. Ha ha hah." Halfway out the door, a tennis shoe smacked Dallas in the ass. "Hey I felt that!" "GOOD," came a muffled scream.

Dallas did a fireman's slide down the stairs onto the lower deck, landing right between the "fighting chairs." He liked what he saw. Looking straight back, his little French seaplane was tethered twenty feet back. He looked left and there was the 51' Morgan sailboat rigged even with the transom of the Chief's Hatteras. To his right was Bob's 36' Scarab, rigged the same way as the Morgan. "Oh Boy!" Dallas said comfortably from one of the fighting chairs he had slid into. "This is perfect! Now as long as we don't get flown over too many times by the boys from Customs or the "Don't Expect Anything" crews, we are good to go!"

The engine cowlings were lifted off, and Dallas could see nothing but elbows and assholes when he looked for Bob and the Chief on Bob's boat. "Jeeez, what the fuck do we have here?" Dallas yelled down into the transom area. "Hey, man, so ya decided to come from the whorehouse to the workhouse? Is that what that fuckin mess is you two have down there? A workhouse? Hahha . . . But seriously, is anything wrong Bob? Is there, Chief?" The Chief stood up and looked at Dallas. "Nah, he was just running a bit hotter than normal, and I can fix that with a little tweak of the carbs. That and a couple new fuel-water separators, which he happens to have. It seemed the old fuck is still thinking ahead." "Who you calling a "Fuck?" The "old" part, OK . . . But I ain't no "Fuck!" Got it?" Both Dallas and the Chief answered at the same time "Oh, we got it. Now fix whatever the hell ya gotta fix, button it up and let's eat and have a few drinks! Especially since you got here early. By the way, you're gonna tell me how you did that over dinner and drinks." "Oh! You liked that, huh?" Bob quipped. "Well hell yeah I like it, but don't be burning yer damn Scarab up having done it!" "Nah, I'm good Dallas." Bob quickly answered back. Dallas turned away and said, "I know Bob, I know . . . That's why you make the big money, Bob . . . I know." "Chief?" Dallas said. "Get him and that Scarab running hot, right? We are gonna need that boat at its best, OK?" "Yeah, man! Give me thirty-five minutes and that fucker will fly!" "OK, you're the man with the wrench in his hand. When I need it," Dallas said, "and I'll need it, we will have to be on the move in an hour. Can we do that?" The Chief, wiping the sweat off his face, looked around and said, "I can have us on the move in less if we need to be." "No, that's cool, an hour is close enough. Thanks Chief." "OK then, boss, an hour it is." "Now come on and let's eat and have that drink! Bob, you too!" "Just give us ten minutes, Dal . . . I'll bring him up with me, OK?" "Yeah, OK, ten minutes." Dallas stepped off and up. On his way he looked around again. "Man, this is a mini-navy! Jeeez! Here we come Chance. I just hope you're still in one piece when we get there . . . Fucking Skeets!"

Dallas walked into the main salon. At the chart table, he laid out the charts he had brought up from the plane. The main one was of the Western Caribbean. It showed all the islands west of the center of Cuba and south, as well as the Gulf of Mexico west of and north of Cuba. In the chart tube Dallas also had tide and sounding charts for the Gulf of Mexico coastal regions. He flipped through the charts until he came up with a set of three. These were all of the country of Belize, the only English speaking country in the region. All three of the charts were identical, with notes handwritten with arrows, times, tides, and points along the coral reef systems where boats would be able to navigate ingress and egress with ease. All these points had G.P.S. coordinates to be used during a storm or at night. Dallas knew that the coast of Belize was a dark place, and without the daylight landmarks like mountains and beaches, it can be almost impossible to penetrate the reefs. Dallas knew by compass and dead reckoning where to get through, since he had done it many times before, but the Chief and Bob were both going to need a set of these navigation charts. "Even if we make a move toward the coast in daylight, it's still a bitch," he thought.

The call for dinner finally came. The Chief, Sonata, Dallas, Janis and Capt. Bob all took seats wherever they could. As promised, there was a ton of grouper fillets, steamed and split spiny lobster tails, a five-gallon bucket of amazing Trinidad jumbo pink shrimp and a Cobb-style salad with garlic toast. Of course the sink was full of beer on one side and some very expensive wine in the other. Dallas picked out a bottle of red. He looked at the label "OK! Someone must have ROBBED my cellar for this to be in here . . . Janis?"

Skeets and Fernando drove the last little way into the hills above Belize City. Skeets had a spot all picked out, just above the city docks. "From here I can see all the boat traffic, in and out, you know Fernando?" He looked over at his partner. Fernando was stone-cold passed out. Skeets shook him. Nothing. He shook him again. Nothing. He leaned over and screamed in his ear, "Hey you dirty little spic Bastard. WAKE THE FUCK UP!!" Nothing. Skeets got out and walked around the car, throwing the car door open. "Now get up!" and grabbed Fernando by his arm and pulled. Fernando "Kinda-Sorta" fell out of the car onto the road. In his hand, which was clenched, Skeets saw the tops of two syringes. Skeet leaned over him and felt for a pulse. Nothing. "Why you stupid little junkie fuck!" Skeets said, slightly lower this time. "You went and fucking *died* on me? Is that what you just did? Jeeez fucking Christ!" He kicked Fernando hard in the ribs. Then kicked him twice more. "Stupid fucker! That shit was for the kid! You dumb Bastard!" Skeets now went into a very dark place. He kicked the body one more time and started to look for a place to put him along the road, all the while watching for other cars, and people . . .

Skeets had parked on a hill, in a small pull-off, sort of like the kind of place you would use to fix a flat, or get a quickie from a whore. It was a hilly jungle area where the drop was about seventy-five feet. At the bottom were trash, and tires, and probably other bodies . . . So Skeets dragged his little spic friend about fifteen feet and stood over him. Looking down at him, Skeets nervously looked around. Not seeing anyone, or any headlights, or anything very much except the city lights and the port below, he very unceremoniously gave Fernando one good-bye kick, and listened as the body bounced along the trees and rocks until a resounding "thud" echoed back. "Hmmm," Skeets said aloud. "That is gonna leave a mark!" He turned and went back to the car. He spent a few minutes going through Fernando's bag, and his area in the car. All he found was about three hundred bucks, a few more syringes, and a rather large haggle of the heroin that killed him. "Fernando, this is it, huh? This is the sum total of yer miserable little junkie life, eh?" Skeets, being the good cop that he was, threw away all evidence of one Fernando Diego Corazon. Skeets looked at his name, and sighed. "For having this last name ("Heart" in English), you sure the fuck didn't have much, that's for sure . . . OK," Skeets mumbled again as he lit the little pile of a life on fire on the gravel behind the car.

Skeets kicked out the fire and scattered the ashes. He moved the car into a more favorable position to watch the docks, went to the trunk and pulled out a small Uzi .380 machine pistol and a bottle of 18-year-old rum, compliments of the Amada household bar. He still sat and stared at the empty seat next to him in the car and just shook his head as he drank. "Asshole! Here's to you!" and took a large pull on the bottle. "Ah, fuck you! I don't need you anyway!" Skeets leaned back and tried to relax. "After all, this could take a while. Who the fuck knows when Streeter will show? All I do know is that he will . . . And sooner than I probably think . . ." He semi-closed his eyes. "We'll see in the morning, and that's only a few hours . . . Fucking Fernando!" And passed out himself.

Assistant Director Cox and Special Agent Sands had arrived from Carl Brewster's house via the Director's jet the day before. They had set up their quarters in a decent hotel within minutes of the city docks. Cox was pacing the floor, thinking aloud, while agent Sands sat in a comfortable chair that overlooked the main street along the Gulf of Mexico. They had a decent room with a decent view, but as usual, it was what a "Director," a man of rank, was used to. Even with Special Agent Sands there, they would be hard-pressed to actually see or hear any new boats coming or going. But still Cox paced – He knew it, knew that he was too far from the action . . . Agent Sands had a few local snitches on the payroll, but it was the same old story. In Belize, as with all islands and countries south of the border, their nickname was still "D.E.A." – the "Don't Expect Anything" gang. And "gang" was right. That's how the D.E.A. operated outside of the country. Some had or have been out so long in the field they had to operate that way. Anyone who cooperated with them knew it had to be "M.U.F." (money up front), or when a bust did go down, if they hadn't been paid, they weren't getting paid. Or they got an "Oh Amigo, or Brother, next time, next time . . ." Assistant Director Cox knew that it was the agents putting that change in their own damn pockets. That's why he personally rotated as many agents around as possible as often as possible. But you can't do all of them, and it takes a great deal of time to gain the trust of the locals.

This was his biggest problem right now – Dallas Streeter paid better than he did, and all the locals knew it. But he had to keep in mind that this was not really about "drugs." Not this time. It is about a rouge agent gone bad, really bad. And it was about some kid who was kidnapped by Skeets, one of his own gone bad agents. One that was handed up to him on a silver platter by Dallas Streeter, and he had let escape. He had told Dallas to stay out of it! And by doing so, he knew that by telling him, it was like hiring a mercenary, especially since it was family. Cox wasn't there to really find Streeter.

Cox was there to find Skeets. Before he killed the kid. And Streeter, if he could. This was why Assistant Director Cox paced the floor . . . "Where was Skeets? Because wherever he is, Streeter will not be far behind." Cox knew that with Dallas Streeter's connections and his payroll, it was just hours now. Cox looked over at Sands. "Hey! What's the latest from the docks?" "Well, I'm not sure. But I am sure of one thing. I need more cash if I want to know the things I'm asking . . . I have to pay upfront. Period. Cox looked at the floor and said, "get that small case with the wheels on it, the red one from the plane. Go get it for me please."

Agent Sands looked at the two envelopes thrown on the table in front of him. Each had $2500 US dollars in it and next to each was five forms to be filled out. Sands reached out and picked one form up. "Excuse me? Huh? You want me to fill these out?" Cox laughed and said, "It's your job, remember? I still have to account for funds used in the field, Sands. That's what makes us different. We have what's still called accountability. Look don't give me a hard time, just fill out the goddamn forms and get moving!"

Sands gave his boss a glare, and under his breath he said "all this shit for five grand? Ya mon, it's little wonder we can't keep up, let alone catch up." Agent Sands then sat down and filled out the forms. While he was filling them out he was thinking, "accountability, my ass . . . Just who the fuck is he kidding? I wonder if he was still accountable for his Vietnam service?" He thought, "yeah, right, this prick was Special Op's in the Air America trans-dope highway in and out of Laos and Cambodia. The "Rice for Rifles" brigade that went bad, really bad. Oh yeah, Assistant Director Cox had a past. The word is he was so vested in Ernie Skeets for one reason, a dark reason. Skeets served under him in Nam!" Sand's still didn't get the Dallas Streeter connection. "Why? Why hadn't Cox taken out Streeter when he had the chance in Great Inauga in the Bahamas almost two years ago?" He thought, "man, whatever it is, it's got to be something . . . I don't even know if I want to know.

Streeter has got to have "weight" on Cox. He's got to!" With this
thought he was sticking the five grand in his dirty kakis, and lightly
slammed the door on Cox while he was on the phone talking in
code to who-the-fuck-ever somewhere in the Crib basin, just like
he probably had done in Laos a not-to-very-long time ago . . . What,
15-20 years ago?

"I'll start in the bars. I need to find my guy. Maybe he has heard
of new people who have floated in. I find Dallas's crew, I'm gonna
find Skeets not too far away, that's a bet. It's all timing now. I have
to be a witness. Or in it!"

Skeets woke out of a feverish dream, still in his car. His foot
jerked forward and his middle toe, which is slightly longer than his
big toe, jammed into the neck of the rum bottle he had thrown on
the floor the night before, up to the second joint. "What the Fuck!"
He yelled. "Fernando, you asshole!" and looked over for him. "Oh,
that's right . . . You can't hear me at the bottom of that cliff, can
ya? Asshole!"

"Ah, shit," he said as he opened the car door and swung out his
foot, his toe still stuck in the rum bottle hole. He sat there looking
at it. The sunlight twisted through the bottle in his eyes as he turned
it this way and that way. "Goddamn!" He snatched his 9mm off the
seat next to him. He pointed the gun at the bottle, but then thought
better of it, and flipped it over and used the butt to try and break it
at the neck. His toe was purple in the mid-morning light. He closed
his eyes. The sound left no doubt that the bottle broke, but it broke
off cleanly at the neck, leaving Skeets with a jagged glass ring on
his toe. "You have got to be shitting me! C'mon, man." He put on
his other shoe and limped away from the shattered bottle on the
ground. "OK . . . OK . . ." He bent down and found a rock and
placed it under his new "toe ring." Again taking his 9mm, he swung
on it. Blood, lots of blood from a backed up purple toe misted his
face and arms. "Oh fuck, oh fuck, that hurt, oh, oh . . ." He couldn't
see his toe for all the blood. "Christ!" He hobbled back to the car

and grabbed a dirty t-shirt, took out a pocketknife and made some quick strips, and wrapped it tight. He leaned back across the seat and stared at the ceiling of his car. "Fuck it! I'm done . . . I'm going back to Amada's house and kill that little fuck Streeter! I'll have my revenge and, while I'm at it, I'll kill fuckin Amada too and everyone in the house! I am DONE! He slammed his fist on the steering wheel. DONE!"

Chapter 12

A hundred miles offshore, the same sun had come up at the same time. It had been decided after dinner that the "move" was on. Everyone was awake and sobering up fast, Janis and Sonata were getting the Morgan 51' ready, Dallas, Bob and the Chief were in a huddle, all eyes and ears as they broke out the guns and cash, each taking what they thought they would need and carrying it to their boats. Capt. Bob was going in the lightest, and he was going in first. It was his job to hit the city docks, check out the lay of the land and radio Janis on the Morgan to tell her what slip at the dock to use. If no slips were good, he would direct them to the anchorage offshore. This would mean using the dingy to get off and on the boat, but also would give them some wiggle room if they had to move fast.

Dallas and the Chief cast off Bob's Scarab first. Bob held up his radio and waved them off. Dallas and the Chief climbed the ladder to the fly bridge to get a better look at them as both boats now left under their own power. Dallas waved at the ladies one last time, holding up his radio also. Everyone was quiet as they left. Everyone knew they had jobs to do and that the fun was over for a while. The Chief looked at Dallas. He cracked a smile, and shook his head. "Ya know D, I let you get me in some "fubar" places, and here we go again!" "Oh shit Chief! What would you do without me?" Dallas took the binoculars away from his eyes. "You know damn well that if the tables were turned I'd be right here for you!

We live for this shit. Not *this* shit, with Chance, but just the jazz of it all and you know it . . .." The Chief started his mains, they roared to life, drowning out the gulls that circled the boat and Dallas. He looked over at Dallas and smiled. "Hey, don't you have a plane to catch?" Dallas looked at his watch; he shook it and held it up to his ear. "I don't know," he yelled back. "I can't hear my watch! I think it may be broke!" The Chief throttled back the engines, and laughed as he said, "Get the fuck off my boat, would ya?" Dallas broke out in laughter, saying, "OK, I'll do a recon and get you on the radio in a couple hours, OK?" Steely-eyed, the Chief said, "look, don't fuck around and try and be a hero, OK? Are you packing?" "Yeah, I'm fine . . ." "You have enough fuel?" "Yeah, I'm fine . . ." "OK then, let's pull that mosquito up to the boat and get you out of here. The flyover's start soon, and I suspect Special Agent Cox will have a plane up there, too . . . Ya know?" "Ya mon! Let's do this thing!"

They both slid down the fly bridge ladder, grabbed a line and pulled in the little seaplane. Dallas leaned over and popped the hatch. The Chief meanwhile held firm while Dallas popped into the seat. The Chief could see a flurry of action inside as Dallas flipped breakers, switches, adjusted the wheel and buckled in. Dallas gave him a thumbs-up and the Chief set the plane adrift . . . From the lower console, the Chief throttled forward and steered away to the right. This gave Dallas a straight shot out. There was no need for his little electric fan; he just fired up his flight engine. The Chief looked back and watched, thinking "you wouldn't catch me in that fucking flying VW . . . Oh hell no!" Dallas sat there warming up the engine, and then hit it. He had a nice little headwind for lift.

The Chief finished tying up the loose ends left from everyone's boats leaving. This was the hard part for him. He was alone now. He had orders, too. He was supposed to move into sight of land, but no closer. He was the mother ship. Everyone relied on him as of the moment they cut loose. If someone broke down, if someone ran aground, if someone got boarded, et cetera, et cetera. . . He had all his radios, scanners, scramblers, depth, speed, G.P.S. and single side band government frequencies dialed in. He was the "floating fortress" of the effort to free Chance Streeter, Dallas's wayward brother. And if the Chief thought it necessary, he would mount the 50 calibers on the foredeck and drive the fucker right up to the beach!

Capt. Bob was now within sight of the coast. At seventy mph, he was in reach of the city docks while the Morgan, coasting in at twelve knots (14 mph + -) was at least 6 - 7 hours out. This would give him enough time to look over where he and the Morgan would put in. At mid-day, the mountains were shrouded in clouds. "It's freaking hot," Bob thought as he strained to see the coast outline. An offshore wind was blowing up a good spray along the reefs that fronted the coastline. He knew the closer he got, the better the visibility, so he took a compass reading, checked his charts, tucked his pistol under his shirt and headed in. Janis and Sonata were taking it easy, each sported a new bathing suit and already were on their second bottle of wine for the day. The Morgan had a pre-set autopilot, so they just sat back on this floating cocaine corpse of a boat and left the driving up to the magic that was autopilot. They knew that when they got close to wherever that someone would show up and take over. At least they hoped they would . . .

Frank Amada stared out at the "Gulfo de Honduras" from his second story, wondering when the older Streeter would make his move. He wondered if Dallas knew he was keeping the younger Streeter safe – That the kid was really no longer a hostage, but a houseguest. He also knew Skeets would be back for him any time now, and he had to play the part of prison guard. He didn't want to kill Skeets. "This is for Streeter to do, no? I don't need no extra heat for that," he thought. "So I play along and bring them two together

and dey kill one another or not . . . I jus have to give Streeter enough
room and he do it. Streeter wants him dead, this I know, but he
gonna have to do it himself." "Raul! Beta ca! I need my radio . . .
Raul! I say I want my radio. It's time to reach out to Streeter and get
this over. I have to tell him that I "expect" him!"

Skeets tapped the brakes a bit. "Shit, as long as I'm here I might
as well slide down around the waterfront and have a look around."
He coasted down the hilly streets through a shitty part of town,
always taking the back streets, checking every face for the familiar
one. Not a lot of white guys in this part of town, so when he saw a
white one he automatically slowed down. When he got to the first
stoplight, he took a hard look at a guy coming out of a small bar.
He wasn't white, but Skeets recognized the walk. "No fuckin way!"
Skeets hung at the light and let it change and stayed put. "That is
that fucking guy – the fucking agent from the Bahamas! What's
his name? Ahh, Chris . . . Sands! That's it! It's him . . . Fuckin guy,
always over-dressed! Those damn Bahamians. Shit! Well shit . . . If
he's here, so is Cox!"

Agent Sands had just laid out the last of Assistant Directors
Cox's (or the agency's) generous allotment of operating cash to a
scumbag that he knew was once also on Streeter's payroll, too. He
strolled down the street, the air full of humidity and the stench of a
small group of horses, the flies so thick they made an audible hum
above the din of the street. He stepped around a vagrant with his
hand out, into the street's gutter. He felt the breeze of a big car go
by, looked up and saw it had three bullet holes in its trunk. "What
the fuck was that?" He strained to get a look at the driver, but he
only saw the head of a white guy with a bad haircut. A big guy. Ugly.

It was at this point that Skeets half-assed attempt to run over
Sands just pissed him off even more. "Fuck it . . . I'll swing past the
docks and head back to Amada's house. I have unfinished biz there.
If the boys from the agency are in town, you can bet Streeter and
his fuckin crew are, or are close. Yup, and if they are here, I'm not!"

Skeets had a thousand-yard stare in his eyes as he drove. "Fucking Fernando!" In his mind's eye, he still stood at the cliff, kicking Fernando's ass off, over and over. Then as if by magic he was back on the sailboat in the Bahamas, Streeter shooting him in his knee. He subconsciously touched it. He turned on to the coast road and only slightly checked the boats on his left. He didn't see anything that looked out of place. Just the usual crap and the usual suspects. He had a few hours before sunset and wanted to get the drop on Raul and his few security guys back at Amada's house. If that meant posting up and waiting, so be it. "This way, I can check and see if Streeter or his old buddies from the D.E.A. were also sitting on the place." His knee was hurting and so was his back. He looked over at the empty passenger seat and saw the corner of a baggie tucked in the crack. He reached over, tugged it out and held it up in front of him. "Hmm." The bag had what he thought was a gram or two of the "horse" Fernando had been riding in it. He held the steering wheel with his knee and tapped out a small portion onto the web between his thumb and forefinger. The stabbing pain in his knee hadn't bothered him in some time, but kicking Fernando off the cliff must have re-torn his scar tissue. He hesitantly brought up the dark brown powder to his nose. "Ah shit, I can do this . . . This little bit will only kill the pain." Yeah, and did it! He wiped his nose, sticking his pinky finger up his left nostril and wrung it out. "Oh shit! That stings, and that taste – fuck!" He tossed the rest of the baggie on the floor of the passenger seat and resumed driving with his hands. "Now I'll deal with those assholes!" He still had a few hours before sunset . . .

Dallas reached the coast a hundred miles southeast of Amada's beach house. He circled a small fishing village but decided not to land there. He looked at his fuel and saw he was still good on that, but the sun was going to set in a few hours and he knew he'd have to put down somewhere. Just where was the question. After flying along the coast for twenty minutes he heard of all things over the hum of his engine the sound of a telephone ringing. "What the hell?" He looked over at his satellite phone on the passenger seat; the red light indicating service was blinking. "Man, only a half dozen people have that number! Who the fuck would be calling me on that?" Reaching over, he knocked off a pile of dirty clothes and turned it around so he could see the incoming number. "Wait a second, I know that area code!" Without a lost second he picked up the receiver and spoke, slowly, "Why hello Francisco! Long time no speakie. What's on your mind? Still up to old tricks? How's the wife? And why are you calling me? I'm not late with that boat am I?"

"Hey Streeter! How ya doing man? I'm just calling to say hello." Dallas and Frank Amada were both very cautious men. Neither one gave a hint of what both knew was going to be said – They both already knew. "Yeah ah Dallas," Frank's accent still heavy after all these years. "Are you going to be on time with my boat? No problems, is there? I'm just wondering, jew know . . . Is everything alright?"

Dallas was holding back now. He wanted to reach through the airwaves and grab old Frankie's fat neck! But he held back, always the "dance" first. "Ah, no Frank, no problems. I seemed to have "misplaced" something and was wondering, though, if you might help me find it? And yes it's bigger than a bread box!"

"What? What's that mean, "bigger than a bread box?"" Frank calmly asked.

"It means I'm looking for something, and can you help me find it? And it means "how much?" if you can, Frank. Oh, and Frank, I know you know what I'm talking about here, no?"

Amada chuckled a bit as he said, "ah jew know I have this *"thing"* at my house, and somebody bring me dis *"thing"* and I really don't want it. But dis guy says it's very important, jew know? But I don't want a problem, so I say, Dallas, you come and take this *"thing."* I know you want dis *"thing"* very much, and just leave the boat where I can find it and everything be all right. But jew has to tells me when you coming, OK?"

"Why Frank I'm in the area as a matter of fact . . . So I'll come get this *"thing"* and then I tell you where the boat is, OK? Oh and Frank . . . I hope this *"thing"* has a pulse in good shape when I come, or I'm gonna sink that fucking boat on your front lawn! Frank, listen to me . . . I'll call you back in twelve hours. By then your boat will be close and I will be closer . . . When I call back, you're gonna have my *"thing"* ready, so deal with whoever brought my *"thing"* before I get there. We don't want a mess, you and I, do we?"

The answer was slow in coming back. "No, we don't want a mess. This is my house; I don wan no problem in my house. But I don know where dis guy at right now . . ." Amada stumbled for words. "Dallas, jew call me back. OK?"

"Yeah, OK Frank, "I call you back, twelve hours Amada . . ."

"Hey, hey Streeter what kind of boat you in? I jus wanna know, I never hear a boat like that before. It sounds like you have a fast boat."

"I do Frank . . . I do." Dallas hung up. "Shit, if that ain't something! That fuck calling me." Dallas thought that was just in time. "Fucking prefect timing, too! HA! He's scared and that works!" He picked up his mic and switched back to radio. "OK, time to get this show over," he thought to himself. "On-Line – On-Line – come in, On-Line. Whisky Tango – Whiskey Tango . . ."

"Yeah go ahead, Dal. This is On-Line."

"Hey Chief, time to move . . . You have those charts we went over? Please start the execution of plan "A." Have all ready by 04:30 and everyone in place. Make the calls. I'm going to be setting down as soon as I am in within walking distance of Amada's beach house. Roger that?"

"I got ya Dallas . . . Will start the move a.s.a.p. and will have all things in place for your next call."

"OK Chief, have those two women off the Morgan, have Capt.

Bob pick them up and set the autopilot to the pre-determined G.P.S. location with the throttle set at one-third, or to arrive at 05:30. Have sails dropped before, and wire it as we discussed . . ."

"Roger that Dallas . . .. I can't wait! Man-O-Man, is she gonna go . . ."

"Oh Chief, yeah I just got off the horn with Amada himself. So it really is on . . .!"

"OK . . . So good luck!"

Dallas looked at his watch, 6:27 pm. He was hungry as hell, his ass hurt and he had had enough of this bullshit to last another lifetime. The sun wasn't going to set until around 7:30 or so, but he had to find a nice little spot to put the "duck" down without too much attention. He checked his position as he flew the coast. He knew this coast pretty well from the past, and kind of had a spot in mind not more than a few miles from the beach house – a nice little inland lake. It was a "crocodile sanctuary," and he knew that if it was the same as the last time he saw it, it would be perfect. It had a nice foot path in and out, with small gates he could get over, and would also keep out most of the curious and horny. All he had to do was not get his ass eaten as he got off his puddle jumper. He also knew that the caretaker had in the past taken bribes for air drops into the lake, so he was glad he had some cash just in case. He might even pick up a meal from the guy if he was around. Then it would be a little walk, and a little recon and then decide if it was to be a "whole lot of shooting" or not . . . If I got to Amada before Skeets showed back up for his prize, then things might go a little smoother. If Frank wasn't an asshole and actually helped that would be nice, but I'm not counting on anything, and all bets are off if Skeets was already there. "I'll just set up and watch the place for a spell. If I can't get in the easy way, then I'll call in the troops. Fuck it! I'll call them in anyway! Now let's find that lake . . . Oh, and something to freaking eat!"

Skeets drove away from the city; its silhouette was fading in his rearview mirror and the mountains on the right were still encased in some clouds. He wanted to stay off the coast road and head away from being spotted by any possible "un-friendlies" that might be out on the road looking for not only him but any of Streeter's crew as well. He was just over a hundred miles from reaching the beach house and sneaking up and killing everyone in it. But as the fastest he could drive on these shit roads, he might as well have been three hundred miles, because it was going to take him till after midnight to get back. Then he was going to sit up and watch the place before he made his move, just to make sure that everyone was settled in for the night.

Skeets felt like shit, his leg was aching and he had a low-grade fever from the malaria he got a year ago from the mosquitoes he slapped all night long while waiting to rip-off some of Amada's rivals down in Panama in the canal zone. The "H" he snorted before he left to come back had worn off. He reached down to the passenger floor and grabbed the baggie again. He had found it got rid of all the pain, but didn't know it only masked the fever he was running. He started to guzzle water that lay in half-empty bottles all over the front seat, and finding the half-empty bottle of old rum, he drank that too. Taking a bigger snort this time, he waited for the first signs of relief. He thought to himself, "shit, another five hours and I'll be there at this rate." He swerved his car to miss a pothole and banged into a concrete abutment and that's when he heard it . . . "Goddamn it!" The car pulled to the left and his front tire was shredded from the jagged concrete he had just hit, the whole sidewall was gone. Ernie banged his head against the steering wheel. "Oh fuck! C'mon! Now? This shit happens now? Fucking Fernando! I know it's you! Cocksucker! . . . Jeez!" Sweating, getting off on the "H" and in pain, he pulled the car off the road on the side of the oncoming traffic. "Goddamn country!" He got out and screamed. "Your whole fucking country is a shithole!" His voice echoed through the hills, mocking him. The toe that he'd gotten stuck in the broken bottle top hole started to bleed again when he kicked the tire. "Oh fuck no, not this too!" . . . He looked at his machine pistol on the seat. It was starting to look good to him, but he shook his head and limped back into the car and made a new bandage. "Well this is going at put me back a few more minutes, I guess."

Frank Amada hung up his satellite radiophone. He set it on the table on the deck outside the French doors and walked inside. "Raul! Hey beta ca! I wan jew to wake that kid up . . . How much of that shit has he been doing? Have jew been cutting him back?" Raul had a stupid look on his face. "Ah but Mr. Amada sir, you told me to keep him comfortable, so no, not really, I give him what he says he wants." "Raul, I told you that to take him off the stuff, not jus give it to him! . . . Go clean him up for Christ sakes! The older Streeter is coming soon. If he gets here and see this shit, Oy mano, I gonna tell him it's your doing! Yours and Skeets! Now go clean him up, now! After that get my wife and put her in a car, have what's-his-face drive her to our airport and the plane. Have him wait there with her. Tell that dumb ass to take a gun or even two guns, OK? And that we will be along shortly. Now go! Get out of my sight! Go stand guard after you get that kid cleaned up. I think Skeets is coming back and I know that Dallas Streeter is coming! . . . I don wan mi casa shot all the hell up! Understand? Oh, and get a money bag ready and put it in my bedroom, too, with a small Uzi, the 9mm Corto, extra clips too. Go! Thank you, Raul. You are a good man." Raul was caught off guard at his boss's tone. "Thank you, Hefe!"

Dallas, now finding his way, noticed the landmark he had been searching for – a small river outlet into the ocean, which also had a very small village on the beach next to the river's delta. The color change was the dead giveaway, where the river emptied into the ocean he could see, even in the fading light, the distinct brown washout of mud from the hills and actually from the "Croc Lake." He knew from flying in nearby that he would have to be careful of the electric fence submerged at both ends of the lake. The fence served two purposes - one was to at least try to keep asshole poachers and their boats and drag lines used catch the crocs that like to dive and lay on the bottom when disturbed out; the second purpose was that the net was not just across the lagoon, but was akin to a "shark fence" to keep Bull Sharks from easy access and an easy meal. Mainly, it kept the croc's in the little lake or lagoon. A small shock usually did the trick, and over time the animals became actual pets for the keeper of the sanctuary. They all had names and distinct personalities. Most had been hand-fed all their lives, and were used to the person that fed them. Dallas understood from what he had been told that they really liked horsemeat. So the trick for Dallas was now landing on this lake and stepping off into anything but an "overly friendly" crocs mouth.

Dallas gently brought the little seaplane in on a soft head wind and barely rippled the surface. As fast as he could, he cut the main engine and brought out the electric steering motor. It was almost dusk. He could see a small light on in the nearby trees. It was a shack, and that was a kind description by any means. But being Dallas, he motored right over to it and hit the throttle hard at the last minute to make sure he ran aground as far as he could on the marshy embankment. To his surprise, no one came out. He waited a minute and shut down the plane, lights off, motor stored, and gun in waistband. He popped the hatch.

Dallas grabbed a duffle bag and stepped out. He stood real still for a moment, just listening to the sounds around him. The humidity and smell of the stagnant water surrounded him, held him tight – he felt forty pounds heavier. He took a step forward and almost at the same time two huge splashes, one on each side, made him jump and pull his pistol out of his waistband. "You won't be needing that!" a deep island voice with a British accent said in a loud whisper. "In fact, put that goddamn thing away. Now!" Dallas slowly turned in the direction of the voice. "No, if it's all the same

to you, I think I'll just hold on to it if ya don't mind, friend . . ."
Dallas was speaking slowly, with all the authority he could muster.
"Well you don't need it! Now put it away, and just who the hell are
ya to be sliding up into two of my breedin' crocs mounds, eh? They
get pretty upset when ya do stupid shit like that, fella. Lucky they
didn't make a snack out of ya . . ." Dallas interrupted him. "Excuse
me, are you the ah, ah, ranger or whatever?" "Yeah something like
that. You're on private property, you know," the voice answered.
Dallas replied carefully, "yeah I know, I've been here before, a long
time ago." "Ya have, eh? Doing what?" The voice got a tone to it
that was just a hair darker. Dallas answered with the only thing
that came to his head. "Are you the same guy that was here when
this place was just getting started? About three-four years ago?" "I
am, so what?" The voice still had that darker tone. Dallas slowly
pulled up the duffle bag. "Well here, let me refresh your memory."
Dal zipped open the bag. He reached in, his money was in stacks of
five thousand each, and he also felt the grips of his two other guns
next to the cash. He pulled out two stacks. "Last time I was here I
think the parking meter ran about a thousand dollars an hour, no?"

Before the voice could answer, Dal threw down two stacks at
the voice's feet, or what he thought were feet. "Here! This is ten
hours of time on the meter . . . Now I won't be here that long, but
you just keep the difference, OK?" The voice answered. "You're
bothering my crocs!" Dallas threw down another stack of five
grand. "Will that un-bother them? For a while? Friend?" . . . Dallas
was in his element. In the bush, the only thing greener than the trees
was cash. The voice said, "well, you got twelve hours. If you ain't
gone in twelve hours, I'm gonna burn your pretty little plane and
sink it in the swamp. You read me, friend?" Dallas, still standing,
tried to see who it was that voice belonged to, but just couldn't make
out anything more than a shape. "Yeah, OK! Twelve hours . . . I
read ya." Dallas zipped up the bag, but still held his gun. "OK, I'll
be out" . . . Not a word came back. "I said I'd be gone in twelve" . . .

Nothing. Just like it was a ghost, it was gone. "Ah fuck, time to move on I guess." He threw the bag over his shoulder and made like a tree and left the smell of rotten flesh and swamp behind him as quick as he could walk. The road that led away from the lagoon was hardly driven; grass grew in the center but the wheel tracks were visible in the din of the evening light. He figured, "I'll get to Amada's beach house at around midnight."

Raul rolled Chance over. "C'mon you, get up! I have to clean you up, we think you brother, cousin, uncle whoever the hell he is will be here soon." Chance reached for the already "fixed" syringe on the nightstand. Raul said, "OK, but dis is the da last one! You need to be sharp tonight and this shit rots your little brain I think, so make it quick, we have to get started." Chance half sat-up. "What do you mean somebody is coming? Not that bastard Skeets, now that I have this – Chance slipped the smooth, hammerless Smith & Wesson out from under the crack in the bed. He pointed it amateur-ly at Raul. Raul slapped it away, and then hit Chance with a backhand to the forehead. "Hey Vato! Don't jew ever point that at me again! I will stick it up your ass so fast . . . You know better, I know you do. Now c'mon, do your shit and let's get you cleaned up. Even if Skeets does come, never let him see that gun. Don't wave it in his face, don't say I gonna kill you . . . You no say nothing. When he turns his back, you shoot him right here!" Raul took his finger and put it to the base of his head. "You kill the head and the body dies. Got it? "Chance got a sick stomach all of a sudden. "Yeah Raul, I got it."

Chapter 13

"**N**o moon tonight," he thought as the Chief set his autopilot with the G.P.S. system. "Good, I'll have no silhouette on the water." He had told Capt. Bob to grab the females off the Morgan and put it under tow until they got closer, then he was to cut the Morgan free with throttles and autopilot set up so it would get where it had to be before dawn. He was then supposed to drop the ladies of at a small village on the coast. Dallas knew his ole lady would have a minor shit fit, but the place had a great beach and a bar the stayed open all night. This fact would be a plus in so many ways. Belize is beautiful in late April.

Once Capt. Bob hooked back up with the Chief, it would be time to wire the boat, and then take up a nice spot just off shore about a mile. A mile seems like a long way on land – on the water, not so much. Just far enough so when the shit hit the fan later, the view will be "killer" and they'll be able to swing in and effect a timely pick up of the last men standing. "Hopefully it will be our guys" he thought. The radio crackled. It was Capt. Bob. The Chief looked down at his watch. "OK, 7:57 pm." He spoke clearly into the mic. "Bob . . . OK man . . . I'll read you my G.P.S. location. After you drop the ladies off, I hope you can get in there. High tide isn't for 45 minutes, so be careful and keep your powder dry! That means "No you can't go in and have only "one beer."" Bob spoke up. "Roger that, going to find them and put it under tow after I drop them off.

Or kick them off, whichever is easier, they are not going to like this, you know?" "Hey Bob, just fill up Janis and Sonata's carry bags with as much wine off the Morgan as they can carry. Tell 'em to have a seat and eat something and not to worry, we'll be right back, OK?" "That seems like a plan, I'll radio in as I approach your position Chief. Give me a couple hours, around 11-ish, OK?" "Right, oh and Bob, keep your eyes open for other boats, or whatever is in the area, OK?" "Ya mon! I will do jus that, see ya in a few hours . . . out."

With no moon, Dallas used his little pocket light as he moved along the access road. Having not really been out of that plane in hours and hours made him feel the humidity and closeness of the bush. He reached the main gate, or what served as one. It was the type cattle ranchers use – a framed three bar deal with a chain and lock. At the ends were posts and barbwire that led in both directions. He slipped through the middle gap and was on the main road. He checked his watch and thought "time-time, I gotta move . . ." Without another thought he broke into a fast-paced walk/jog. His back was killing him. All those hours sitting down, cramped and awake was making this the hardest part of this deal so far. He reached into his backpack and fished out a pill bottle. Without breaking stride, he opened it and ate the contents. The Perc's tasted like chalk he thought as he quickly took a sip out of the water bottle off his shoulder. He tossed the empty pill bottle to the side and picked up the pace a bit. Dallas kept telling himself, "only two miles . . . only two miles." . . .

Back at "Casa de Amada," Frank Amada came down the stairs. Raul stood just outside the door that led into the garage. The garage door was open and Frank's Land Rover was backed in, ready to go. Frank stopped at Chance's door, knocked and let himself in. "OK young Streeter, you do what Raul tells you!" Chance looked at Amada. "Where you going?" he asked. "Oh, not very far. Somewhere I can watch. This is between agent Skeets and your family. You just do what Raul tells you, understand?" Amada turned away. "I'll be watching!" he said over his shoulder as he disappeared into the darkened hall. Chance heard a car start and pull off. He closed the door and locked it, finished putting on his shoes and sat on the edge of the bed, fingering the satin finish on a weapon he had never used. Life was feeling very real .

A fly spec on the horizon line of the Gulf of Mexico grew larger as it appeared to a conch diver headed in with his dinner-size load to his home dock at the small fishing village that Dallas had over-flown hours before. It looked to him like just a couple boats headed in to somewhere, and seemed to nowhere in particular.

The Chief sat comfortably on the fly bridge. In his ears he could still hear the sounds of music and laughter, or thought he could, the boats now empty with the Morgan 51' under tow, both devoid of any of the commotion that had filled them over the last three days. The sun was setting far to the west, only half above the waterline. He kept one eye on the water ahead and one eye on his G.P.S. position. He couldn't help but wonder if Dallas had landed safely and was making his way to Amada's beach house. All he knew was that when that call came in, he was going to climb aboard the Morgan and start her up, set the autopilot and the timer on the charge that was going to set all hell loose as close to Amada's beach house as possible! He looked around in all directions. "Ah, what a nice night for fireworks!" That little smile crossed his lips, and he shook his head. "What a waste of a good boat and a hell of a lot of good blow!" He leaned in and turned up the volume of the VHS radio. The drone of his engines was now starting to ring in his ears, and the absence of other people seemed deafening now.

Capt. Bob and his Scarab weren't going anywhere fast. Janis and Sonata made sure of that. The fight started before they even got to the docks. All the way in, Janis and Sonata drank bottle after bottle of wine, and with each one they finished, the screaming got louder. After the third bottle of red she turned around from her seat in the bow and threw the empty at Capt. Bob. "You are not going to leave us anywhere, asshole!" Bob stepped out of the way and the bottle smashed against the starboard engine, leaving a gash in the engine cover. "The hell! Don't throw that shit at me!" Bob screamed back above the roar of the engines. "Hey Bob! Go fuck yourself. You're not dropping us off!" "Oh yes I am!" The shouting match ended abruptly when Capt. Bob threw the boat into neutral and the momentum almost dumped two drunk women off the bow and sent loose, open bottles of wine all over both of them. They both went sprawling onto the deck face first. Janis helped Sonata up, and they both armed themselves with full bottles. "Oh Shit! . . . No don't even . . . But it was too late – a bottle of 1964 Rothschild hit Bob in the side of the head, knocking him out cold. Janis turned and looked at Sonata and shrugged. "Serves him right, asshole!" Sonata walked around the center console and bent down and looked at Bob. "Janis? I think you really hurt him." "No, he'll be fine." Janis said calmly. "No really! Look!" Just above Bob's right eye, blood was starting to run down in a clockwise circle, "Oh damn! Get me a towel, Sonata . . . Dallas is gonna kill us . . . and some ice, too!"

Dallas had made his way down the access road onto the main road rather quickly. He knew the clock was ticking and had no time to slow down now. He figured he had about two full hours before the sun started rising. He knew Skeets would be showing up back at the house to tie up loose ends, since he hadn't been able to find him in the city. All Skeets found in the city was a dead Fernando and some old friends from the D.E.A. Fernando . . . Well, Skeets dealt with Fernando in a very Skeets-like manner – He just tossed the little junkie fuck's body and belongings off that cliff above the city very un-ceremonially onto the garbage dump below. He had spent the rest of his time in the city dodging his old friends from the past who were loving the thought of getting their hands on his neck.

At this moment, Skeets was pissing and moaning about his back, his shoulder, his lack of sleep, the Streeter brothers, Frank Amada, the D.E.A. chasing him, "prol here!" and any number of shits that could go wrong. "Christ, I need another Percocet or even a nose full of the other shit! Anything to just take the edge off." At least he knew there is booze in the house! Skeets mind was a confuckulation of some very twisted shit.

Dallas crossed the main road into the sawgrass, scrub pine and palmettos. He could smell the fresh ocean air and could hear it as it swept through the brush around him. He climbed the small dunes through the sea oats, and the smell and humidity of the gulf blasted him in the face. The sea oats gently swayed in the onshore breeze. From the top of the sand dune he could see Amada's casa. It was a little bit more than three hundred meters to his right. He looked at his watch – 3:40 a.m. on the nose. He reached into his carry bag and fumbled for his binoculars. Once found, he flipped the battery powered night and rangefinder to the "on" position. He scanned the horizon line in the gulf. "C'mon Chief, where are ya buddy?" . . . With his radio, which he hadn't let go of since he left the plane, he "clicked" the mic several times. The chief spoke slowly and clearly. "Hey Dal, he said in a low voice, are you good?"

Dallas spoke back in the same low tone. "Yeah, I'm good. Right where I wanna be, but I can't see you yet." "Here, this might help!" The chief reached over and flicked the mast spreader lights on and off three times. "There, ya find me?" "Oh yeah, brother!" Dallas said. "You're good ta go! Is the boat wired?" "Of course it is; that's a stupid question!" A chuckle followed and trailed off. "Hey Chief, did ya have any problems with the ladies?" "Jeez! What do you think? Nope, none at all!" Dallas muttered into the mic, "yeah I bet . . . So where's Capt. Bob?" The Chief sorta said, "yeah well . . . You know Bob . . . He likes that flair for the dramatic, so I imagine he'll be showing up either after the shit starts or come zooming in right on time."

"So what time we gonna start this party?" the Chief asked, sheepishly. Dallas spoke extra clear. "Listen, here's the deal" . . . Dallas was interrupted by the sound of a go fast boat. "Is that Capt.

Bob? Chief?" "Yeah, Dal!" the Chief yelled into his mic. Dallas could hear the Chief shout over to Capt. Bob to "kill those damn engines, will ya? I'm talking to Dallas here, OK?" Dallas could hear the Chief ask Capt. Bob, "hey, what happened to keeping this thing quiet? Shit Bob! Now cut those off! Thank you! . . . "OK Dallas, what were you saying?" Dallas asked the Chief to get Bob on board so he can hear this too. Bob climbed aboard the Morgan, and Dallas started to lay out the night's fun . . .

Dallas, having cleared the palmetto scrub, worked his way up the last of the wind-drifted dunes. He looked to his right and could see the Amada house just down the beach. He reached into his pack and pulled out his small 50 x 70 Nikon glasses. First he checked out the house, which appeared to be empty. Some lights were on but not very bright. No movement at all in or around the building; a couple cars in the drive but Amada's main ride wasn't there. He noticed that the garage door was open. This didn't look right. Then he saw the glow of a cigarette in the shadow. "Ah, no shit, that's Raul . . . I'll bet on it . . . Amada must be still in the house. He's probably upstairs in his safe room watching everything on his home security cameras," Dallas thought. "Oh hell, Frank wouldn't miss this for love nor money." He hated Skeets just as much as Dallas did. "Oh yeah, Frank has a front row seat!"

Dallas lay on top of the dune. He was now looking at the Morgan and the Chief's boat about a quarter-mile out. He picked up his hand-held radio and hailed the Chief. "Hey Chief, you there?" The radio crackled back. "Oh hell yeah, and Capt. Bob is right next to me. So what's the plan?" "OK Chief, this is the deal. It's what? About 4:45 a.m?" "Ah, yup! That's close," the Chief responded. "OK Chief, you have the Morgan loaded and wired, right? So I want you and Bob to start her up and send her towards the beach. "What's the range on your radio control? You aren't going to lose contact or any dumb shit like that, right?" The Chief spoke slowly. "Dallas, you know me better than that. Don't you worry boss. I

press these buttons . . . And you sit back and watch the show!"
"OK Chief. I want you to tie off the helm and send that bitch right
up on to the beach, or until it runs aground. But we have a bit of
good surf, so try and time it so it rides right up and lays on its side.
I want it to look like it drifted in, like a couple idiots didn't anchor
her out and she dragged in. Get it Chief?" "Oh, nice touch," the
Chief radioed back. "This way, if that fucker Skeets gets here, and he
will be soon, by daybreak I wager, he'll maybe go down and have a
look! . . . But no matter what, no "Boom-Boom" til I give the word,
OK? We have to be clear on that. He might drag Chance down to
the boat, thinking "well here's how we get out, we'll sail out!" Shit!
So no "Boom-Boom" til I say!"

    "OK, Boss! . . . You just say the word! There's enough "Boom-
Boom" to blow out a ten-foot hole and vaporize that boat. No
worries, Dallas. We are gonna back off this bitch and send her on
her way then." . . . "You do that Chief, nice and easy, nice and slow.
Just have it on beach just before dawn." "Right O, Chief standing
by." . . . The Chief clicked off, looked at Capt. Bob and didn't say
a word. He pulled open a console cabinet and reached inside and
with two fingers he slowly tugged out a 1956 Mouton Cadet, labeled
from the "House of Philippe de Rothschild" in black pencil, and
in red stencil "Private." In black pencil it read "Bof bottle," which
loosely translated means "Bullshit bottle" or "Possibly Laughable."
It depends on the translation – the French have a wicked sense of
humor to the point and have no problem sharing it, even at the
expense of vainly and squarely doing so to themselves. So the Chief
and Capt. Bob opened the very expensive bottle and thumbed their
noses at this known fact by using a marlin spike to push the cork
down into the bottle. They poured the loose, fractured smaller
pieces of cork on the deck and passed the bottle, and time, between
them as they watched the Morgan 51', with only it's mast light on,
motor off into the darkness towards shore.

    Dallas now having had a good look around, and checking out

Raul's garage position one more time, slipped over the dune and headed towards the beach. The surf was pounding softly with a regular beat. He covered the two hundred yards to the beach break, and his footprints disappeared behind him with each lap of a wave. He stopped and squatted as he pulled out a Sig 9mm, his small Uzi .380, and one very special Colt .380 govt. series 80 Mustang, and slipped clips into all. The Uzi he slung over his shoulder, the Sig he stuffed in the front of his shorts while he slid the Colt. .380 into the small of his back under his shirt. He discarded the travel bag, but kept his Nikon binoculars on a tether around his neck. From his conversations with Amada on his way up, he got the feeling that Amada and his crew were wanting to stay out of this, and had from the beginning, so Raul was watching for Skeets, not him. The lack of Amada's main ride in the drive could mean only one thing; that he had cleared the house of his wife and housekeepers. No reason for them to possibly get all shot up. He had mixed emotions about approaching Raul – he was probably jumpy enough – so Dallas decided to just move around as quietly as possible, try the doors and unlock a few if locked. He wanted Skeets full attention on the Morgan 51' listing in the surf, and if at all possible he wanted Skeets to actually go check it out, because once Skeets saw that boat he would know that Dallas Streeter was so close that the hairs on Skeets neck would be standing erect.

Dallas stood at the waterline, the smell of the beach break and warm salt water brought back memories of different times in his life, good times and bad times all swam through his head for a few seconds and he found himself walking towards the steps that led down from the deck above. He looked around at all the angles, saw a security camera and stopped. It had a dim red light on top. He took a couple steps towards it, stopped, and waved the open palm of his left hand into it. To his surprise the security camera tilted up slowly, and then back down. "OK Frank," Dallas thought. "I hope you have a comfortable chair!" Dallas opened the French doors to the dining room and walked in. "At least you keep a clean house Frank, even on your worst days. I'll try not to fuck it up too bad" was his last thought about housekeeping. Dallas knew the layout of the Amada beach house – stairs on the left went to bedrooms upstairs, kitchen off to the left, pantry at the back of the kitchen. He walked to it straight away and looked inside. Nothing. Dallas ran up the steps to the bedrooms. All the doors were open, even the master bedroom. But he knew Amada had a safe room behind the clothes at the back of the walk-in closet. He ducked out of the master bedroom and stuck his head in each of the other bedrooms, and bathrooms, and closets. Nothing. One bedroom looked like a Tijuana whorehouse and smelled of one smell he had smelled before. Liquor bottles, dirty clothes . . . "the smell of filth." Dallas didn't linger. He knew only one fucker on earth smelled like this brand of shit, "Ernie Skeets," ex-beat cop, ex-D.E.A. agent turned full time piece of shit for hire.

Dallas skipped down the stairs, hooked a left and slowly walked down the stairs that led up from the garage and housekeeper's quarters. He walked slowly, his 9mm with the hammer half-cocked and a round in the tube. "Jeez, I don't want to shoot Raul by mistake, or Chance!" He cleared the bottom of the steps and came to the first bedroom door on the right. He tapped with his fingernail and whispered "Chance, you in here?" Nothing. He moved down and across the narrow hall. He tapped again, this time with the old rhythm, "beer and a cigarette, two bits." Only an American would get it. And whispered again. "Chance, you in there?" Dallas put his ear against the door and tried the handle . . .

Dallas felt something cold and round with a slight echo of a trigger cock inside with a distinct Latin ring about it. "Mr. Raul, I do believe?" "Why Mr. Streeter, I do believe!" came back, only this time without the aid of a Colt Desert Eagle eight-inch barrel as an amplifier. Dallas slowly turned and faced a man in his fifties; a little on the dark side, but in great shape as men in their fifties go. Raul spoke first. "Yes, I'm here to make sure Skeets does not harm the boy. But I am not to get in the way of either you or Skeets. . . Only to protect the boy, period! When Skeets shows up, it's between you and him! Mr. Amada wishes you well. He has grown tired of Ernie Skeets, and wishes you "Good hunting.""

"No Shit!" He does, does he? . . . OK, I know he has the house all camera-ed up and won't miss a thing." "Yes, the younger Streeter is in this room." Raul pulled Dallas back away from and just down the hall. "Here this is the key to the room." Raul spoke in quiet tones. Obviously he did not want Chance to hear what was going to be said, "OK, Dallas . . . Can I call you Dallas? . . . When you open that door prepare yourself, for after seeing his two friends shot dead in the desert by Fernando, Skeets partner, and then being turned into a heroin addict - At first he struggled against it, he really did, Dallas, but after being held down and injected over and over, naturally he broke, and now he is but a shadow of the kid I saw for the first time." Dallas looked down and took the key from Raul's hand. "Anything else I should know?" "Yes, I gave him a gun . . . a C.I.A. special. An air-weight, no hammer, point and shoot." "Does Skeets know about it?" "No! I also gave him a hand-cuff key." "A hand-cuff key?" Dallas looked up this time. "You mean that fucker had him hand-cuffed?" "Yes," Raul answered. "For many, many days, and the whole time in the trunk of his car from Arizona." "Oh. OK Raul, thank you, I have the picture now. Thank you again, and of course Mr. Amada" . . . Dallas waved at the camera with a little red light on top at the end of the hall. "Yes," Raul said. "Mr. Amada can also hear everything." "OK. Then Raul, I have to speak with Chance for a few moments, so if you could go please and watch for Skeets" . . . "I'm sorry Mr. Streeter, from this moment on, you are on your own! Good luck"

Raul disappeared into the darkness. Dallas heard a door close and that was it. "Fucking really? OK, I came in on my own, so what the fuck's the difference?" Dallas put the key Raul gave him in the lock and turned it. He whispered Chance's name several times from behind the door. "Jeeez, Chance with a fucking gun, all doped up, seen his two buddies shot dead and left in the sand face down" . . . All these thoughts raced through his mind as he stuck his head out from behind the door. "Hey! Chance! It's Dallas! I've come to get you!" "BANG!" A bullet ripped a hole in the door just above Dallas's left shoulder. "WHOOO! Chance, it's Dallas! Now put the gun down!" Dallas ducked a little lower behind the door and heard a faint, "Dallas?" . . . "Yeah! It's me, man!" "Dallas, is it really you?" Dallas heard this like from someone on the verge of passing out. "Put the gun down, Chance . . . Put it down on the bed" . . . Dallas heard a real weak "OK, it's on the bed."

Dallas opened the door all the way without going in, and stood in the doorway. With the gun on the bed, he rushed in and grabbed Chance up in an all-encompassing hug. Dallas sat Chance back on the bed and looked him over. He brushed the hair out and away from his face, and saw a gaunt vacant and pale twenty-four-year-old. "What the fuck did you get yourself into?" Dallas asked "I, I don't know, it happened so fast . . . and then they were dead. He killed them in the desert. Why did he have to do that, Dallas?" Dallas knew. Dallas knew the answer before it was asked. He looked at his watch. Christ, it's almost fuckin 5:00! I gotta move! "Chance . . . Hey, listen up! Your life might be riding on this, son. So snap outta it . . . You have to listen!" "Yeah, I'm here. What's the plan?"

"We really don't have a plan, we have events." A confused look came across Chance's face. Dallas grabbed Chance by the arm, picked up Chance's pistol and put it in his hand. "Do you have any more bullets than what's in here?" Dallas flipped it open. "Fucking four bullets left" . . . Jeez . . . Here we go!" Dallas swung it shut with a resounding click. "Chance, you stay right fucking here in the room! This is why –Skeets is gonna come in this door at the end of the hall from the garage. He's gonna want to check on you first. In case you haven't figured it out, he's holding you to get to me, or more to the point, my money! He'll kill you to get me to pay, or rather he will hurt you real bad, and I mean he will hurt you. So you lock yourself up tight as "Dick's hat-band" and only speak to him through the door! Does that mother fucker have a key, Chance?" Chance was looking around, and it wasn't for a key. He was flopping the pistol around this way and that. "HEY! What the fuck are you looking for?" Then Dallas saw it. On the sink vanity were several needles and a big spoon. Next to all that was a good-sized bag, and in the bag was the dope Chance has been doing. Dallas went in to the bathroom and looked it over. "So this is the shit, huh Chance? And what I bet by now is you can't even function without this Crap! Can you?" Make no mistake, Chance Streeter was a smart kid. He was top of his law school class back at Arizona State. "OK," Dallas said, "you made it this far on it, let's hope you can finish the night. So you and your monkey do what you need do to function. And if that fuck Skeets crashes through that door, empty that .38 into his chest. But not me! It's my plan that Skeets is going to be so busy with other shit going on that he is gonna temporally forget about you . . . How's that?"

"Dallas" . . . "Never you mind, I'm leaving now. LOCK that fuckin door and be quiet. I'll be back for you, I promise. Just do as I say, Chance, OK?" "OK! Sit tight, no noise, just me and my monkey!" . . . "That's right, just you and your monkey." Dallas closed the door, turned and waited to hear if Chance locked up. He did. "OK, Skeets, where are you?" Dallas peeked over the stairs and could see a sail boat mast in the back yard. He smiled.

Chapter 14

D awn was just breaking as Ernie Skeets drove the last two miles along the highway next to the beach. He was playing with his guns on his lap when one slipped between his legs on to the floor of the car "Goddamn it!" he yelled at the empty seat next to him. "This shit is all your fault, Fernando! But no . . . You had to fucking overdose! You piece of shit!" Skeets picked up his .45 and shot a hole in the passenger side door. "There, take that, Motherfucker! I know you're still here! How was that last bounce before you landed in that steaming pile of shit at the bottom of that cliff, anyway? Was it as good for you as it was for me?" This is the way it had been since Skeets hadn't slept and did dope and coke for the last three days. Actually it was four days since he was drinking and driving the streets of Belize City, where he almost ran over D.E.A. agent Sands, but who's counting all the days since they were melting into one big blur?

Thanks to Ernie Skeets, the boys from the agency, the D.E.A., were about fifteen miles behind him now. Skeets was clueless at this point. All he knew was that all of a sudden, in the direction of Amada's beach house, a sailboat mast flashed in and out between the dunes and coconut palms. "What the fuck?" He rubbed his eyes and slowed down a bit so he could maybe get a better glimpse of it. "No shit! It is a mast, but why the fuck is it laying at a forty-five-degree angle to the beach? STREETER? Or maybe a drug boat of

Amada's caught at low tide?" Skeets slapped himself hard across the face (as if this would wake up a mind that was over the edge). Skeets couldn't take his eyes off the mast, and missed the driveway turn on to Amada's property.

Dallas sat and watched. He had heard the errant gunshot echo that announced Skeets arrival. He sat in a deck chair that he dragged up onto the roof of Amada's beach house. "Take the high ground." Something that he had lived as gospel since his early days as a lookout for the Haffler brothers in his twenties. "Oh, this is better than I hoped, that fuck is so preoccupied with the boat he is gonna fuck up, and when he does . . . I'm going to be right there!" Dallas pulled his radio out of his back pocket. "On-Line . . . On-Line" . . . This is your captain speaking, do you read? Over."

"Oh yeah! We are On-Line . . . Waiting instructions . . . (The Chief by the sound of his voice was on point this morning) "OK, please stand by . . . I have eyes on target. And please switch frequency on radio at this point. Switch to Trinidad number one." "Roger that Boss, switching to T-1," was all that was said between the Chief and Dallas.

Dallas watched as Skeets backed up, almost putting himself in the ditch. He spun the tires and sped up the drive. As Skeets drove up, Dallas moved around the roof. He wanted to come in through the master bedroom window. While he was upstairs when he first got there he had left the master bathroom window just cracked enough to get a couple fingers in to pull the three foot by four-foot-long horizontal sliding window open. Dallas didn't even know why he did this, and when he was working the window open he thought, "jeez if this kinda shit isn't force of habit, then what is?" Dallas knew that Frank Amada was probably only feet away from where he stood, in his "safe room," getting a sick kick out of watching this. Yeah, "The Island of Dr. Maru" he thought – watching, waiting, on the phone making side bets! "Hey Frank," he looked into a small round camera mounted in a dark corner of the walk-in closet doors.

"Don't bet against me, you fuck. You see that Morgan sailboat up on your beach? The camera tilted up and then back down. "Well Frank, you know the thousand kilos I have of yours, the ones I'm supposed to deliver? Huh? Those and that Morgan 51? Boy am I'm glad I have been paid up front!" The camera started tilting up and down, and then in a new move, right to left and back again. "Oh shit, Frank, I see I got your attention! Hahha . . . Well Frank I'm giving it all to Skeets! Well, sort of . . .That is . . . Just stay in your room Frank! Things are gonna get messy in the house. I hope you didn't fire your housekeepers! Hah ha, Jeeez!" All this time, Dallas watched Skeets get out of that mess he called a car. Fucking bullet holes in the trunk, a big-ass exit hole from the bullet he tried to kill Fernando's ghost with . . . "Hey Frank," Dallas leaned in close to the camera. "Where is that junkie fuck Fernando anyway?" The camera went right and left again. "What, you don't know Frank? OK! . . . I gotta go Frank, nice talking with you. Never mind the mess when it's over! You can have the Morgan 51; it's a present from me to you for at least keeping Chance alive til I got here. OK?" The camera nodded one last time, and Dallas was already gone.

Skeets slammed his ride into Park. The morning light hadn't yet lit up the inside of the garage, and he searched the car for his now-missing glasses amongst all the trash that filled it just like a sixty-three year-old hoarder that you would find on some nice street, in a nice home from the looks outside, but on the inside is a sweater that has been buried under an eight-foot pile of half eaten pizzas and a bag of fish sticks that never made it to the freezer, because the freezer was under a pile of the same shit as all the rest. Skeets could see without them, but across the room he could only make out shapes. "Far-sighted" is what the doctor called it thirty-odd years ago when he last had then checked, and it had only gotten worse. "I need my fucking specs!" He moaned as he rummaged through all the half-eaten tacos and bean dishes. "Goddamnit!" He stumbled upon a box of .45 shells and stuck those in his pocket. "Fernando!

You're fucking with me!" . . . Skeets also found a bag that had a bunch of dope in it. He settled into the seat and poured it out on to the armrest, bent over and snorted it, sounding like a pig at a trough.

All this time Dallas spent finding the secret door Amada had that led down to the laundry room off the garage. While at Amada's during a party a few years ago, Dallas got laid on these steps. So he knew it well . . .

Skeeets mind was all over the boat that he had seen driving up the road. Now that he was getting high he became even more fixated on it. "I wonder . . ." he thought, and slammed the car door so hard that it just bounced back open. It didn't latch and swung back open again as he made a quick walk into the garage and in the door of the house. He did stop for two seconds and with the butt of his .45 hit Chance's door and yelled, "I'll be back for you cocksucker! I'll be back!" He almost bolted up the stairs and through the dining room and out the French doors, but stopped short, looked around and when he saw he was alone, he hit the fridge and grabbed a beer, wiped his nose and then walked out on to the deck that overlooked the Morgan 51, now completely laying on her side. Skeets scratched his head with his gun barrel. "What the fuck is this?" Then he noticed a note. It was addressed to Frank Amada. Skeets ripped it open. He had to close one eye – he was so high that everything was double or crossed up. It read . . .

> *Frank, look I know we have had our troubles, but here's the "Load" as promised. Keep the Morgan 51. It's all there – the thousand kilos . . . Plus I hope you can get my brother from Skeets with as little problem as possible! Please help me! . . . Chance is a good kid . . . Call me when you secure his freedom. "p.s." The money is there, too.*

> *Dallas*

"Oh, no shit!" . . . Skeets downed the beer and walked over to the stairs that led down to the beach. "So look at what I got! All I have to do is wait for the tide, and push this fucker off the beach! . . . And kill Amada if he shows up. And that spic Raul. Fuck it, Amada's wife, I'll rape first, then kill her . . . Now let have a look at this boat, no, at *"my new sailboat!"*"

Dallas sat at the top of the hallway stairs, radio in his hand. "Hey Chief! You there? . . . "Yeah, Boss I'm here" . . . "Well I think he is gonna take the bait! As long as he doesn't double back for a shot at Chance . . . No! Hold on . . . He's walking towards the boat . . . He's two hundred feet . . . one fifty . . . C'mon, you motherfucker, another hundred feet! C'mon . . . Get ready, Chief! He's almost there! . . . FUCKING-A Chief! . . . BLOW THAT FUCKER NOW!!! NOW!!! NOW!!!"

The Chief looked over at Capt. Bob and winked. Here goes everything!" And pushed the button on the cigarette-sized box. "Hey Bob! He did say "Now," right?" "Uh, yup" . . . As the words left his mouth the Chief and Bob didn't hear it. Being just at the horizon line, it takes a few seconds for sound to travel about the four miles to where the "On-Line" was sitting. But they sure did *see* it! "Now that was cool, Bob . . . The Chief brought up his binoculars, as Bob did the same. "Oh! That was very cool indeed!"

Dallas, who was lying on the stairs on his elbows and chin, only able to see the top half of the Morgan 51, was shaken, as the whole house was, and slid down the steps to the bottom. "Christ Chief! You weren't shitting! Fucking-a, "BOOM- BOOM" is right!" Dallas slowly crawled back up the steps to the top, and this time stood up, more like "leaned" up, and could see a fucking white-out of exploded Coke starting to settle and drift in the wind. The French doors that led out to the deck were blown in . . . In fact, all the front glass picture windows were blown in. Shards of glass were embedded in the walls; the dining room table was flipped on its side . . . Dallas walked around and climbed over things to get out to the deck. "Where was Skeets? Where was Skeets?" Dallas from above searched the beach below. Half blown-open kilos of coke were everywhere, even on the deck at Dallas's feet. Pieces of yacht lay in a 360-degree circle, the waves playing with them like bathtub toys. Only three feet of hull remained of the Morgan 51, and it sat in three feet of water, easily floated out if Skeets still wanted to do that. Dallas went up to the roof. From there he hoped he would see maybe a piece of Skeets, or blood, or something! Nothing. Dallas wasn't real keen on the idea of going onto the beach at all. "Fucking Skeets! You can't even die right, you fuck!" Dallas climbed down. Actually he went in through the master bedroom's bathroom window again. The first thing he noticed was a large crack in the wall over the bed. He looked quickly into the camera above the walk-in closet – it still had the red light on. Dallas smiled for the camera; it didn't take but two seconds for the camera to move back and forth in a way Dallas took as a "Oh, Hell, No, you didn't!" Dallas took the back steps down to the garage laundry room. He peeked out. "Hmm, No Raul. But that don't mean anything, sneaky bastard."

Dallas moved across the garage to the hallway door that led to the housekeepers' and Chance's makeshift cell. He got to Chance's door. He used the same "shave and a haircut" tap on the door. He made out a mumble, and said, "Get your shit, we are leaving! NOW!" Dallas stepped away from the door to the stairs, thinking he heard something up there. He turned around. "OH FUCK! Where did YOU come from?"

Dallas was looking into Ernie Skeets "head." Directly into Ernie Skeets head; where his right eyeball was now gone. Where just above that his eyebrow and *three inches of his skull* was gone! Ernie had a what looked like a big,.45 cal pointed at Dallas's head, and was shaking badly. In Skeets shoulder was the top half of a broken-off red wine bottle. It was embedded and a small trickle of blood was ironically coming out of the open drinking end. This was about all Dallas could stand. He spoke to Skeets. "Can you hear me?" Nothing . . . Obviously Skeet's was deaf from the blast. He was about drop Dallas. He pulled the .45's hammer off half cock to full . . . . For the first time, Dallas was actually looking at his imminent death. There had been many, many close calls . . . But he had a feeling about this time in his gut! A wobbly Skeets put the gun against Dallas's forehead. Dallas closed his eyes and shouted "DO IT Motherfucker!" Skeet's smiled, mumbling. Dallas cracked an eye open - Ernie had no teeth left! Dallas burst out laughing!

Just as Dallas laughed a gunshot rang out . . . "HE MISSED!" . . . "CHRIST HE MISSED!" Ernie Skeets went down on his knees, and three more gunshots rang out! Dallas looked up. Chance Streeter stood in a trance, still pulling the trigger! Dallas reached out and grabbed the gun. "It's over! . . . Man. It's OVER! CHANCE!!" . . . There were tears . . . Lots of tears as Dallas gave him a bear hug. "It's over, man! You saved my life, man! That fuck was gonna kill me sure as shit. How he survived that blast, I'll never know. You owed him that for your friends. And for yourself."

Dallas helped Chance back into his room and sat him down. "OK, we have to get the fuck out of here NOW! Where's all your shit? Like your wallet, like your passport, like everything you came in here with?" "It's all in Skeets room upstairs. It has to be, Fernando took it all and Skeets told him to put it in the drawer, so it has to be in his room. "OK, stay here. Take this." Dallas handed him the small black Colt automatic he had pulled from the small of his back. "You know how to use this? Here." Dallas took it and clicked the safety off. "If anyone comes in that door . . ." "Oh, man!" Chance protested. "I'm going with you! I know what my shit looks like. So let's go! "Well, OK," Dallas said. "Hey, don't trip on any bodies. It's bad form! Ha-ha!" "That's funny Dallas . . . Really?" "Just stay close and make this fast. You search the room, I'll stand guard. This place is gonna be crazy with the heat and everyone else that saw or heard that this morning. I, *we,* have to be gone in no more than five to seven minutes. NO SHIT and no screwing around. Find it, or don't! Five minutes!"

Assistant Director Cox and agent Sands had stopped for gas on the coast road. Sands, while chatting up the locals, was told about some strange "Boom" that happened about two hours earlier. They cut the gas stop short when Sands told Cox about what sounded to him like an explosion up the coast. "Oh Fuck! What did Streeter do now?" Cox wondered out loud. "We don't know it was Streeter. It could be anything," Sands spoke out. Cox said, "Listen, Agent Sands - It's Streeter! And its Ernie Skeets! . . . Now get your ass on the road, and just don't kill anyone or anything on the way, OK?" "Yes Sir! Ass on the road, hands on the wheel!" "Don't get smart mouth with me, agent. This is Frank Amada's house, remember that. And we have no back-up! . . . And those were the last words spoken in that car.

Dallas stood outside while Chance actually found his wallet and passport. "Christ, will miracles never cease?" Dallas sighed, as the both took the back stairs down into the garage. Of course, that was not all Chance found while tossing the room. While in the dark on the stairs, Chance stuffed a baseball-sized ball of his "monkey's favorite" down his pants. They both cleared the garage. Dallas turned around and, in a final thank you, waved and smiled into Amada's security camera mounted above the garage in the left corner. "Hey Frank! Adios, you almost-helpful motherfucker! WE ARE EVEN! . . . Call me!"

"OK, kid, follow me! And keep the fuck up if you still want to live. We are not outta the woods yet." . . . Dallas set the pace. He looked back. "HEY! Move your ass! We gotta plane to catch!" Chance, in between gasps, said, what?" Dallas said, "you heard me!" They made it to the road. Chance was breathing so hard that Dallas turned and "shushed" him. "Quiet and listen . . . OK, let's go . . . Follow me." Dallas moved as fast as he could without losing the kid. They cut a hard left and came out on the lake access road.

"Where's this go to, Dallas?" "Goes to a crocodile farm, and the caretaker is a little off the wall, so if we see him, you don't say shit! I'll handle him . . . I think my parking meter may be over by a few thousand bucks. So just let me pay the man and we will be on our way . . . "By "pay the man," you don't mean kill him, do ya?" "I'm not even going to answer that! What the fuck, you think I just go around killing people? No, I'm going to let YOU kill him! . . . You're the killer! I just watched you shoot an ex-D.E.A. Agent in the head FOUR times . . . "He was a D.E.A. agent? Oh fuck, I'll get the death penalty for sure!" "Ha-ha. No, he was a very bad man. Ex-D.E.A., wanted by the federal government for at least a dozen murders and kidnapping you. Yes, he was wanted for your case and your friend's deaths. We, and I say we because we just did the world a big favor, and we did their job for them. So no, Chance . . . It's all good what we did. Of course we made a mess doing it . . . But my crew has always had a flair for the dramatic. And now you are a member of my crew. No way can you go back to school; in fact, no way you can go back to the states for a while, pal . . . Hey, there's the plane!" "That's no plane!" "Hey Man – Careful, she's sensitive. And besides, she is your only ride home!"

"Jackass!" "Ah, excuse me?" (Oh Shit! There's that voice, that un-mistakable voice from the dark!) "Yeah, ah but you're pulling on my airplane, and it's bothering my crocodiles, and we can't have that at all. It's breeding season and I didn't fly in and bother your parents while they were doing their thing, or land all up in the O.R. while your momma was giving birth to you now, did I? No I didn't, to answer my own question. Now what can I do for you? You two gentlemen appear to be lost. This here place is a government owned and operated, privately funded nesting facility for the "North American Salt Water Crocodile," and you must have missed the signs that say "No Trespassing," et cetera and so on."

Dallas looked at Chance and said, "I'm gonna try one time." . . . "Excuse me sir, but the reason I'm pulling on this rope is because

It's MY rope attached to MY plane. I know the parking rates here on this fine bit of water, and even finer crocs. I know I came in a little early in the morning, but that is why I paid the price last night for only the best of what you had to offer . . . Do you remember that transaction? Your neighbor Frank Amada just over there and one of your public benefactors recommended your little piece of paradise, and I paid in cash."

"Well sir, I do not see Mr. Amada with you at this time, and while I do remember a late-night transaction, I'm not sure it was on this here airplane. Now if-in you had paper title on this plane here, I am sure we could come to a "mutual understanding" . . . "Yes sir, if I had some papers I think" . . . Dallas reached over and pressed into the water proof keypad the seven-digit lock code. "Hey, hey! Just what are you doing, Mister? I want you to stop that and step away from my airplane!" Dallas just looked at him the whole time, smiling. "But I'm getting you the papers on this airplane that you want! You do want the papers on this plane and all. You see, we are in kind of a hurry and really need to go." Dallas motioned to Chance to get in on the other side. Ole Croc watcher Jim had walked over to his little cabin, undoubtedly to get a gun. Dallas opened the hatches and had even reached in and brought up the electric fan for pre-take-off moving. But Dallas also had his Colt Mustang Series 80 .380 cal. With that he had 10,000 dollars in a bag, a clear shoe bag. He figured if one didn't work, the other would and the crocodiles would have a great meal tonight!

Ole Croc Jim reappeared, and quicker than he had been moving also. He had no gun, or weapon of any kind. It seems he went and made a phone call. He told Dallas that he was very sorry! And if he would be so kind and please remove his airplane, and all people with him as fast as possible . . . That it would be just fine, and to have a happy and safe flight home, or wherever they were going. And that he was to refund any and all money that may have changed hands.

Dallas couldn't take the groveling any longer. "Hey! Forget about it, I'll just go now and you have a nice day. Oh, there's going to be a whole lot of people, I mean a WHOLE LOT . . . And if you would like to have this donation, on one condition, and that is you only saw me real late at night and you could never, ever, be able to recognize me – cause it was so late and you have no lights because it disrupts the crocs breeding an all!" "Wow! Sure, I can tell them that and I would not even be lying . . . And this is a lot of money! Maybe I can buy me an airplane like this one." Dallas's last words to him were "I can see it now – "Crocodile tours by air!" Bye-Bye! Remember now – Not a word!" Dallas jumped into the cockpit. Chance was fiddling around with the harness, finally figuring it out. "What now, Dallas?" "Ha-ha-ha! What now? Sit back and enjoy the ride, that's "What now!"

Dallas pushed the electric steering motor to max. He cleared the overhang and was coming about. He taxied to the near end of the lake. Chance, looking out the window, noticed three rather large crocs in the plane's wake. Old ones, big ones and toothy ones. "Jeez, Dallas. Look!" And pointed at them. "Ha-ha-ha! Yeah, so? Something to remember this lake by. Ha-ha-ha! Now sit back and enjoy. The first time in this is always the best!" Dallas went to the main engine and hit the gas. Chance grabbed the edge of the seat and stared ahead as the lake whizzed by and at the last moment the little boat became a plane. Dallas, not used to the extra weight, had to pull a bit harder than normal, and those trees he came in over seemed a little taller . . . But that was at night so maybe they were. He took a heading to the northeast, away from the coast road far enough and low enough that any traffic on the road or along the coast would not be able to see him. He grabbed the radio and started his call . . . "On-Line – On-Line," if you recognize this voice please acknowledge and respond, over" He made this same call one more time without a break for the On-Line to have responded. Now he waited. He heard a garbled response. "Shit I'm too low!" He brought the nose up and climbed another seven-hundred-feet. "OK, On-Line, let's try that again please!" As the Chief's voice boomed into the cabin, a wave of relief washed over Dallas "This is On-Line, do you have the package? Repeat, do you have the package?" . . . Dallas, almost giddy, looked over at his brother. "Yes, On-Line, I have the package, and am requesting G.P.S. delivery zone. Please switch to secure channel number fifty-seven." (Which meant switch to channel seventy-five). "OK! On-Line waiting G.P.S." the Chief's voice said. "Sending now." "Hey Chief, do a quick check on distance, too – I am running distance left in tanks here." While this was being done, Dallas and Chance hooked a ninety-degree right, taking them south and about to cross the main coast road. Dallas told Chance, "you look left, and I'll look right. Tell me if you see any Government traffic, or anything that looks like a convoy." "I don't see anything Dallas." "Ah, but I do! We just missed them by ten minutes at the most! There, see?" Dallas was pointing at a fire truck at the end of a row of other trucks and S.U.V.'s . . . "Ha-ha-ha! FUCK YOU!!!" Dallas screamed, and got back to the radio. "OK Chief, read me those G.P.S. coordinates and I'll let the computer-aided autopilot bring us in."

Chance, who had never seen the ocean before from the air, just stared out at the change from shallow coral reefs to the line where the deep water started. He didn't speak more than a half dozen words; all he could do was try and process these *Last days in May.* Days he wouldn't, couldn't, ever be able to forget. All of a sudden the radio was alive. "We have you in sight Dal, two – three degrees to starboard. Damn, son, we almost missed you! What, I bet you're only flying thirty feet above the water!" "Sorry, but I had to do radar evasion coming out of that place. It was starting to get crowded, if ya know what I mean. Thank the gods I'm so small I probably looked like fly shit on their radar screens, maybe like the "Mexican Air Force" (Pelicans). OK, I see your and Bob's boats!" Dallas did a three-sixty around the big Hatteras and the smaller go-fast of Bob's . . . He lined it up and brought it in on fumes.

"Christ, Chief I hope you saved me a bit of AV gas, cause I'm gonna need it!" "Oh, Hell, just tie that bitch up and get on board! You're home, boy! It's been a hell of a week, just a hell of a week!"

Epilogue for the "Long Ride Home"

Janis and Sonata's Ride

Needless to say, neither Janis or Sonata were around for the show and "Boom-Boom." But they had a wonderful and safe time spending lots of cash staying in the best hotel they could find. They had an ample supply of the best wine in the world and gambled Dallas and The Chief's money away all night long every night. Until Marboy finally found them. Marboy was flown in after Capt. Bob decided that both Dallas and The Chief might want to see their wives alive again. If not sober, at least drunk and alive. Both were picked up after a radio call to the On-Line. They both pampered and got very possessive of young Chance . . .Hitting on him like the "Cougars" they are. The Chief did not get back the wife he had left behind – Janis had seen to that with a quickness. But Dallas got his back "intact"– every bad habit, every mood swing, every bit Janis!

Chance's Ride

It wasn't but one day at sea, slow going on the way to Cuba as it was with the seaplane under tow, before Dallas discovered his little brother's stash of "H." Dallas wasn't upset as one might think. He confiscated it and started a two-week detox program at sea. You just don't lock someone up, and you especially don't lock up family, who through no fault of their own got turned into a victim. That was the case in this story. Happily, the detox worked, on a physical level. Dallas knew it would be many months on the island, his new home for more than a little while, before his mind shut off the desire, wanting, and craving . . . It would be a long haul, and everyone knew it, and all were going to be a part of it, like it or not.

Chance didn't talk about or even mention his friend's names. It was his cross to bear, and everyone knew that to and left him alone. Some day he would. Dal knew it and never pressed him.

Marboy's Ride/Looking for Carl Brewster

The plane waited offshore while the On-Line went into Cuba and arranged a rather expensive deal with an old military friend during a lunch at Hemingway's Marina just outside of Havana. The fuel was good and clean. Dallas said his short-term good-byes, put Marboy in the passenger seat, fucking scared to death and sure he would die, but in the plane none-the-less . . . Dal dropped off Marboy at the Mo-Bay Yacht Club, or rather down the beach, said his farewells and promised to be in touch. Dallas flew around and found an old beach he knew well. He had someone to see that lived up the mountain a way – Carl Brewster – Mountain Militia Man "extraordinaire." All Dallas found was a burned-out shell of what was once a Jamaican paradise. No sign of Carl could Dallas find, except one fresh boot track on the side of what was a garden that Carl once grew the finest orchids in and on the trees that had surrounded it. He looked at the boot track and smiled. Only one person on this island notched the letter "C" on the center tread of his left boot and a letter "B" on the right. Not obvious. If you didn't know what you were looking at, you would never have a clue! "Only one track, though." Deep inside, Dal had his gut feeling, but who knows? Carl is getting old, and all these years in the jungle alone left Dallas with one big question mark and the knowledge that the years had not been as kind as his dearest friend had been to him over the many years and countless tears un-shed. Carl has always been a dark guy, that's why he moved to the island right after Vietnam did the number on his head that it did. But he had always been there, "blood-gore-guts." He was always the stand-up, go-to guy.

AmadaAmadas Escape

Frank Amada, house blown to shit, the end of operations as he knew it. Frank escaped down a slide that was installed into his safe room. While it was never intended or expected to be used, this day it carried him deep under his beach house to a tunnel that had been built a few years ago for stashing tons of the trade's supplies. It ran under the dunes for almost a thousand feet. It came up with some effort on his part to a waiting Range Rover that Raul had taken right after the last he and Streeter had exchanged pleasantries in the hallway outside Chance's holding room. They drove the mile and a half to his waiting wife and plane. His whereabouts are unknown.

Capt. Bob's Ride Home

Capt. Bob and his Scarab "Go-Fast" . . . He decided that he would help Dallas keep Chance on the right track back on the island, and if things worked out, with the two hundred grand Dallas was paying him, was giving serious thought to starting a new life, while he watched the deep blue pass and the dolphins ride the wake of The Chief's Hatteras. "What a life he thought . . . Could this be?"

The D.E.A.

Assistant Director Cod and Special Agent Sands. Just like it has been for years, so many that Cox has now stopped counting the years of near misses. They arrived on scene an hour to the minute after the place burned. Cox called in backup and forensics to do a search for "whatever" and "whoever" might be toast in this. At one point, Cox said, "fuck, what's the use?" Agent Sands looked back and said, "I am officially asking for "leave." Going home to the islands, maybe see my family, go fishing." "When are you coming back?" Cox asked. "I don't know, Director, jus don sir. I's jus don knows," he said in his best native tongue.

Dallas and The Chief

Dallas and The Chief, along with a new edition to the clan, arrived "one by air" and "one by sea" about the same time back at the half-moon-shaped house on the cliffs. Janis and Sonata were the first ones off the boat. They almost ran up the dock and stairs, only to be greeted by Goliath the Iguana in the pool, with several of his lady friends sitting in the fountain waterfall and around the edge of the pool. The screaming started, and both Dallas and the Chief could hear it from down below. They cracked a beer and burst out in laughter. "Good at be home, eh Daly?" The Chief asked in a sarcastic voice. "No shit! Nowhere like home, Martin" (Dal used the Chief's "given" name for the first time in years). Dallas continued. "Where else can you hear that? and pointed up to the pool. Anywhere but home?" . . . "Yup, man, it jus don't get any better than this! Hey what day is it?"

"I think it's one of *"The Last Days in May,"* Dallas."

The End